W9-CFJ-740

"I am not looking to make a marriage." She might as well be clear on that matter with Ashe from the beginning.

"Not tonight anyway." Ashe laughed at her defiance. "That doesn't mean we can't explore other interesting avenues of association."

"I decide for myself. You don't have any claim on me," Genevra asserted, although her body knew the latter statement to be something of a lie. Ashe did claim her attentions—in a way that transcended their connection through the estate.

Ashe's long fingers reached out to stroke a cheek. "And what have you decided, Neva? Have you decided to allow yourself the pleasure of a night? It is too late to deny it. I see the desire in your eyes. And not only tonight. I've seen it before, in the conservatory. I intrigue you and you intrigue me. I would gladly give you the one night your body is asking for."

* * *

How to Ruin a Reputation
Harlequin® Historical #1108—October 2012

Introducing a deliciously sinful and witty new trilogy from

Bronwyn Scott

Rakes Beyond Redemption

Too wicked for polite society...

They're the men society mamas warn their daughters
about...and the men that innocent debutantes
find scandalously irresistible!

The notorious Merrick St. Magnus knows just
HOW TO DISGRACE A LADY
September 2012

The untameable Ashe Bevedere needs no lessons in
HOW TO RUIN A REPUTATION
October 2012

The shameless Riordan Barrett is an unequalled master
in
HOW TO SIN SUCCESSFULLY
November 2012

Be sure not to miss any of these sexy men!

How to
RUIN
a Reputation

BRONWYN SCOTT

entertain, enrich, inspire™

If you purchased this book without a cover you should be aware
that this book is stolen property. It was reported as "unsold and
destroyed" to the publisher, and neither the author nor the
publisher has received any payment for this "stripped book."

Recycling programs
for this product may
not exist in your area.

ISBN-13: 978-0-373-29708-5

HOW TO RUIN A REPUTATION

Copyright © 2012 by Nikki Poppen

All rights reserved. Except for use in any review, the reproduction or
utilization of this work in whole or in part in any form by any electronic,
mechanical or other means, now known or hereafter invented, including
xerography, photocopying and recording, or in any information storage
or retrieval system, is forbidden without the written permission of the
publisher, Harlequin Enterprises Limited, 225 Duncan Mill Road,
Don Mills, Ontario M3B 3K9, Canada.

This is a work of fiction. Names, characters, places and incidents are
either the product of the author's imagination or are used fictitiously,
and any resemblance to actual persons, living or dead, business
establishments, events or locales is entirely coincidental.

This edition published by arrangement with Harlequin Books S.A.

For questions and comments about the quality of this book
please contact us at CustomerService@Harlequin.com.

® and TM are trademarks of Harlequin Enterprises Limited or its
corporate affiliates. Trademarks indicated with ® are registered in the
United States Patent and Trademark Office, the Canadian Trade Marks
Office and in other countries.

www.Harlequin.com

Printed in U.S.A.

For my dad and Nancy, just because
it's been a long time since I've dedicated a book to you.

Hugs and love to you both.

Author Note

The Rakes Beyond Redemption trilogy is a chance to look at three gentlemen of the *ton* who are transformed for the better by crisis. In Book One, *How to Disgrace a Lady,* Merrick faces personal financial ruination and a test of his long-dormant sense of honor when he's placed at the heart of a sinister wager to transform the retiring Alixe Burke into the *Toast of the Season.* In Book Two, *How to Ruin a Reputation,* Ashe has to cope with the aftershocks of a death in the family. And in Book Three, *How to Sin Successfully,* Riordan grapples with becoming an instant father when he inherits his brother's two young wards.

These are three Regency-style crises that often served to shape families and destinies in nineteenth-century England, but their situations find echoes in modern society: economic hardship, loss and changing family structures in which, more and more, extended family are stepping in to raise children while parents work, often far from home, to make ends meet.

I thought this was a fitting theme, given the current economic situations around the world and what they mean to regular people like you and me. In the past few years my family, like so many others, has had to decide what's really important to us about where our money and time are spent. What will we give up and how will we change our living habits to accommodate our needs?

In *How to Ruin a Reputation,* Ashe is faced with that same decision. What is he willing to change in order to keep the things and the people that are important to him? Up until now he'd envisaged and lived a fairly self-centered life. He'd never imagined a time when his father was dead and his brother no longer a bulwark of respectability to shoulder the mantle of the earldom. Now the earldom is his—if he dares to claim it. Ashe is not an ideal hero. His father, worried that Ashe might be the heir after all, has made some provisions in his will in order to protect the estate and the earldom's legacy from the prodigal second son. Death does not make Ashe perfect—he's not suddenly transformed into a bulwark of familial stability. He is filled with regret, and he does set out to make things right, but it's not an easy road for him—especially with the nominally perfect Cousin Henry waiting in the wings to take over the estate should Ashe fail.

There are secrets revealed and tests to pass along the way for Ashe in his journey to recognize his true potential. Fortunately, as on any good journey, there is someone to help. For Ashe, that mentor comes in the form of Genevra Ralston, an American heiress who understands his trials and failures better than he thinks, because she has secrets of her own—secrets Ashe will delight in uncovering as he faces the greatest trial of all…a rake falling in love.

Happy reading—I'll see you out there!

Drop by my blog at www.bronwynswriting.blogspot.com for updates on new titles and sneak peeks.

Prologue

The dim interior of the sickroom bristled with contentious silence. 'The will must be changed.' The old earl fairly shook in his chair with the force of his statement.

'I heard you the first time,' Markham Marsbury, solicitor to the Earl of Audley over the past ten years, responded with a patience born of long practice. The earl wasn't his first client who'd had last-minute doubts about his final arrangements. But the earl's requests might be the most irregular.

'You disagree with my decision,' the earl challenged, sounding more like his usual irascible self than he had in months. Perhaps it was a good sign, Marsbury thought hopefully. Perhaps the old man would get better one more time. Goodness knew the earldom could ill afford to lose him now. On the other hand, he knew better. Anyone who had been around lingering death knew the signs: a sudden rally, a brief explosion of energy that might last a day or two—then nothing.

'Yes, I disagree, Richard.' They'd become friends

over his decade in Audley. 'I can understand wanting to make the inheritance into a regency, a trusteeship of sorts. After what happened to Alex, it's a logical course.' Marsbury shook his head. 'But to divide the governance into shares and leave fifty-one per cent to *her* makes no sense. You have two viable male heirs hanging on the family tree, one of them your second son. For goodness' sake, Richard, she's not even British. She's American.'

'She's what the estate needs. She's already proven it in the year she's been here,' the earl broke in with vigour, unwilling to hear his position maligned. 'Some American thinking will rejuvenate the place and she's become the daughter I never had.'

And maybe even a substitute for the son who had not come home in ten years. 'Ashe will come home,' Marsbury put in. But he got out his papers and his ink and began to write. He recognised the signs of early intractability. There would be no dissuading the earl.

'Not while I'm alive,' the earl said matter of factly. 'We quarrelled and he made his position very clear.'

Then the son was a lot like his father, Marsbury thought privately as he finished the codicil and brought the paper to the earl. He held the older man's hand steady as he signed. The earl hadn't been able to write on his own for some time. Even with help, the signature was a barely legible scrawl.

Marsbury sanded the document and carefully placed it with the other papers. He reached out to shake his friend's hand. 'Perhaps there will be no need for this, after all. You look better today.' He offered a smile.

The smile was not returned. 'There is every need for it,' the earl barked. 'I've done what needs doing to bring my son home. I know my son. What he wouldn't do for me, he'll do for Bedevere. He loves Bedevere and he will come for that reason alone.'

Marsbury nodded, thinking of the other two names on the codicil, the other two 'shareholders' named in the trusteeship. His father's death would bring the errant son home, but knowing Bedevere was surrounded by enemies who had been positioned to snatch it up should he falter, might be enough to make him stay.

'I'll see you tomorrow.' Marsbury snapped his writing case shut.

The earl gave him a wan smile, looking more tired than he had a few minutes prior. 'I rather doubt that. If you mean to say goodbye to me, I would suggest you say it now.'

'You are far too stubborn for such maudlin talk,' Marsbury joked, clasping the old man's hand one last time.

Stubborn as the fourth Earl of Audley was, Death was ultimately more so. It was with no surprise that Markham Marsbury received word over his morning coffee the next day that the earl had passed away shortly before sunrise surrounded by family and one Genevra Ralston, the American in whose hands the fate of Bedevere now resided. Markham called for his writing things and dispatched a note to London, hoping it would find Ashe Bedevere and bring him home with all possible haste.

Chapter One

Sex with Ashe Bedevere was one of the 'Great Pleasures' of the Season and not to be missed, which explained why Lady Hargrove was favouring him with a splendid pout and a peek-a-boo glimpse of her bosom beneath a carefully draped sheet in hopes of persuading him to stay.

'Surely a few more minutes will not matter,' she protested with a coy look, letting the sheet slip ever so provocatively over the curve of her hip.

Ashe shoved his arms through the sleeves of his shirt, dressing rapidly. Whatever he'd found appealing about Lady Hargrove's feminine assets earlier in the evening had vanished in the wake of the note that had come for him. He pulled on his trousers and favoured her with a sinful smile designed to placate. 'My dear, what I had in mind for us takes more than a few minutes.'

The promise of deferred pleasure was enough. Ashe eased out the door before she could argue, all his thoughts fixed on one goal: getting to Bedevere, the Earl of Audley's family seat. Never mind that Bedevere was three days' ride away. Never mind he hadn't any idea of what to do once he got there. Never mind he could have answered numerous requests to return home in the past years and hadn't. Never mind any of it. This time it was different. This time, the solicitor had written two desperate sentences. 'Come home. Your father has died.'

Ashe sprinted the last few streets to his rooms on Jermyn Street, fuelled by a sense of urgency and impotence. He'd always thought he'd have more time.

Three days later

God and the devil in the details! Ashe swore none too softly and pulled his bay stallion to a jolting halt. *This* was Bedevere land? More to the point, this was his father's land? He could hardly reconcile the weed-choked fields and broken stone fences lining the roadway with the once-fertile fields and immaculate roads of his youth. He'd seen plenty of the devil since he'd ridden on to Bedevere land and not much of God. How had it come to this?

A sharp pang of guilt stabbed at him deep and hard. He knew the answer.

It was his fault.

The current summons home wasn't the first, but it would be the last. Ashe could have come home long before when the first bout of illness had settled in four years ago. He could have come home when his brother had gone round the bend two years ago for reasons still unclear to him. But he hadn't and an extraordinary consequence had occurred as a result: the timeless fortitude of Bedevere had faltered, proven fallible at last. He'd waited too long and all this ruin could be laid at his feet.

It seemed an ironic twist of fate that he was now poised to be the curator of a place he'd so willingly fled in years past. The place had been perfect then, so unlike his imperfect self. It was less perfect now and he was still flawed—a broken king to rule a broken Camelot.

There was no use in putting it off. Ashe kicked his horse into a canter for the last ride home. His trunks would have arrived yesterday, signalling that he was not far behind. The aunts had probably been up since daybreak, anticipating his coming, and they would all be waiting.

All *four* of them. He was their protector now, a role he felt ill suited to play. He supposed that was part of the Bedevere legacy, too; the Bedevere women didn't marry men who had the foresight to provide beyond the grave and the Bedevere males hadn't much luck in living long enough to do it for them.

The rough-kept lands preceding the park were a blessing of sorts in that they prepared him for the sight of the manor. Ivy crawled rampant across the formerly pristine sandstone of the hall's façade. A shutter hung loose from a second-storey window. Flowerbeds were overrun with plants that had long outgrown their intended shapes. Nature was having its way with the once-orderly estate.

Years ago, it had been a point of pride that Bedevere Hall, seat of the Audleys for four generations, was the gem of the county. It might not have been the largest home—Seaton Hall was bigger just a few miles to the south—but Bedevere was by far lovelier with its comely gardens and well-appointed views. From what Ashe could see trotting down the drive, there wasn't much of that left now.

Ashe dismounted and steeled himself for what lay inside. If the outside looked this bad, he could only imagine what had taken place inside to allow such decay to be permissible. A lone stable boy ran up to take his horse. Ashe was tempted to ask him about the state of things, but decided against it. He'd rather see it all with his own eyes.

Ashe doubted he'd even finished knocking before the door swung open and time stalled. Gardener stood there, as tall and sombre as Ashe remembered him, perhaps a bit greyer, a bit thinner, but very much the same. Growing up, Ashe had thought it was funny to have a butler named Gardener and a gardener named Smith, who looked to be long gone from the state of things.

'Mr Bedevere, welcome home.' Gardener bowed, 'I am sorry for the circumstances, sir.'

For a moment, Ashe almost looked behind him to see who else had followed him home—the greeting had been so very formal.

'This way, sir,' Gardener said. 'You are expected.'

Ashe followed Gardener down the hall to the drawing room, making mental notes as they went: bare hall tables, faded rugs and curtains. There was a shabbiness to the house. But most striking was the emptiness. There were no maids polishing the staircase, no footmen awaiting errands. The usual bustle of the hall was silent. There was Gardener and the stable boy. Presumably there were more, including a cook, hopefully, but Ashe didn't want to presume too much. It didn't look promising.

Ashe paused outside the drawing-room door and took a deep breath. Beyond those doors lay a responsibility he'd eschewed for years. He had his reasons. It was a mean act of fate that all his efforts to avoid it had come to naught. The Bedevere legacy, the one thing he'd tried so hard to escape, had landed quite squarely in his lap anyway. Perhaps it was true that all roads lead home in the end.

'Are you ready, sir?' Gardener enquired. With years of impeccable service behind him, Gardener knew how to read his betters and had given him a few seconds to prepare himself.

'Yes, I'm ready.' *Or not.* Ashe squared his shoulders.

'Yes, sir, I believe you are. Ready at last.' Gardener's eyes held the twinkle of approval.

'I certainly hope so,' Ashe replied with a nod of his head. He could see Gardener's rendition of the tale below stairs already, full of admiration about how the young lord had ridden in, taking no time to fuss over his appearance after a long ride. Instead, he'd gone straight to his aunts.

Gardener had made a habit of seeing the best in him

in his youth. Gardener would make him out to be an angel by evening. But if he was an angel, he was a very wicked one. Heaven forbid anyone at Bedevere ever learn what he'd been doing the moment the message of his father's demise had arrived. In hindsight, 'aggressively flirting' with Lady Hargrove seemed akin to fiddling while Rome burned.

Gardener opened the door and cleared his throat. 'Ladies, Mr Bedevere.'

Ashe stepped into the room, noticing the difference immediately. The curtains were faded, but the best of what was left in the house had been brought here. There were vases filled with flowers on the side tables, pillows on the sofas, little knick-knacks set about the room for decoration. Ashe saw the room for what it was: an oasis, or perhaps bastion was a better word—a *last* bastion of gentility against the bare realities that lay outside the drawing-room doors.

His eyes roved the room, taking in the surprising amount of occupants. His aunts were not alone; Leticia, Lavinia, Melisande and Marguerite were settled near the fireplace with a man he didn't recognise, but it was the woman seated just beyond them, by the window overlooking the garden, who held his attention. She was of uncommon loveliness—dark-haired with wide grey eyes framed by equally dark lashes against the creamy backdrop of her skin. Even in a crowded London ballroom she would stand out. Ashe suspected she'd chosen her seat away from the others in an attempt to be discreet, a task her beauty no doubt made impossible under the best of circumstances. Today, in a room peopled by elderly ladies and a middle-aged man, there was no opportunity for obscurity.

Ashe approached and gave his aunts his best bow. 'Ladies, I am at your service', but his gaze kept returning to the corner. Her comeliness was not all due to her good looks. It was in the way she held her slender neck, the straightness of her shoulders, both of which said, 'Notice me, I dare you.' For all her delicate beauty, she was no shy maiden. He could see it in the jut of her chin and the frank stare of her gaze in spite of her efforts at anonymity.

Leticia swept forwards, white-haired, regal and perhaps more fragile than Ashe remembered. They were *all* more fragile than he remembered, except for the siren at the window. She'd been watching him since the moment he'd entered the room, no doubt wondering and assessing, just as he was now. She was no one he recognised, but apparently she was important enough to be invited to his homecoming. More importantly, she'd been invited into the household in the aftermath of a significant death.

Ashe was cynical enough in his dealings with the world to be suspect of such an invitation. The aftermath of funerals were private matters for families, a chance for the bereaved to mop up the particulars of the deceased's life, re-organise and carry on. The weeks after a funeral were intimate times. Strangers were not welcome, although strangers invariably came in the hopes of grabbing a scrap from the table. Lovely, dark-haired females aside, Ashe had a word for those importunistic people: carrion.

Leticia took his hand. 'Ashe, it's so good of you to come. I am sorry we could not wait to bury him,' she said softly.

Ashe nodded. He knew that, counting the time it had taken for a message to reach him in London, at least six days had passed since his father's death. Even with all haste, he'd known he'd miss the funeral. One more regret to heap on an already laden platter.

'Come meet everyone. This is Mrs Ralston, our dear Genni.' She gestured fondly to the lovely creature at the window. 'She's been our rock in our time of need.'

Genni was far too girlish a name for the woman. She rose and extended her hand, not to be kissed, but to be shaken. 'It is good to meet you at last.'

Ashe did not miss the note of censure in her tone, so subtly hidden no one would notice it except the intended recipient—or was that his own guilt-plagued imagination imposing its own frameworks?

'Mrs Ralston, a pleasure, I'm sure,' Ashe returned drily. Whoever she was, she'd already inveigled her way into the aunts' good graces. He doubted she was a companion, at least not a successful one. Her demeanour was far too confident to play that submissive role and her clothes too fine. Even the simple lines of her afternoon gown of forest-green merino were cut with the perfection of a high-class dressmaker; the lace trim at her collar and cuffs was demure, but expensive. From the looks of Bedevere, affording that calibre of companion made the point moot. But it raised others. If she was not a companion, what was she?

'Genni has bought Seaton Hall for restoration.'

'Is that so?' Ashe said politely, but his speculations ratcheted up a notch. That probably wasn't all she meant to take advantage of. A woman choosing to take on the responsibilities of an estate alone was quite unusual. Perhaps there was a husband at home? Leticia didn't make it sound as if there were and there was no more information forthcoming. A young widow, then. Interesting. *Young* widows often had the most peculiar histories, some of which didn't necessarily include husbands.

Leticia moved on to complete introductions. 'This gentleman is your father's solicitor, Mr Marsbury. He's generously stayed on until your arrival so the estate can be settled.'

Ashe extended a hand, taking Mr Marsbury's measure. He was an older gentleman, bluff and florid, reminding Ashe of a country squire. 'Thank you for your timely note. I hope you haven't been unduly inconvenienced.'

Marsbury's demeanour was as firm as his handshake. 'It's been no trouble. It made more sense to wait for you to arrive since everyone else involved is already here.'

Ashe gave 'Genni' a cool glance. Did the unfamiliar beauty have a stake in his father's estate? A kaleidoscope of unpleasant scenarios ran through his mind— if she was a widow, was she a late-life lover his father had taken? Did she hope to be provided for?

With that pile of satiny black hair and the delicate sweep of her jaw, Ashe had no trouble believing she could entice even the most resolute of men into a proposal, a difference of thirty years in age notwithstanding. Ashe raised his eyebrows in query. '*Everyone* else?'

Marsbury met his gaze evenly. 'Your cousin, Henry Bennington.'

Cold suspicion took up residence in Ashe's stomach. 'What does my cousin Henry have to do with anything?'

'Henry has been a great support these past months.' The beauty spoke up from her station by the window. Ashe imagined he saw the quicksilver lightning of emotion flash in the depths of those grey eyes. Did the beauty carry a *tendre* for Henry? Henry of the blue eyes, golden hair and manipulative manners?

Ashe met her gaze evenly over the heads of the others. 'Forgive me if I find that hard to believe. Cousin Henry's only notable distinction, other than his penchant for collecting literature, is being the nearest male heir should my father die without surviving issue; a prospect, I assure you, he has long dined out on.' Most especially, Ashe knew from London gossip, in recent years when Ashe's brother, Alex, had no longer been a contender and Ashe's own lifestyle seemed destined to place him on the explosive end of a jealous husband's pistol.

Marsbury folded his arms across his broad chest and coughed to indicate his disapproval of Ashe's comment.

'Mr Bennington will join Mrs Ralston and ourselves in the study where we can discuss everything privately.'

Ashe noted Mrs Ralston looked up with surprise that was rapidly masked. An act, perhaps?

Ashe turned his hard stare on Marsbury, his voice firm with command. 'Yes, we certainly shall.'

So, the reading of the will was to involve the three of them. Certainly not the *ménage à trois* he was used to, but the dynamics were the same: two on one. Ashe wondered if the delectable Mrs Ralston and Henry had cooked something up together. She'd been quick to defend him and that had raised Ashe's suspicions.

Whatever webs his cousin had been weaving in his absence, Ashe wanted it understood that Henry Bennington had no authority here, nor did pretty, dark-haired Americans. Ashe Bedevere had returned.

Chapter Two

The elusive Mr Bedevere had returned. The room fairly vibrated with the evidence of it even after he'd departed with Marsbury. Genevra was not sorry to see him go. In a span of minutes he had unnerved her as few people could. She needed time to gather her thoughts and settle her surprise over the summons.

Genevra turned her attentions out the window, giving the aunts some time to digest their own excitement over Bedevere's arrival. He was the kind of man who stirred excitement wherever he went. Power sat on his broad shoulders as comfortably as his travelling cloak. But she'd met powerful men before. What had disturbed her most was the sensual potency of him. He wasn't just confident, he was seductive. His devil-dark hair had been windblown and rakish, his green eyes as hard as jade when he'd looked at her, his very gaze seeming to penetrate her innermost thoughts with an intensity that had sent a *frisson* down her spine.

If she could get through the reading of the will, she

would make sure to avoid Mr Bedevere when at all possible. Perhaps there'd even be enough chambers done at Seaton Hall for her to move back home. That would certainly help her keep Mr Bedevere at a distance.

'We shall have a party!' Lavinia exclaimed to the others. 'Cook can fix pheasant and we'll put flowers on the dining-room table.'

A party at which Mr Bedevere would be the guest of honour. Genevra turned from the window, her hopes of quick and immediate avoidance sinking a bit further.

Melisande gasped. 'Do you think we should? We're in mourning.'

'It will be private, no one will know and it's not as if there will be dancing afterwards,' Lavinia said staunchly.

She held out a blue-veined hand to Genevra. 'Isn't our nephew a handsome one? I told you he was.'

Genevra smiled and took Lavinia's hand. If the ladies wanted a party, she'd give them one. The past months with the ailing earl had taken a toll on them and not one of them was a day under seventy. She'd ridden over daily to help and had eventually moved in to stay over the winter to be of assistance while Seaton was undergoing renovations. Henry had already taken up residence by then and she'd meant it when she'd said Henry had been a support, which was more than she could say for the errant Ashe Bedevere.

Perhaps the allure of an inheritance had finally been the carrot to bring him home. Whatever had brought him, he was here now. Having taken his measure, she'd do best to keep him at arm's length. Forewarned was forearmed. She'd finally got her life back together. She'd learned her lesson. She wasn't about to let a handsome man turn her life upside down again.

The study was getting crowded, Ashe thought uncharitably. He'd barely seated Mrs Ralston when Henry made his entrance, striding towards him, hand outstretched, a wide smile on his face. 'Cousin Ashe, it's so good of you to come.'

Ashe didn't trust that smile for a moment. Most of the trouble Ashe and his brother had ever found themselves in could be laid at Henry's feet. Henry had a habit of making others pay for his misdeeds.

'So Aunt Leticia has already told me.' Ashe replied drily. Had there really been that much doubt? Ashe made no move to shake the offered hand. He was gratified to see that his lack of a polite response gave Henry a slight pause.

Henry regrouped and took an empty chair, smoothing his hands on his trousers in a nervous gesture. 'I would have been down sooner to greet you, but I was taking care of some estate business.'

'It's my home, *cousin*, I don't need to wait on an invitation.' He would not tolerate being treated as a guest in his own house. Nor did it sit well that Henry had sailed in here and commandeered the estate. Well, no more.

Ashe moved to take the upper hand. 'Marsbury, let's get on with your business.'

Marsbury settled a pair of spectacles on the bridge

of his nose and folded his hands on the desk. 'Gentlemen, Mrs Ralston, as you are aware, circumstances are somewhat unusual in this case. The earl has died, but his oldest son has suffered a nervous breakdown that has left him incapable of overseeing the estate. The title will, of course, transfer to the legitimate heir. Mentally incapable or not, he is still a recognised peer. Alexander Bedevere is officially the fifth Earl of Audley until his death. Should he die without a legal son, the title will pass to you, Mr Bedevere. This is all very regular. However, in the meantime, there is the estate to consider.' Marsbury eyed them over the rim of his spectacles. 'In his present condition, the current earl cannot be expected to manage the estate or its finances.'

Ashe was listening intently now. He'd known the title wouldn't be his, he hadn't wanted it. He was perfectly happy being Mr Bedevere, London's finest lover. But now, he sensed that Bedevere itself was in danger. The cold pit in his stomach spread a little deeper.

On either side of him, Mrs Ralston and Henry had their own reactions; Henry's eyes contained a barely concealed expectation while Mrs Ralston's hands were white from their iron grip on the arms of her chair. Henry was excited, but Mrs Ralston was cautious, perhaps even alarmed and trying to hide it.

Marsbury went on, 'The former earl petitioned the crown for a regency to be granted, not unlike the regency granted during King George III's illness. The petition was granted a few months before Audley's death.

Under a regency, your father was free to appoint any guardians or trustees he saw fit.'

'What the hell does that mean?' Ashe growled.

'It means, cousin, that Bedevere, in the common vernacular, is up for grabs.' Henry was all nonchalant insouciance.

Marsbury cleared his throat in censure of the indelicate translation. 'Not exactly, Mr Bennington. I think it will become clearer if I read the settlement straight from the will.'

Marsbury withdrew a sheaf of papers from his valise and began to read. 'I, Richard Thomas Bedevere, fourth Earl of Audley, being of sound mind and body on the twenty-fourth day of January, eighteen hundred thirty-four...'

The date pierced him. This codicil Marsbury read from was not some long-standing document. The alteration had been made the day before his father's death. Ashe shot Henry a speculative look. Had Henry talked his father into something absurd? Had Mrs Ralston? Sick, desperate men were fallible creatures. Perhaps more than one person had got their talons into his father.

The first part of the reading covered what Marsbury had already relayed concerning the transfer of the title. It was the second part that garnered Ashe's attention.

'During Alexander Bedevere's lifetime, the Bedevere estate shall be managed under a regency overseen by the following trustees who have been allotted the following shares of influence: to my son, Ashton Bedevere, with whom I regretfully quarrelled and have not seen since, I leave forty-five per cent of the estate in the hopes this will inspire him to embrace responsibility. I leave to my nephew, Henry Bennington, four per cent of the estate in the hopes he will understand he has got his due reward. Finally, to Genevra Ralston, who has been like a daughter to me in my final days and who has inspired me with her vision of a profitable estate, I leave fifty-one per cent of the estate.'

Ashe went rigid at the implication. The estate he'd been reluctant to assume had suddenly been lifted from his shoulders, but Ashe did not feel relief. He felt anger. He felt resentment. Had his father thought such an arrangement was what he'd want? Or had his father thought something else altogether less altruistic? He could divine those reasons later. Right now his brain was calculating at lightning speed and discarding scenarios about this particular three-way regency. Had he been meant to align with Henry?

Henry's four per cent did nothing for him. Aligning with Henry would only give him forty-nine per cent. Clearly his father did not mean to achieve a reconciliation between him and his cousin from beyond the grave. It served as further proof that Henry was no good and his father suspected it. From the insult-red beet colour of Henry's face, Henry knew it too.

'Four per cent! That's it? After all I've done this past year?' Henry burst out. 'I gave up a year of my life to come here and look after him.'

'No one asked you to make that choice,' Marsbury said calmly. 'Surely you chose to look after your uncle out of a sense of familial duty and not out of misplaced avarice?'

Well done. Marsbury rose a notch in Ashe's estimation. Henry glowered and stood up, making a hasty departure on the premise that he had a meeting elsewhere. That left only Mrs Ralston. She was beautifully demure, her gaze downcast, effectively hiding what must be a barrage of thoughts. She'd just inherited, at least temporarily, a controlling share in the governance of an English estate. Was she shocked? Was she secretly pleased that all had come out as she'd perhaps so carefully planned?

'Mrs Ralston, I would like a word with Mr Marsbury,' Ashe said, assuming she would be well-bred enough to hear the implicit request for privacy. She did not fail him.

'Yes, certainly. Good afternoon, Mr Marsbury. I hope we will have the pleasure of your company on happier occasions.' Mrs Ralston seemed all too relieved to quit the room. Perhaps she was eager to go up to her rooms and do a victory dance over her good fortune. Or perhaps she was eager to sneak off and celebrate with Henry at his supposed meeting. Together they could rule Bedevere at least during Alex's life, which should by rights be a long one. It had not escaped Ashe's mathematical attention that fifty-one plus four gave Henry a lot more control of the estate through Mrs Ralston. Of course, forty-five plus fifty-one maximised his own control of the estate quite nicely.

It was all becoming clear. Whoever wanted to control Bedevere had to go through Mrs Ralston. His father must have thought highly of Mrs Ralston indeed.

Marsbury set down his papers and folded his hands calmly as if he told sons of earls every day how they'd been essentially cut out of their father's will.

'Mr Bedevere, I think you come out of this better than you believe at present. You will inherit in due course should your brother's life end prematurely, whereas Mrs Ralston's tenure will terminate at some point.'

Marsbury had said absolutely the wrong thing. Ashe fought the urge to reach across the desk and seize Marsbury by the lapels in spite of his earlier favourable outlook towards the man. 'Is that supposed to console me? Because I assure you, it does not. There's nothing I'd like better than to have my father alive and my brother restored to his right mind.'

'Mr Bedevere, I can see you're disappointed.'

'I'd say disappointed is an understatement, Mr Marsbury. Let's be clear about this. I am mad as hell and, for the record, nobody takes what's mine, not an upstart American who has somehow weaseled her way into the family, nor my cousin.' Growing up, Henry had always been a snake in the grass as far as Ashe was concerned. He was *not* getting his hands on Bedevere. Henry would run through the estate within a year.

Apparently most of Marsbury's clients took bad news sitting down. Having no idea how to respond to the blunt remark, Marsbury cleared his throat again and glanced meaningfully at the documents. The man was positively tubercular. If he cleared his throat one more time, Ashe thought he just might leap across the desk anyway.

'Don't think I cannot see what my father has done.' Ashe fixed Marsbury with a hard stare. 'He is mandating marriage without saying the words. The man who weds Mrs Ralston will gain control of her shares upon marriage.'

'That is your construction,' Marsbury said firmly.

'And Henry's too, no doubt, once he arrives at it,' Ashe said coldly. Henry had never been quick. 'It will be a race now to see who can woo the lovely American to the altar.' He paused in contemplation. Every scrap and speck of human nature went back to motives, his father's nature notwithstanding. 'Can you tell me, Mr Marsbury, why my father would have wanted that?'

Marsbury cleared his damned throat. 'Bedevere needs an heiress, sir.'

Marsbury's announcement was the final *coup de grâce*. Ashe felt the quiet words like a blow to the stomach. Bedevere was debt ridden? How was that possible? His father had always been a strict and diligent steward of the funds. Sometimes too strict for a young man about town, but Bedevere's coffers had always been full.

'How bad is it?' He'd not anticipated this. But neither had he anticipated contesting Henry for his own inheritance.

Marsbury met his gaze, his tone matter of fact. 'The money is all gone. Your brother went and lost it a few years ago in some fool land investment that turned out to be a swindle.'

'The Forsyth scandal?' Ashe said with no small amount of disbelief. Three years ago, London had been rocked by the land swindle. It had dominated the newspapers. Shares of a Caribbean island had been sold to merchants and nobles looking to invest in New World property. The problem had been that the island did exist, but it had turned out to be swampy and infested with tropical disease. The shares were valid, but worth nothing. Ashe knew several people who'd lost money, but he'd never imagined his brother would be caught up in it. Alex had always been too intelligent, too reserved for rash behaviours.

Marsbury nodded in confirmation. 'That was the major one.'

Lucifer's stones, there'd been others? The sensation of guilt returned. If he'd come home when first asked, he might have caught his brother in time. Three years past would have put the incident right before Alex's breakdown. Perhaps his brother's faculties had been failing even then to have taken such an unprecedented risk.

'Are you sure there's nothing left?' Ashe put the question to Marsbury.

'I've looked over the books. Mr Bennington has looked over the books. No stone has been left unturned, or in this case, bled.'

Henry had looked over the books? Henry had known Bedevere's assets and worth right down to the last farthing and done nothing? Arguing Henry had known and done nothing made Ashe look like a hypocrite, even to himself. In the years of Bedevere's demise, he had done nothing either. Yet it seemed as though Henry's crime was the worse. He had been unaware, but Henry had *allowed* it to happen.

'Can I challenge this will?'

Marsbury sighed and shook his head. 'You can appeal the process, of course, but this was a special dispensation from the crown and there is legal precedent for it no matter how unusual the situation. I do think it will be a waste of your time and energies.'

'Energies better spent pursuing Mrs Ralston?' Ashe supplied with a dose of sarcasm.

'Yes, if you want to keep Bedevere.'

Ashe clenched and unclenched his fist at his side in an attempt to hold on to his temper. Again, there was the subtle implication that he did not have to assume Bedevere unless he chose to. He could leave it to Mrs Ralston and Henry. It would stay in the family and perhaps Mrs Ralston's American ingenuity would protect it against Henry's inherent stupidity.

Ashe sighed. It was time to talk about the American. 'What did Mrs Ralston do to earn my father's regard? Did she think to marry him at the last moment, but having failed to do that decided to influence the will with her apparent fortune?' His tone left no mistake as to what kind of 'influence' she might have wielded; the kind women had wielded against men since Eve.

Marsbury, who'd managed to stay cool throughout

the difficult interview, did look nonplussed at that comment. He was from the old school. One could talk about money baldly with other men, but one did not bandy about slanderous consideration regarding the fairer sex.

'Mr Bedevere, Mrs Ralston could buy Bedevere ten times over if she had a mind to.' Marsbury's voice was cold as he gathered his papers into a folder. 'Her "apparent" fortune is quite tangible, I assure you.'

'You have to understand this all comes as a shock to me.' Ashe held the man's gaze.

Marsbury took off his glasses and leaned back in his chair. 'Shock or not, it boils to one common denominator. You, Mr Bedevere, are in great need of an heiress and there's one practically living next door with a shipping line and a hundred thousand pounds to her name. I'd call that a pretty piece of serendipity if I were you.'

'That's where we differ, Marsbury.' Ashe fixed the solicitor with a hard stare. 'I'd call it suspicious.' This was starting to look a lot like a conspiracy: an estate that had been allowed to fail, coffers that had suddenly become prey to a string of bad investments, a recently altered will and a rich American living in Henry's pockets.

The next question was—at whose door step did he lay the blame? Mrs Ralston's? Henry's? Were they both in it together? Maybe he was too cynical. Maybe the conspiracy was his father's—one last attempt to order his wayward son's life to specification. His father had thrown down the gauntlet even on his deathbed. Marriage to a woman of his father's choosing was to be the price for Bedevere, for his wildness, for ever having left. Ultimately, whose conspiracy this was didn't matter. The only thing that did matter was what he was going to do about it. Would he sell himself in a marriage of convenience to save Bedevere?

Chapter Three

The aunts were all in it together. Genevra had seen their conspiracy for what it was: matchmaking. She would do almost anything for the old dears, but she couldn't do that. The last thing she was looking for was male attention even if it came with a set of broad shoulders and mossy-green eyes.

Genevra smoothed the skirts of her evening gown one last time before she entered the drawing room. The gunmetal-silk gown was one of her favourites and she'd need all the confidence it afforded if she was going to withstand the probing gaze of Mr Bedevere and the romantic hearts of the old aunts.

Dinner would be a polite battle on two fronts, even if there wasn't the issue of the estate between them. The announcement this afternoon had been most unexpected. Not once had the old earl offered any indication of his thoughts. He'd been intrigued by the American management practices she'd shared with him and she'd known he held her in high esteem. But to leave her the majority share in the estate had not occurred to her.

She appreciated the honour the old man had done her and she would do her best for him. He had been a father to her when she had no one. But taking on the estate also meant taking on other complications, not the least of which waited for her on the other side of the drawing-room door. Mr Bedevere would not be happy or complacent about the current arrangements.

Genevra stepped into the room and her eyes fixed on the man standing at the fireplace mantel. Surely the old earl had not been blind to the implications created by giving her fifty-one per cent. He'd all but set her up to be a target for his errant son should the son decide he wanted the estate. She liked to think she was sighting her enemy straight away, but she would have noticed him regardless. How could she not? He stood there surveying the room, surveying *her*, like a king from his throne. Washing away the road dust had done nothing to diminish his aura of power. It was the hands she noticed first. Long, elegant fingers negligently wrapped about a preprandial drink in a way that conjured up the most decadent of thoughts. She couldn't help but wonder what else he could do with those hands.

Quite a lot if his eyes told the wicked truth. She'd stared too long and he'd caught her. Genevra blushed. A slow smile on his lips said he was making her accountable for it. She looked away from his face with its straight Grecian nose to avoid the forthright heat of his gaze only to find her eyes travelling down the length of his well-apportioned body. Good lord, she couldn't look him in the eye, and no self-respecting lady should look at him *there* where her efforts had landed. She'd try his face again—that was where *normal* people looked at each other, after all.

Then he spoke without a hint of animosity, his tone more reminiscent of bedrooms than drawing rooms. 'Mrs Ralston, allow me to properly welcome you to Bedevere. There wasn't time earlier.' He might as well have said, 'Mrs Ralston, allow me to properly welcome you to sin.' How many women had he led astray already with that voice? She'd never encountered such a blatant sexuality before. Yet she knew precisely what it was; it was dangerous and it drew her as thoroughly as a magnet draws iron filings.

Years of hostessing for her father and then for Philip saved her from an utter loss of words. 'I am pleased to make your acquaintance at last, Mr Bedevere. Your aunts have spoken of you often.'

Genevra managed a curtsy, determined to do her best for the aunts. Tonight was to be a party. The ladies were dressed in their best silk dinner gowns that had seen more fashionable days, but their spirits were high. The aunts, herself, Henry—all of them deserved a slightly festive occasion. Henry! Genevra's mind tripped back over its thoughts.

She'd been so distracted by the handsome newcomer she hadn't realised Henry was missing. 'Will Mr Bennington be joining us tonight?' Genevra's eyes swept the room guiltily in case she'd simply overlooked him. Not that anyone would overlook Henry with his good looks and guinea-gold hair.

'No, dear, Henry had an appointment to dine with the Brownes at the vicarage,' Leticia offered.

Genevra furrowed her brow, trying to recall the appointment. 'Mr Bennington didn't say anything yesterday about it when we went out walking.' Nor had Vicar Browne when they'd stopped by to deliver some items for the sewing circle.

Leticia waved a hand in airy dismissal. 'He said it came up rather suddenly this afternoon. But our Ashe is here now.' There was no chance to say more. Gardener announced dinner and there was a potent moment when Genevra thought the dark god at the fireplace was going to offer her his arm to go into supper. Instead, he turned to Leticia. 'Shall we, Aunt?'

The regal Leticia giggled for a moment like a young girl. 'It's been an age since anyone's taken me into supper, young scamp.' She took his arm and said with a wink, 'You have two arms, don't you, my boy?'

'Mrs Ralston, would you do me the pleasure?' He was all polished English manners in his dark evening clothes, but the eyes that held hers weren't mannerly in the least. Those eyes seemed to be studying her from the inside out, a decidedly uncomfortable predicament that left her feeling as if she was standing there naked.

The Bedevere dining room was turned out in its best; the long dining table was set with the Bedevere china and crystal and a vase of hothouse flowers graced the centre, courtesy of Lavinia's greenhouse efforts.

In the friendly light of candles, one could forget the worn surroundings. There was a whisper of Bedevere's past glory here, of what it must have looked like in more prosperous, happy times, Genevra thought. Mr Bedevere seated them all, giving her the spot on his left and Leticia the seat on his right. At least the devil had manners aplenty, she'd give him that. But manners and good looks made her wary. Philip had had just such a way about him and, in the end, he'd not been so very fine.

'Are you enjoying Seaton Hall, Mrs Ralston?' Mr Bedevere enquired politely after a creamy bisque had been set down in front of them.

Genevra smiled. Seaton Hall was one of her favourite topics. 'Very much. There's been quite a bit of work to do on the gardens, but I hope to have them finished in time for summer.' The gardens were the first stage in a much larger plan she had to turn Seaton Hall into a tourist business. If Mr Bedevere was willing, she could do the same here and help the estate generate funds. He really shouldn't object. The estate was in need and his ten-year absence made it plain that he didn't live here. The experiment would hardly inconvenience him.

Bedevere cocked a dark eyebrow her direction. 'Won't you be going up to London for the Season in a month or so? I would have thought the entertainments of the city would be vastly more appealing, especially after a long winter in the country.'

There was no question of being in London. There was too much work to be done here. It was an excuse she'd long relied on and in time it had become the truth. Besides, the only reason to be in London was to catch a husband. In London, she would attract too much attention and someone was bound to dig up the old scandal. Genevra shrugged and said with a great show of nonchalance, 'London holds little allure for me, Mr Bedevere.' London could keep its prowling bachelors. Her brief marriage had not recommended the institution worth repeating.

He held her gaze over the rim of his wine glass for a second longer than was decent, long enough to cause a note of silence. When he spoke, his words were deliberate and commanded everyone's attention. 'Why is that, Mrs Ralston? London is generally held to be one of the finest cities in the world. For myself, I've lived there for several years and have yet to grow bored with it.'

Genevra had the vague feeling she was being quizzed, tested. There would be more questions she'd rather not answer if she didn't take the offensive now. She shot him a quick smile, 'Well, that's just it, isn't it? We can't all live in London. Someone has to hold things together in the country.'

There was the slightest movement of his dark brows in acknowledgement of her sweetly delivered barb. '*Touché*, Mrs Ralston,' he murmured for her ears alone, leaving Genevra to wonder if her subtle attack had done her more harm than good.

Genevra turned her attentions to the aunts. It was far easier talking to them than it was their nephew, but that didn't mean she wasn't aware of Mr Bedevere's eyes on her, seeking answers as if he intuitively knew the answers she'd supplied were blithe smokescreens for the truth. It was impossible. He'd only just met her.

He couldn't possibly guess she was here because this was her refuge, because the rural backwaters of Staffordshire was one place where scandal couldn't find her.

The rural backwaters of Staffordshire were full of surprises these days, not the least of them the elegant young woman on his left with her piles of dark hair and exquisite figure shown deliciously in a gown of gunmetal silk.

Ashe decided by the fish course that Mrs Ralston would have been a pleasant delight under other circumstances. Watching her converse with his aunts about their watercolours and embroidery had pleased him.

By the time pheasant was served, however, all that pleasantness had begun to work against her. Her answers about her presence here had been vague earlier and far too non-committal for his tastes combined with the fact that she was almost too good to be true.

Ashe watched her with stealthy objectivity as she cut into her pheasant; here she was, beautiful, rich, apparently disposed to a genteel temperament that pleased his aunts, and living practically next door *precisely* when he needed an heiress to save Bedevere.

His father's intentions couldn't be more blatant. The only thing more transparent was his aunts' matchmaking efforts. If the efforts hadn't been aimed at him, he would have found them humorous. The old dears weren't even trying to be discreet as they flaunted Mrs Ralston's charms shamelessly course after course. But always Ashe's thoughts came back to the one idea: when things were too good to be true, they probably were.

All through dinner, he'd looked for a defect: a nasty table manner, a poor conversation ability, an annoying habit. He was disappointed to note that, in spite of her American upbringing, she used the correct fork, carried on flawless conversation without the slightest stutter and hadn't a single bad habit visible to his critical eye.

It all begged the question: what was an attractive heiress doing *here* of all places? In his experience, such a paragon of marriageable womanhood should be in London, American or not. There was no reason for her to be in the country. That in itself was a point of intrigue. Why would she be here when she didn't have to be?

There were really only two answers that came to mind: she was hiding, which carried all sorts of unsavoury implications, or the likelihood that she was fortune hunting—title-hunting, to be exact. That was the only fortune Bedevere had to offer these days and she had to be well aware of it.

Beside him, the mysterious Mrs Ralston laughed, a wonderful throaty sound with a hint of smoke, a laugh made for evenings and candlelight. She shook her head at something Melisande had said and the candles caught the discreet diamonds in her ears. *Expensive* diamonds. It had been a long time since he'd been able to afford to give a woman such a gift. They sparkled enticingly, lending her an air of sophistication.

It was all too easy to see how his father might have

been fooled by her. It was also all too easy to see what she might have been after with her diamonds and elegance; perhaps she'd thought to marry his father before he passed away, no matter what Marsbury thought. That strategy having failed, she'd now opted to stay on and wait to snare the title eventually through the sane second son. It wouldn't be the first time someone had traded themselves for a title. One didn't have to be a sick man to find Mrs Ralston's charms appealing. His own growing fascination with their dinner guest was proof enough of that.

Ashe drained the rest of his wine and set his glass aside. Wedding and bedding aside, it was time to uncover her secrets before things went any further, a task Ashe thought he'd might enjoy just as much as uncovering her.

'Mrs Ralston, perhaps you'd do me the pleasure of a stroll in the conservatory. I seem to recall it used to be lovely by moonlight.' No time like the present to start with that uncovering.

His suggestion was met with great enthusiasm from his aunts and he had a sudden vision of all of them traipsing through the conservatory, a scenario hardly conducive to seducing one's secrets.

'Genni has made so many improvements to the conservatory,' Lavinia put in. 'She saved the roses last summer when they came down with aphids. She mixed up a special spray.'

'Well then, Mrs Ralston, I don't see how you can refuse. Shall we?' Ashe rose and offered her his arm.

Walking brought her close to him, her skirts rustling against his trouser leg with the sway of her motion. She smelled of lemongrass and cassia as she walked beside him. It was a telling scent, not the standard lavender or rosewater worn by so many of London's débutantes. The sharp spicy edge of lemongrass was not an innocent's perfume. It was a woman's perfume: a smart, confident woman's.

At the entrance to the conservatory, he moved his hand to the small of her back and ushered her ahead of him. He left his hand there, comfortably splayed. Touch invited confidences and he wanted hers very much.

His intuition hadn't been wrong. The conservatory *was* beautiful. Moonlight streamed through the glass roof and the scent of orange trees lingered enticingly. A small fountain trickled in the background.

'This is my favourite place at Bedevere.' Mrs Ralston tried to walk ahead of him, a step too fast for his hand to remain at her back. Ashe closed the gap with a long stride, his hand remaining unshakeable at her back. He was making her nervous. Good.

'I can see why, Mrs Ralston, it's very lovely.'

Chapter Four

He was most definitely making her nervous. Not even an innocent débutante would believe he was talking about the conservatory with a remark like that. Especially not after the way he'd studied her with his eyes all through dinner, stalking her without moving from the table or after the way his hand had loitered so deliberately at her back. What was worse, his attentions had aroused her. She was honest enough to admit it, to herself at least.

'This place holds the heat in winter. The glass makes it possible to trap the heat from the sun.' She was rambling out of some desperate need to minimise the tension that had sprung between them. 'Your father liked to come here when he was well enough. Henry and I would bring him and spend the afternoons reading.'

She stopped suddenly and faced him, realising she hadn't offered any condolences. It had seemed the wrong thing to do amid the gay atmosphere of the aunts' dinner party. 'I am sorry for your loss. Your father was a good man, a brave man.'

'Was he?' Mr Bedevere's green eyes narrowed in dangerous disagreement. 'Pardon me, Mrs Ralston, I don't need a stranger to tell me about my father.'

A person of less fortitude might have flinched under the cold words. She squared her shoulders and met his gaze unswervingly. 'Forgive me, I thought perhaps it would ease your grief to know he died well.'

'Why? Because I wasn't here?'

There it was, the crime she'd charged him with at the dinner table—absent Ashe Bedevere who couldn't be bothered to come home. It seemed wrong that she, a mere stranger of a neighbour, had seen more of the earl in his last days than his own son had.

'Surely you knew how grave his situation had become.'

'Is the pun intended, Mrs Ralston?' There was a terse set to his finely carved jaw and a hardness to his gaze that matched his rigid posture.

Genevra bristled. Handsome or not, it was ill mannered of him to think she'd engage in witty word play in the midst of a delicate conversation. 'No. The pun is not intended. Was your absence? Intended, that is.'

His eyes glittered dangerously, his tone forebodingly quiet. 'I must inform you, Mrs Ralston, I find this an unsuitable topic of conversation between two people who have barely met.'

Genevra tilted her chin upwards a mere fraction, letting her cold tone convey just the opposite. 'My apologies for any untoward assumptions.'

His eyes were studying her again, the hardness

gone now, replaced by something else more feral. 'You shouldn't say things you don't mean, Mrs Ralston.' The faintest hint of a wicked smile played on his lips. The dratted man was calling her out, fully aware she hadn't really apologised.

'And you, sir, should know better than to scold a lady.' Genevra opted for the high road.

'Why is that?' He stepped closer to her, the clean manly scent of him swamping her senses, his nearness hinting of the muscled physique beneath the clothes. He was all man and there was no place for her to go. She'd backed herself against a stone bench. This was nothing like being with Henry. Henry was the consummate companion, comfortable, never imposing. There were no prickles of awareness like the ones goose pimpling her skin right now.

'Because you are a gentleman.' At least he was dressed like one. Up close, she could appreciate his impeccably brushed jacket stretched elegantly across an impressive breadth of shoulder and the rich cabernet hue of his waistcoat. But other than the clothes, she had her doubts.

'Are you sure?' His voice was low and she was acutely aware of the long curling strand of hair he'd wrapped around one finger. He gave her a sensual half-smile, his eyes roving her face, flicking down ever so briefly to her throat and perhaps slightly lower. His attentions were perilously arousing.

'No,' her voice came out in a hoarse tremor. She wasn't sure of anything in that moment, least of all how they'd arrived at this point. They'd been talking of his father. But the conversation had wandered afield from the comforting solace she'd intended to something else far more seductive and personal.

'Good, because I can think of better things to do by moonlight than quarrel, can't you?'

His next move startled her entirely. Before she could think, his hand was at the nape of her neck, warm and caressing, drawing her to him until his mouth covered hers in a full kiss that sent a jolt of heat to her stomach.

The kiss was all hot challenge and she answered it without provocation. The arrogant man was far too sure of himself. He needed to know he wasn't completely in charge. His tongue sought hers and the kiss became a heady duel. He tasted of rich red wine against her lips. His hands were warm against the fabric of her gown, massaging, pressing her to him, making her aware of the hard lines of him and the most sinful invitation his body issued. She arched her neck, letting his kiss travel the length of her throat. This was not the hesitant kiss of a moonstruck dandy. This was the kiss of man proficient in the art. The kiss promised fulfilment. If she took the invitation, she would not be disappointed.

Her arms were about his neck and she breathed deeply of him. If temptation had a scent it would be this: the understated mixture of sandalwood and vanilla combined with the clean smell of freshly laundered clothing. Genevra nipped at his ear, eliciting an entirely male growl of appreciation. She was not the only one intoxicated by the duel.

Without warning, Ashe stepped back, releasing her, his eyes a smoky green. It was his eyes that held her attention. They were surrounded by long soft black lashes, but the green orbs were hard and assessing when he looked at her. They were not the eyes of a man in the throes of desire, although his body argued that to the contrary.

'I don't know what you're doing here, Mrs Ralston, but I will find out.'

'What makes you think I'm doing "anything"?'

'A woman doesn't kiss like that unless she wants something. Badly.'

It took a moment to comprehend, so unexpected was the comment. 'If I were a gentleman, I would call you out for that.' Genevra fairly shook with rage. She'd never been so insulted. If he wasn't careful, she'd call him out anyway.

'We've already established there are no gentlemen here at present,' he drawled. 'And you, Mrs Ralston, are no lady.'

Genevra stiffened, her temper rising. If she couldn't call him out, there was one thing she could do. She slapped him right across the face.

In the retrospection of a sleepless night, Genevra understood she'd slapped him as much for her behaviour as for his. She *should* have been indifferent to that kiss. Instead, she'd been so flustered that she'd ordered her carriage and set out for home, finished renovations or not. She'd not spend a night under Ashe Bedevere's roof.

She had still been berating herself as she tossed and turned through a sleepless night until she'd finally given up and risen at dawn, her mind more than eager to ponder her behaviour while she watched the sunrise from her window.

There were several reasons she could offer as to why she'd given in. First, there was the element of surprise. She hadn't been expecting such an audacious move on his part. Second, she was lonely. Except for the company of Ashe's aunts and Henry, this part of Staffordshire wasn't exactly a hotbed of society.

These were good excuses for her momentary lapse, but none of them could disguise the reality. She'd let her independent streak get the better of her. He'd baited her and she'd taken the lure, unable to resist the challenge. He'd been testing her again as he had at the table, but it hadn't been the test she'd expected. She'd thought he'd been testing her mettle. It hadn't been until afterwards when he'd spoken those insulting words that she'd realised he'd still been probing for answers as to why she was here in this place of all places and why his father would give her controlling interest in the estate. Answering his challenge as she'd done had not been the best way to allay his concerns.

She hoped the slap had conveyed her intentions as readily as his hot gaze had conveyed his. He was a seducer of the first water, used to getting what he wanted. But in this case, he would not succeed in seducing her fifty-one per cent out of her. His game was far too obvious, even if his kisses had been nothing short of dazzling. Never had anything roused her so thoroughly or so immediately. The stirrings of such emotions was a risky pot. Kisses could cloud a woman's mind, make her forget certain realities. She'd learned her lesson with Philip. He'd only wanted her for her father's money. Bedevere only wanted her share of the regency.

Genevra rose from her chair and prepared to dress. Debating herself over Mr Bedevere's kiss was accomplishing nothing. What she needed was activity to purge last night's memories. Time in the garden overseeing the new landscaping would be just the thing to distract her.

Chapter Five

Henry heartily wished for a distraction—a bird hitting the glass panes of his benefactor's prized French doors, a servant spilling hot coffee on someone's lap. Really, anything would do as long as it took the gentlemen's eyes off him. Breakfast wasn't his favourite time of day, especially when he had bad news to report. All eyes at the well-set table fixed on him. The meal had long been finished. It was time to discuss the business for which their host, a Mr Marcus Trent, had invited them all.

'Well, Bennington, we've had our kippers and ham. Tell us how the will went yesterday. Are you in full possession of the trust?' Trent was a florid figure of a man with blunt manners honed in a merchant's world. His sense of competition and honour had been honed in a different world—however, a darker, more dangerous world where one took what one wanted at the point of a knife if need be. For all the wealth and fine trappings surrounding Trent, he was no gentleman. Henry had noted at the beginning of their association not to run afoul of Trent's good humour. He very much feared he was about to do so.

'There is good news,' Henry began cheerfully. 'My uncle did indeed set up a trusteeship for the running of the estate, as I told you he would.' They needed to remember he had been right about some things. If it weren't for him, they wouldn't even have this opportunity to begin with.

Trent's eyes narrowed dangerously. 'Who is the trustee, Bennington?'

Henry looked at the four other men assembled, sensing their growing worry and, with it, their growing distrust of him. Of them all, he was the outsider. These five men had done business together before. 'Three of us were named trustees: my cousin, Ashe, myself and the American, Mrs Ralston. We've all been given a share of influence when it comes how the estate is to be managed.'

'What precisely is your share?' Mr Ellingson, the group's accountant, spoke up from the far end of the table.

'Four per cent,' Henry offered with feigned pride. He'd been livid over the slight all night. How dare his uncle reward him with so little after a year of his devotion. But Henry would be damned if he'd let this group of cut-throat investors see that disappointment. He went on to spell out the details of the other portions given to Ashe and Genevra while Ellingson stared at him thoughtfully, doing sums in his head.

'This is not what we agreed upon,' Trent put in after

Henry had finished. 'You said Bedevere wouldn't come home, that he'd want to sell his shares, that he'd be lucky to receive any shares at all when you got through kowtowing to your uncle.' The others murmured amongst themselves up and down the length of the table. Henry fought the urge to squirm. He'd been wrong about Ashe and therein lay the crux of his troubles. He'd wagered Ashe wouldn't come home.

Ellingson spoke up. 'There's only one thing for it. Bennington needs to wed the Ralston widow. Marriage will secure him the majority interest in the estate. Her control will pass to him upon marriage and give him fifty-four per cent.'

Trent nodded with approval. 'The Ralston chit is perfect.'

Henry's blood chilled a degree at the potential direction this conversation was heading. They were going to mandate marriage, *his* marriage, as if it were of no major import. 'There's always a possibility she'll refuse me.' Henry hedged.

The table roared with congenial laughter. 'You're too handsome to be refused, Bennington.' The man next to him clapped him on the back and Trent tossed a bag of coins on the table. 'Buy her a pretty bauble and be done with it, Bennington. We're an "I do" away from untold wealth. It would be a shame to falter here at the last.' Trent surveyed the group. 'Let's meet again in a week and see how our young Romeo is progressing.'

Henry smiled and pocketed the bag of coins, but he didn't miss the implication of Trent's dismissal. He had one week to secure the promise of matrimony to a woman he'd not choose to marry of his own volition. Since yesterday, his prospects had been steadily going downhill.

Henry took the long road home, giving plans a chance to settle in his head. He would change clothes, then he would call on Genevra. The thought of pursuing her left a sour taste in his mouth. He had cultivated her friendship of course during the earl's illness because it pleased the earl. The old man had doted on the pretty American. But Henry had seen right away how outspoken she was, how she would be the most non-compliant of wives. She would never give him full control of her money, even if she did happen to fall in love with him. He'd have to beg every shilling from her. It would be like asking his father for an allowance all over again. But it would be worth it, he reminded himself. There was much to be gained.

On his suspicions, a bore hole dug four years ago on the outskirts of Bedevere land had produced a promising sampling of lignite, indicating a rich deposit of coal beneath the land. It stood to be the most plentiful coalfield in Audley, a piece of Staffordshire known not only for its hops and gardens, but for its coalfields as well. The possibility of attaining such wealth demanded extraordinary effort and the men he'd partnered with weren't afraid to go to extremes. But so far, the extremes were all his. Aside from the money Trent's cartel had put up, the risks had all been his. They hadn't spent a year currying favour with the old earl, nor were they now facing a forced marriage.

He had to keep his eye on the goal. He would go courting today and keep in mind the purgatory of those consequences would last only a short while.

It had been a hell of a day and it was only two o'clock. Ashe pushed a hand through his hair, not caring that the action caused his hair to stand on ruffled ends and leaned back in the leather chair. At least here in the study he had the privacy he needed to think. There was so much to think about, it was hard to know where to start.

He'd spent the morning going over the estate books, trying to get a sense of where to start first, assuming he'd come up with some funds. Did he start outside with the gardens or inside with the most-used rooms? Maybe he didn't start with the house at all. Maybe he should start with the tenant farmers in ways that would generate income.

Ashe sank his head into his hands. He didn't know the first thing about managing an estate and there was no one to ask, unless one counted Henry. It would be a cold day in hell before he took that option. Ashe shut the leatherbound ledger. The numbers in the columns didn't add up and there were bills to pay. Surely the horses listed as sold last autumn hadn't gone for so little. The value posted in the ledger was half their worth. His father had kept prime cattle and knew their value.

Ashe pushed back from the desk. The morning

hadn't been an entire waste. He'd done what he could with regard to bills, which had amounted to writing assurances to those who held Bedevere's outstanding accounts telling them all would soon be remedied. He wasn't sure *how* he would see it remedied, but they didn't need to know that.

He'd also sent off letters to London. One was a private message to his closest friend, Jamie Burke, asking him to look into Genevra Ralston's background on the off chance that someone had heard of the American. That much money surely wouldn't go undetected by society no matter what its nationality. If he was required to marry her, he wanted to know who she was and if there was any detrimental scandal attached to her name. It wouldn't have been hard to hide such a thing from his father, but Mrs Ralston would find he was a bit more worldly than his father.

The second was about money as well. He'd enquired about the potential of a loan, as futile as such an enquiry seemed. Ashe was under no illusions. If he could not prove he was the predominant regent, no bank would advance him any funds.

Why does it matter? ventured the devil on his shoulder. *If you don't get the estate, why do you care if it goes to rack and ruin? If Henry wants it, let Henry figure out a way. If Mrs Ralston wants it, let her buy your shares and be done with it.*

Because it's the right thing to do, regardless, answered the angel on the other.

Because it's my home, Ashe thought. Because he'd

spent his life proving his father wrong. He wanted to prove his father was wrong here, too. His father and he had had their differences. Those differences had driven him away years ago, but he could not believe his father hated him that much, believed in him that little, to wrest Bedevere from him. Then again, his father had not planned on losing Alex. There'd never been a need for his father to consider leaving Bedevere to him. If only he could talk to his father one more time, try to explain why he'd had to go.

The devil on his shoulder wasn't satisfied. *If you want to save Bedevere stop brooding over books you can't make sense of and start wooing that pretty heiress at Seaton Hall. You need money and she's got 'piles' of it.*

Genevra Ralston.

All his thoughts seemed to come back to her. In and of herself, she was enough to keep a man busy with all her mysteries. Woman in hiding or brazen fortune hunter, it hardly mattered which. Both spelled trouble. It was a matter of how much trouble he was willing to tolerate along with her money. And trouble was a surety. Last night had established that without equivocation.

He'd not dreamed she'd respond so ardently to his advances. He'd meant to warn her that she played with a man who was out of her league. He knew women and he knew their games. Just because he loved women didn't mean he trusted them. They were as brutal as men when it came to getting their way.

His head ached. The estate wasn't the only thing that

needed sorting out. There were emotions he hadn't expected to feel, and answers he desperately wanted. What had really transpired at Bedevere in his absence? What had really happened to his brother? He would have to find time to see Alex soon, although the prospect was one he dreaded.

A knock interrupted his thoughts and Melisande poked her head around the door. 'There you are, Ashton.' Only his aunties called him that. Not 'Ashe' like the ladies in London, who claimed he could burn them to cinders with one smouldering look of his green eyes.

'You've been cooped up in here for hours.' She clucked disapprovingly. 'You should go for a ride. You never know when the weather will take a turn for a worse this time of year.' She settled herself in a chair across from him at the desk. The chair was large and gave the impression of swallowing up his petite aunt. Old age had made her appear even smaller than he remembered, but no less sharp. She eyed the ledgers.

'Are you making sense of it all?' There was hope in the question. She wanted to hear that all would be well, that things would be better. She wanted to hear he'd found a hidden cache of money or a mistake in the ledger that suddenly rendered them wealthy again. He didn't fault her for it. It was what he'd hoped, too, when he'd sat down with the books that morning, still in disbelief that the Bedevere largesse could all be gone.

Ashe offered her a warm smile. 'There were no miracles in the ledgers. But we'll make our own miracles, I promise.' He would find a way to keep this promise, never mind the string of broken, half-kept promises that littered his past. He had a lot to make up for. He was only just beginning to understand he wasn't the only one who'd borne the consequences of his choices.

'Genni will be our miracle, Ashton,' Melisande said with a straightforward confidence that bore none of Ashe's own cynicism on the subject.

Ashe didn't wish to argue with his aunt, neither did he know how much they knew regarding the will. Was this a comment she made because of their less-than-subtle matchmaking efforts, or because she knew 'Genni's' business acumen would save the estate? Ashe merely shrugged.

The non-committal shrug wasn't enough for his aunt. Melisande leaned forwards and said with force, 'Genni. We all like her and your father thought highly of her. She's the one we want.' He'd never heard his delicate flower of an aunt sound so demanding. At least the outburst had confirmed her motives. She was strictly about matchmaking. She didn't know about his father's arrangement, only her own.

'She might not want me,' Ashe ventured.

'She will. You can be irresistible when you choose, Ashton.' That shamed him. Aunt Melisande meant it with all the goodness of her heart, remembering the pretty child and the handsome youth. She had no idea how 'irresistible' the man had become or how he'd bartered those charms for a price.

Melisande pushed a soft package in brown wrapping paper across the desk at him. 'Since you're going for a ride, I thought you could take this to Seaton Hall. It can be your reason to visit and then you can apologise.'

'Apologise for what, Aunt?' Ashe drawled obtusely.

'For whatever you did to her last night. She's too much of a lady to say anything, but she left so quickly we knew something had happened. I hadn't even had time to give this to her.' A scolding and guilt all rolled into one.

Melisande patted his hand. 'A good apology is never wasted on a woman's heart, Ashton. Your great-uncle could always turn my head with one. Women are capable of great forgiveness if men ask for it.'

'And if we don't?' Ashe teased, taking the package.

Melisande winked. 'Then we're capable of a great many other things.' She rose and made to leave. 'I'll tell the groom you'll want your horse brought around in twenty minutes.'

She shut the door behind her and Ashe let out a laugh. He'd been thoroughly manoeuvred by his seventy-three-year-old aunt. So much for delicate and fragile.

Twenty minutes later, Ashe swung up on Rex. Seaton Hall wouldn't have been his destination of choice after last night. But, Ashe thought with a touch of mischief, it would be rather interesting to see how the stunning Mrs Ralston would follow up last night's slap.

He spurred Rex into a canter and gave the big horse his head through the meadows. He took a jump over a stone fence and revelled at the wind in his face. He took another and let loose a cry of pure enjoyment. There weren't fences like this in London. Anyone could ride in London as long as they could walk a horse through Hyde Park, but this kind of riding across open fields took an accomplished rider.

Ashe came to the road leading to Seaton Hall and reined Rex to a walk. No one in London thought of him as a country gentleman. It had been a long time since *he'd* thought of himself that way, but, buried and ignored, that was the stifled truth. Behind the fancy clothes and elegant manners, he was a product of the quiet rural lands of Staffordshire. Like himself, Staffordshire often struck him as a place of contradictions. The land was riddled with mining and industry, yet a large part of the land had also maintained its rural nature with fields for farming, and its proclivity for beautiful gardens; a proclivity Bedevere had apparently let slide in the last few years, but one that Seaton Hall had embraced with success from the look of things. Roles had been reversed. Under Genevra Ralston's money and careful eye, Seaton Hall had emerged as the belle of the county while the once-elegant Bedevere strangled in weeds.

Ashe turned up the drive, noting with an appreciative eye the trimmed grass of the parkland, the organised flower beds showing early shoots of spring flowers poking through the soil. In a few months, those beds would be vivid with colours. Bedevere had looked like that once. Jealousy stabbed. He wanted Bedevere to look like that again. But that was foolishness, at least this year. One did not waste efforts on pretty gardens when there were bills to pay and mouths to feed. Perhaps if he could get a loan. Right now, everything hinged on money, even his own potential marriage. On his own, with no funds to speak of, what he could do was extremely limited. Once married to Mrs Ralston, an infinity of possibilities lay open to him—one more reason to sell himself in this marriage of his father's choosing.

Ashe sighed. The reasons for marriage were mounting. His desire for freedom, to make his own choice when the time came were starting to look petty and stubborn next to the gains the marriage would give him.

At the door he was told Mrs Ralston was in the back gardens and was shown to a brightly done sitting room at the front of the house where he could wait. If the room was indicative of Seaton Hall's recent fortunes, the American was doing very well for herself indeed. The creamy-yellow paint was fresh, the white-plaster moldings newly painted. Dusky-blue curtains framed the long windows overlooking the front drive. The pillows on the blue-and-yellow sofa were invitingly plump. Best of all, there was a pianoforte along the wall.

Ashe ran his hands along the keys experimentally, noting the full, mellow tones. It must be new if it had the Babcock strings. Curiosity piqued, Ashe gently lifted the lid of the case and peered inside, the old excitement rising. Ah, yes, the soundboard was cross-strung. He couldn't resist.

Ashe sat down and began to play. It felt good, it felt *liberating*. There was no one to judge, no one to impress. This was just for him.

Chapter Six

Bedevere was *here*. The very thought brought a flutter to her usually stable stomach. What did one say to a man one had previously slapped? 'I'm sorry?' 'I hope your cheek isn't terribly sore today?' Obviously the slap had not achieved the desired effect. He'd come to Seaton Hall, clearly undeterred. And here she was, gardening in an old gown in a desperate attempt to forget last night had ever happened.

If she was going to face Ashe Bedevere, she had to look decent. Genevra slid one of her favourite afternoon gowns over her head, a green-and-white sprigged-muslin affair that made her feel pretty and confident. She gave her hair a quick brushing to get rid of any garden debris she might have acquired. It wouldn't do to give that green-eyed rogue a reason to touch her hair again, even if it was under the auspices of picking out a leaf.

Genevra was still trying out possible greetings on the stairs when she heard the music. It was lovely. Perhaps a lieder? It was far beyond anything she could produce. No one had mentioned Mr Bedevere had brought a guest.

At the doorway, Genevra halted in surprise. There was no guest. The musician was Bedevere himself. His back was to her and she took advantage of it, reacquainting herself with the broad shoulders and wavy black hair that skimmed decadently over his collar, too long and too full for fashion's dictates, but just right for him.

The piece ended and Genevra clapped. He started at the intrusion and turned on the bench. 'Please, continue.' Genevra took up a seat on the sofa, relieved that the music had offered a neutral entrée into their meeting. She could smoothly avoid any awkwardness over last night now.

'I am afraid the piano doesn't get much use, but I thought I should have one anyway for musical evenings. Although I must confess, we haven't had one yet for all our good intentions.'

He shook his head. 'I've played enough. It's a fine instrument. It's new, I can tell from the strings. Do you play, Mrs Ralston?'

'Only moderately,' Genevra confessed. 'But I am glad the instrument is a good one.'

'Come here, and I'll show you how good it is.' Bedevere moved to the side, gesturing for her to join him. She crossed the room, unable to refuse the irresistible excitement that hummed about him as he peered into the case. He smelled of wind and vanilla, an entirely intoxicating combination when associated with a man.

'These strings are Babcock's. He patented them a few years back. They're thicker than the old strings, allowing for increased volume.' Bedevere plucked a string inside the case for demonstration. 'And now piano makers are cross-stringing the soundboards to create more resonance.'

With hands like that, she should have guessed. 'You're very accomplished, Mr Bedevere. I didn't know.'

'Please, call me Ashe if you don't mind.'

Genevra recognised the dangerously quiet tones from last night. 'Of course.' She decided not to enquire. She didn't want to spoil this pleasant truce after last night's unpleasantness. 'Will you stay for tea?' She didn't wait for an answer. She went straight to the bell pull. This was England. Everyone stayed for tea.

'I must apologise for dropping by unexpectedly, but I have something for you.' Ashe took a seat and handed her a soft package.

A gift from him? An apology, perhaps, for his prior conduct? Certainly a gentleman would make the effort. A little flutter took up residence in her stomach as she played with the string. In the daylight, he seemed so civilised.

'Melisande asked me to bring it.'

'Of course.' The flutter disappeared. Naturally it wasn't from him. He was no gentleman and slapped men didn't bring gifts. Genevra smiled to cover her mental error.

'It must be Melisande's latest embroidery pattern.'

Genevra held up the cloth. 'Tell her it's lovely. It will do well at the markets this spring.'

'I beg your pardon?' This time he was the one caught off guard and it did things to his face. His dark brows winged upwards, his eyes narrowed in speculation.

'Didn't they tell you?' Genevra folded the cloth up. 'She and your other aunts sell their handiwork at the local markets. Cook even sends some jams. They did quite well last summer.'

'My aunts *sell* crafts at the market?' The look on Ashe's face was incredulous bordering on furious. 'Like *merchants*?'

Genevra replied evenly, 'Yes, like merchants. Like most of the normal world, in fact. Not all of us live in such rarefied circumstances as a British gentleman, dashing around London looking for entertainment.'

A tight tic began to pulse low on Ashe's jaw. Whatever tenuous truce they'd had over the music had evaporated. 'Whose idea was this?' he ground out, thankfully choosing to overlook the other insinuations she'd so carelessly made.

'It was mine,' Genevra said, grateful for the arrival of the tea tray to derail this line of conversation.

But Ashe wasn't ready to let it go like a self-respecting gentleman. 'Why ever would you suggest something like that?' His disbelief was tangible as he took a tea cup from her. She took care to make sure their fingers didn't touch.

'They had no money and you were nowhere to be found.' Genevra allowed her temper to spill over. 'They had to do something and it was a very good something. They were too proud to take so much as a farthing from me. If you must know, people like to buy things that represent the peerage. It's a good advertising angle. It's far more exciting to buy a handkerchief embroidered by a real lady.'

Ashe's dark eyebrows rose. 'And a good deal more expensive too, I hope? Still, they'd have to sell quite a lot of handkerchiefs and jam to support Bedevere.'

Genevra frowned. He was missing an essential component to the effort. 'It's not just about the money. We're expanding to Bury St Edmunds this summer and the aunts are excited.'

'No, *we* are not. I'm home now—those kind of measures won't be necessary,' Ashe said firmly.

Genevra set down her tea cup and fixed him with a stare. She hadn't meant to argue again. She'd meant to behave herself. 'I disagree. It is necessary, even if weren't about the money. Those ladies need to feel useful. This gives them purpose, it helps them feel as if they're contributing.'

'They're English ladies, Mrs Ralston. I don't know that you quite comprehend what that means.'

'They're *people*. I wonder if you comprehend what that means?'

The sound of horses' hooves on the drive broke the ensuing silence. She looked past Ashe's shoulder and felt a wave of relief. 'It's Henry. I'll ring for another tea cup.' Surely Henry would know how to deal with his prickly cousin. She'd certainly made a mess of it thus far. It probably had something to do with a pair of hot green eyes and a wicked smile that only had to flit across those aristocratic lips of his to conjure up illicit memories of a stolen kiss. Goodness knew it was hard to think straight under those conditions.

Henry stepped into the parlour, all smiles and charm until he spotted his cousin. 'I didn't expect to see you here. I'd stopped by to see if Genevra wanted to ride into the village with me.' Henry turned towards her, excluding Ashe from the conversation. 'My monthly shipment of books from London has arrived. I thought you'd enjoy looking them over. But I see you have company.' If she thought Henry would be a neutral buffer between her and Ashe, she was quickly proven wrong. His resentment was barely veiled. In the months she'd known Henry, she'd never seen a poor show of manners until yesterday. Since then, she'd seen two.

Genevra offered Henry a smile, trying to smooth over his lapse in good behaviour. 'I *do* have company. But you're welcome to join us for tea before you go on. I've already called for another cup.'

'Genevra likes Gothic novels.' Henry explained to Ashe with a friendly wink in her direction as he took a seat in the other wing-backed chair. 'I always try to surprise her with a couple in the shipment.'

Ashe was looking at her again in that steady way of his. 'So you like a good romance, Mrs Ralston?'

Even his polite conversation was sensual. She guessed at his innuendo and a hot blush crept up her cheeks. 'I do on occasion,' Genevra managed evenly. He could make of that response what he wished.

'*Mrs Ralston*? When have we ever been so formal among friends?' Henry laughed at his cousin. 'This is Genni, or Genevra if you prefer. I stopped calling her "Mrs Ralston" ages ago. We've practically lived in each other's pockets these past few months, caring for Uncle.' Henry smiled fondly at her and reached across the short distance to cover her hand with his. It was meant to be a friendly, touching gesture, but Genevra sensed undercurrents of something else, as if the display wasn't necessarily spontaneous. It certainly wasn't characteristic. Genevra hated to think this unusual outpouring of affection was motivated by Henry's meagre four per cent. Even more she hated that she was forced to think that way.

'Tragedies have a way of bringing people closer together.' Henry's smile softened as he looked into her eyes for a brief, meaningful moment.

Or tearing them apart. Genevra was distinctly uncomfortable. She and Henry had been perfectly good friends until yesterday. Henry had never intimated he wanted anything more from their association, which had made him all the more attractive to her. He was exactly what she was looking for: an intelligent companion who wouldn't demand more than she wanted to give. She'd tried marriage once and found it not to her liking. She was in no hurry to try it again, even to the amiable Mr Bennington, and certainly not to his less-amiable cousin, Mr Bedevere, no matter how well he kissed.

'We read to your father for hours on end.' Genevra returned the conversation to Ashe, acutely aware that this was the second time Henry had excluded him.

'How cosy,' was all Ashe said.

'Do you enjoy books as well?' Genevra tried again.

'I like picture books.' Ashe gave a wicked grin that left no room for misunderstanding.

'Good lord, Ashe. You're even worse than I remembered.' Henry scowled his disapproval, unwilling to let the second edgy comment pass without censure.

'So are you,' Ashe shot back.

Whatever expectations she might have had of familial love between the cousins were completely vanquished in that single line. Tension thickened like the piano's Babcock strings and Genevra looked about the room for a polite, neutral subject of conversation. Her eyes fell on the instrument against the wall.

'Your cousin played the piano for me just before you arrived,' Genevra told Henry. 'He's amazing.'

Henry arched an eyebrow at Ashe. 'You're still playing? Well, that's something at least. Your rebellion wasn't a complete waste then, was it?'

The tic in Ashe's cheek began to throb again. It was time to get Henry off on his errand before there were fisticuffs in her parlour. Henry hadn't made anything better, but he'd certainly made them worse. 'I'd offer you a second cup, but I fear I've delayed you long enough.' She rose and offered her hand to Henry. 'Thank you for the invitation. It was kind of you to think of me.'

'Then I am always kind.' Henry bowed over her hand and made his exit.

Ashe rolled his eyes, looking entirely at home in the wing-backed chair with his leg crossed over one knee, smashing any hope *he* would be leaving soon. 'That's the most beefwitted line I've heard. My cousin thinks himself a poet. It's ridiculous.'

'It was sweet.' Genevra busied herself stacking the tea things on the tray. Perhaps Ashe would get the message that the interlude was over.

'Do you think so? Do you fancy him?' Ashe asked point blank.

'We are merely friends.' A cup nearly slipped out of her hands at his frankness.

'It seems he'd like to be more than friends.'

'And you?' Genevra faced him, hands on hips. If he could be bold, so could she. 'What are you sniffing around here for? I am sorry if I gave you the wrong impression last night.'

'I assure you, I got the right impression. I can't afford not to. I only have two cheeks to slap.' He followed her with his eyes to the bell pull as she rang for someone to come and remove the tray.

'Is this the part where you regret to inform me I must leave because you have to get back to your projects, but in truth it's because I've spoken too boldly and made you uncomfortable?' Ashe was laughing at her with his eyes, and his mouth, which curved up into a wry, challenging smile, dared her to deny him.

'Only if you don't perceive the need to leave without being asked.'

'And here I was, thinking I might get a tour of your gardens. After all the talk last night of landscaping, I did have hopes of sneaking a glimpse.'

He had her there. Her gardens were her weakness. She loved to show them off. 'Give me a moment to change my shoes.' Genevra smiled. This would be the perfect way to show him his assumptions the night before were unfounded. She had *legitimate* reasons for eschewing London, starting with her gardens.

She showed him the topiary garden first with its trees shaped into exotic animals. There was a giraffe and a horse and an elephant, each set in a corner and surrounded by pansies that would bloom later in the spring. Even without the added colour of the flowers, this garden attracted the eye with its designs. Set between the sculpted animals were spiral-cedar topiaries set in large wooden planters.

'I've tried to copy some Italian designs I've seen in pictures of the Boboli Gardens,' Genevra explained. They walked side by side, but she'd been careful not to take his arm. She did not want to risk rekindling any of the flames from last night.

Ashe stopped to look at one spiralling tree in a planter. 'You've managed to capture it exactly right.'

Her breath caught. 'You've been to Florence?'

Ashe nodded, bending down to look up through the tree's shape. 'All over Italy, actually. After Oxford, some friends and I went. We were all interested in the Renaissance and I wanted to see Cristofori's pianos.' He paused and she thought she saw a flicker of hesitation before he continued. 'My father hadn't wanted me to go. He loved England and didn't see a reason to venture so far from home.' One piece of the puzzle, Genevra thought. One brief insight into the inscrutable, mysterious past of Ashe Bedevere. She waited for more. It would be all she'd get.

'I would love to travel,' she offered to fill the silence. She'd only come to England because her circumstances demanded it in the wake of Philip's death. If things hadn't gone poorly, she might never have left Boston.

'Then you should, Mrs Ralston.' She wasn't sure if that was an affirmation of her desire or a suggestion that she act on it with the utmost immediacy. Was he warning her off? All the better to gain control of her shares.

They came to a patch of garden still under construction. He offered his hand and this time she took it as they navigated the little piles of rubble. 'This will be a corridor of orchard trees and knot gardens, all leading to the fountain,' she explained with a wide gesture of her free hand to indicate the water feature at the end of the lane. She was well aware he'd kept her other hand trapped in his even though the need was no longer there. His grip was warm and solid.

'Gardens are a lot of work for someone who wishes to travel,' Ashe murmured.

She saw the contradiction too late. 'The future is an uncertain creature. There's no sense in *not* doing something in the present simply because the future might provide a different opportunity. If it doesn't, then much has been lost waiting for what might be.'

They'd reached the wide bowl of the fountain. There was no one about, only the sound of the water splashing as it landed in the basin. They might have been the only two people in the whole world. One of his long fingers had begun to trace slow circles on the back of her hand, conjuring up a reminder of how his hands had drawn small circles on her back last night while he'd trailed kisses down her neck.

'It sounds, Mrs Ralston, as if you know a thing or two about loss.' The invitation to confess was quietly issued. The temptation to do just that was potent. Good lord, this was a man who knew how to touch a woman. His eyes were searching her face and, against all logic, she wanted him to kiss her again, to take away the responsibility of answering him. But he didn't. He merely waited, his lips hovering tantalising inches from hers, reminding her of the possibilities.

'I do,' she whispered. She could give him that much at least. Admission wasn't confession.

'Is that why you're here, Mrs Ralston? To seize the opportunities of the present or to hide from the past?'

Chapter Seven

Silver-grey eyes looked away to a spot over his shoulder and then back, a small smile taking her lips. 'Is that what *you're* doing here?'

'I'm not hiding from my past, Mrs Ralston.'

'No, I was incorrect there. You're atoning for it.' The words were not meanly said. Her voice was softly reflective as if she'd just come to the revelation herself.

Her mouth was only inches from his, pink and inviting, her face tilted up to his, so close he could see the obsidian flecks of black in her deep-grey eyes. At this proximity, one might believe she was a well-tempered Pocket Venus. But Ashe had seen her quicksilver eyes flash with temper and other more tempestuous emotions. Yet up close, one could not miss the gentle, porcelain beauty of her features. Nor could one miss the undeniable proof that Mrs Ralston was not as immune as she seemed. A pulse-note beat at the base of her throat, quick and rapid, belying her attraction.

He stepped back. He wouldn't kiss her, not today. She

might think he was in the habit of always kissing her. She might come to take those kisses for granted. That would do his seduction no good if he chose to pursue her. 'You know nothing about me, Mrs Ralston.'

'Or you me.' Mrs Ralston's features schooled themselves into an elegant portrayal of politeness. 'Although you seem content to speculate that you do.' Her implication was clear. She thought him a hypocrite.

She was no coward, he'd give her that. Sharp tongued, sharp witted, Mrs Ralston was not easily bested.

'Are all Americans like you?'

'Are all Englishmen like you?'

Just once he'd like to have her answer a question without another question. It was proving to be a frustratingly evasive tactic of hers.

'My cousin isn't anything like me.'

'No, he's certainly not.' It was said equivocally. Was it Henry who'd been measured and come up lacking or was it himself? They were back to Henry, where they'd started. The conversation had come full circle.

Ashe pulled out his pocketwatch and made a show of checking it. 'Since we're not likely to tell each other our secrets, this seems to be a good place to make my exit. Thank you for the tour of the garden. It was most insightful.' She could spend her evening pondering what insights he'd gleaned. 'I can show myself out.'

He hadn't gone more than twenty paces when she called out, 'When will you be returning to London?'

Ashe turned and said slowly, 'I don't have any plans to return to London in the immediate future, Mrs

Ralston.' He grinned, making her regret the impetuous question. 'Were you afraid you'd miss me?'

She did laugh at that, the same throaty sound he'd heard at dinner. 'Miss *you*? Hardly.'

Ashe resumed his departure and called over his shoulder, 'You will, though. *Adieu*, Mrs Ralston, until next time. There will be a next time. You're going to have to deal with my forty-five per cent whether you like it or not.' If he squared his shoulders a little more than usual and walked a little straighter or with a bit more swagger, it was only because he knew she was watching. She liked to look at him. He'd caught her at it several times. It was a start. At least she wasn't ignoring him, although that could be fun, too, if he had the time for it.

If the stakes weren't so high, he'd thoroughly enjoy flirting with Genevra Ralston and then taking that flirtation a step further, Ashe mused, swinging up on Rex for the ride to the village and the public house. But the stakes *were* high. He could not gamble haphazardly. This was one seduction that had to succeed. He didn't have a choice, no matter what he pretended to himself. There was no question of selling his shares and backing away just as there was no question of meekly accepting his less-than-majority ownership of his own estate's regency. His track record in seduction was impeccable. It was *her* record he was worried about, especially if she had any loyalty towards Henry.

The women he seduced were willing. His partners

understood from the start this was a game just like *vingt-et-un* or whist with its rules and progressions. It was contractually understood that his partners knew where the game ended before they even started. He wasn't entirely sure Genevra Ralston would play by those rules, or that she'd play at all in spite of her hot kisses and fast-beating pulse.

In her case it wasn't enough simply to want him. There was a fortitude to her that suggested her mind could resist the temptations of her heart. To win her, he'd need a strategy that went beyond chance meetings and the thrill of stolen kisses. It bore thinking about. It wouldn't do for the one woman he couldn't seduce to be the woman he had to marry.

But now was not the time. Thoughts of Genevra Ralston's grand seduction had to wait. Right now he had to concentrate on the evening ahead. Ashe touched the pocket of his coat. Inside were tokens of female affection, acquired from his various *affaires* in London: a ruby stick pin, a set of emerald cufflinks, a rhinestone pin. They would be enough to get him a few games of billiards at the assembly hall in town. He would start building his own bankroll for Bedevere. *He* would find the money to pay for improvements. Asking Genevra to advance him funds would only make it more obvious just how much he needed her fifty-one per cent.

Ah, there was nothing like the smell of ale and sweat to bring a man peace. Ashe breathed deeply of the pungent smells as he stepped into the back room of the public house. It might not be the freshest of odours, but it was familiar and right now that was enough. He always thought well when he played billiards. It was a lot like playing the piano. Focusing on the game freed his mind to think about other things with greater objectivity. He needed time to think and to raise funds. If luck was with him, tonight he'd be able to do both.

Like most assembly rooms and public houses in villages across England, the village of Audley sported a billiards table. This particular table, Ashe noticed, was well used to put it mildly. But Ashe had faced better players on worse and tonight he just wanted to play, wanted to lose himself in the game. Ashe scanned the perimeter of the table and found his prey, not that it had taken much. The man was frankly advertising himself as a target.

'Will no one play?' the big man behind the baize table was gloating loudly. The crowd around the table shook their heads after the last victim had been dispatched. Ashe chuckled. He'd seen players like this before. The man had no finesse. He was too obvious with his skill. The trick was to hide one's true skill until it was time to strike.

Ashe stepped forwards and launched the first salvo in his private campaign to restore Bedevere. 'I'll play you.' Tonight, he was going to make money the only way he knew how. It would be better if his usual comrades, Merrick or Riordan, were with him. They could have run the two-friends-and-a-stranger gambit on this fellow. It would have been quicker. But Merrick was happily married in Hever with twin girls and lord only knew where Riordan was these days. Without them, Ashe would have to settle for quiet manipulation on his own.

The crowd stepped back to make room for the newcomer. The heavier man studied him with disdain, already mentally dispatching him. Ashe knew what his opponent saw. He'd planned it that way on purpose—a younger man overdressed for this place with a pocket full of guineas, a veritable rooster for the plucking. He was still dressed in the clothes he'd worn to call on Mrs Ralston. They were riding clothes, to be sure, but they were well cut and made for an afternoon in Hyde Park. *Good*, Ashe thought. *Be as cocky as you like.*

'What shall we play for?' The man eyed him with barely contained greed.

'This.' Ashe placed a rhinestone pin on the rim of the table, drawing oohs from the crowd. The pin wasn't extraordinarily expensive, but it was well made and the rhinestones had the desired effect, catching the light from the table lamp hung over the playing space. He could see the man's eyes flare with interest. *That's right. Keep your eyes on the prize and you'll forget to concentrate on the game.* 'Shall we go best three out of five?'

Ashe played skilfully, losing the first two games and buoying the man's substantial ego. He won the next three, and then the next three. The man gave up, but there was another to take his place. And after that, some enterprising soul had awakened the local billiards expert in the next village over and brought him in at dawn. That match had taken a while before Ashe claimed victory and put a thick roll of pound notes in his pocket, enough to pay wages for a month for anyone who wanted day labour at Bedevere.

He'd played longer than he'd anticipated, but once word got out who he was, there'd be no more billiards games at the local public house. Gentlemen didn't gamble with commoners. Still, there were areas around Audley Village that wouldn't hear the news for a while. If he travelled for a few games, this idea would last. But what else could he do to raise money? That sparked another, long-term idea. If he couldn't gamble at the public house, perhaps he could set up billiards games at Bedevere, after a proper period of mourning had passed, of course. When he got home, he'd see what sort of shape the billiards table was in. He suspected it hadn't been used in years. But that was for later—he'd need some ideas for now. Perhaps an auction, as distasteful as the idea was.

His mind started to whir with ideas. He could clean up Bedevere, make it look respectable enough for entertaining a few gentlemen over an evening of billiards and brandy—cards, too. He could invite the gentry—some squires, their sons, their nephews. He'd have to ask Leticia for a list of people. That meant gardens to pretty up and a few rooms to restore. The idea of restoring the gardens didn't seem so wasteful now. Perhaps for an auction there was furniture in the attics…

Ashe's mind was fully occupied when he stepped outside, cravat undone, coat slung over his arm. The bright daylight hit him full force. He squinted and lost his footing on a loose cobblestone.

'Oh!' The cry came too late. Ashe careened right into a passer-by, taking her and her packages to the ground along with him in a most intimate pile of legs and arms and thighs and skirts.

He levered himself up, aware that the sensation of being on top of this lush female was something his body didn't find entirely unpleasant—or unknown. It was quite funny, really, in the way that irony is funny. Of all the women in Audley Village, he'd managed to crash into Mrs Ralston.

'I'm sorry.' Ashe laughed, making light of the mishap. What else was left to do when one has landed in the perfect matrimonial position atop a lovely woman? On the positive side, he already knew her, which made it far better in some ways than landing on a stranger.

Apparently she didn't share his humour over the incident or his optimism. A stormy set of grey eyes met his and instinctively he knew he wasn't as sorry as he was going to be.

Chapter Eight

His eyes were *tremendously* green up close, and she couldn't imagine him being any closer than he was right now. Nor could she imagine being any more mortified. The source of her mortification didn't come from the fact that his body pressed most intimately against her in a public venue, but from her response. She *should* have been more upset with such familiarity and much less aroused. But, in all honesty, she *was* aroused and, from the feel of him, he shared the sensation. Of course it was all a great game to him, just like that ill-advised kiss in the conservatory had been.

Ashe had risen with a laugh. 'Mrs Ralston, are you hurt? Let me help you up.'

He looked taller and more presupposing than usual from her supine position on the sidewalk. He offered her a hand. She ought to take it, but her stubborn pride wouldn't permit it. She could get up by herself very well, thank you, and perhaps gather her thoughts into some sensible order in the meanwhile.

'Keep your hands to yourself.' Genevra struggled to her feet, trying to look somewhat graceful amid the strewn packages as if she collided with handsome, arrogant gentlemen on the street every day.

He tossed back his dark mane and laughed. 'And my other parts? Should I keep them to myself, too, or do you have need of them?' Genevra blushed furiously. Had he no decency? She was coming to learn Ashe said and did the first things that came to his very imaginative mind.

'Oh, hush up, and help me gather the packages.' They were starting to draw a discreet crowd. This was fine excitement in the sleepy village. Goodness knew what kind of tales would enliven dinner tables tonight.

She took a step forwards, bent to reach a parcel and stumbled, caught only by the firm grip of Ashe's hand at her arm. 'Eager for a repeat, are we?' he whispered wickedly, steadying her. 'In all seriousness, Mrs Ralston, I think you might have done yourself a minor injury.'

'You mean *you* might have done me a minor injury.'

He smiled, all white-toothed wickedness. 'Yes, *I* may have done so since it was I who fell on top of you. There's a decent inn across the street. Let's get you some tea and some rest.'

Now she had no choice but to rely on him and hobble on his arm to the inn, a *different* inn than the one he'd been coming out of, she might add. The presence of a woman's touch was evident in the Sheaf and Loaf. Blue-chequered curtains hung at the front windows and a big-bosomed, bustling woman in a clean apron was eager to seat them in a private parlour—an industrious innkeeper's wife, to be sure.

Genevra did not think her ankle was sorely damaged. A rest would be all it would take to restore her to proper working order, but in the meantime it meant keeping company with the enigmatic Ashe Bedevere.

'Will you be all right, Mrs Ralston?' he enquired after tea had arrived. She smiled over her tea cup. If he could be audacious in conversation, she could be, too.

'In the two days I've known you, you've kissed me, come to my home uninvited and landed on top of me in a public street. Truly, Mr Bedevere, I am beginning to wonder.' She was wondering quite a few things about this man these days; things she shouldn't wonder because one look was really all she needed to know precisely the kind of man he was: a man she should not get involved with.

She'd known it from the first moment he'd blown into Bedevere, travelling cloak swirling on those broad shoulders. His actions in the conservatory that night had confirmed it. Looking at him now, she should not be surprised he'd come careening out of Audley Village's more disreputable public house dressed in the same clothes he'd worn to her home yesterday afternoon. She knew precisely the kind of man he was. A smart woman knew that when a man looked like a rake and spoke like a rake, the man was definitely a rake.

'I do apologise for the mishap,' Bedevere began, giving her that slow smile of his designed to charm. She would not let herself fall for such an obvious ploy. But what a smile it was. It was the eyes that helped the smile right along. Sharp and green like a cat's, the eyes glinted with all nature of mischief. Oh, yes, she understood this man quite well.

'You wouldn't have to apologise if you hadn't been there in the first place.' There was a censorious tone to her voice, although truth be told she was slightly curious to know what had kept him out all night, even if she didn't quite approve.

'Or if *you* hadn't,' he answered easily, passing her the plate of scones. 'I do believe it takes two to cause a collision.'

How dare he make the accident her fault, as if she had wanted all that male muscle to land on her in such a fashion? '*I* was shopping, whereas *you* were coming out of a public house at eleven in the morning.'

He laughed again and she had the suspicion he was laughing *at* her. 'Is that a crime? You say it as if it's a bad thing.'

'It is,' Genevra retorted. 'Just look at you. Just *smell* you.' To her great alarm he grinned and did just that. To her even greater alarm, she could feel herself starting to melt. That smile was beginning to work. Good lord, he was devilishly handsome when he grinned like that.

'Hmmm. Cigar and whisky. A little on the stale side,' he said matter of factly. She had the impression he was enjoying this far too much. She needed to end this avenue of conversation. Whatever he'd been up to, he'd been up to it all night. She wasn't generalising there. His startling green eyes showed signs of sleeplessness and his clothes told their own story.

'Mr Bedevere, really.' She was no prude, but he pushed the boundaries of what could be tolerated.

'That's another thing. I do think we've moved past "Mr Bedevere and Mrs Ralston"—don't you agree?' He leaned over the table, closing the space between them. For a fleeting moment she wondered if he was going to kiss her again.

'I have a confession to make.' Probably more than one—he didn't strike her as precisely the church-going type. 'I usually call women I've, um "landed" on by their first names.' She was sure he did. She didn't miss the plurality of reference.

'Call me Ashe. It's the second time I've asked.' He was smiling again and a small rebellious *frisson* ran down her spine whether she wanted to be immune or not. He did not wait for her to offer the appropriate response. 'And I'll call you Neva,' he drawled, his eyes holding hers.

'Your aunts and Henry call me Genni,' Genevra countered quickly. Even in a morning parlour at an inn, 'Neva' sounded far too sensual on his lips. It was a name she should not permit for her own sanity, if not for protocol's sake. She'd been in England long enough to know better. An English woman of decent society would not allow it.

'Well, that's hardly original, but then again that's the

limit of Henry's imagination,' Ashe said off-handedly, leaning back in his chair.

Genevra laughed in spite of herself. 'Why don't you like your cousin?'

'Oh, no, you don't.' Ashe smiled and crossed his arms. 'No more answering questions with questions. We were talking about your name, not Henry's. We're not changing the conversation.'

Genevra sobered and leaned across the table, all seriousness. 'Mr Bedevere.'

'Ashe.'

She sighed and conceded. '*Ashe,* I can see that you're used to flirting with women and having some success there. I am flattered.' Genevra rose. Leaving was the most effective way of ending a conversation she knew of. 'However, I am not interested in whatever you're offering.'

Matrimony, Ashe thought wryly. The 'whatever' he was offering was far bigger than she suspected. He knew what she thought; he was out to make her his latest mistress. Perhaps she believed he meant to woo her fifty-one per cent out of her. She wasn't far from the mark, but he'd make an honest woman of her in the process. He wasn't such a cad to not offer marriage in exchange for her shares.

Ashe rose to stand beside her, taking her arm and effectively cutting off her lone exit. He kept his voice low. 'Are you certain? You don't know what I'm offering since I haven't made my "proposal" as it were.'

She gave him a cool sidelong look that would have done any courtesan playing hard to get proud. 'I know very well what you're offering, Ashe.'

'Really, and you still refuse?' Ashe murmured. 'I must say either your fortitude is quite amazing or your imagination is not.' Her mouth quirked into a split-second smile before she regained her composure. 'It's all right, you can laugh. I am known for my witticisms,' he assured her.

'I am sure you're known for much more than wit.' She looked him squarely in the eye. 'I am not for you. Again, I must decline your, um, "proposal." Now, if you would excuse me, I would prefer to leave alone, Mr Bedevere.'

'Ashe. We were making progress on that a few moments ago.'

'Good day, *Mr Bedevere*.' There was a stern finality to her voice.

'Good day, *Neva*.'

What a woman. Ashe let her go. She'd be back and she'd be his. Of course, he wouldn't offer her matrimony to begin with. She would reject that request out of hand and likely she'd see the proposal for what it was: an attempt to take control of the estate. He'd start small and tempt her with his gardens. She liked gardens and, with his new endeavour in mind, his had to be cleaned up. The arrangement was really quite symbiotic if presented in the right light. That light was not morning light, however.

Ashe sat back down and finished his tea. His head

was starting to pound after the long night. It did bring him a silent bit of humour to think the lovely and discreet Genevra Ralston's first reaction to his flirtation was that he offered something improperly wicked. It was a delicious bit of irony that the woman who'd scolded him for spending a night in Audley Village's version of a gaming hell had a mind that went immediately to bedding. Not that he was opposed to it. He was definitely up for it, in all ways.

What was *not* delicious was the rather lowering discovery that the one woman he needed to marry was the one woman who had outright refused him before he'd even asked.

Ashe pushed a hand through his hair, catching a whiff of his evening activities. She was right. He did smell, but a bath would have to wait. He had labourers to hire and supplies to order. What a difference a day made. Yesterday he hadn't any idea what he'd do with supplies or workers even if he could have afforded them, but today he did and Genevra Ralston was going to help him whether she knew it or not.

From his table by the front window of the public house Henry had a clear view of Audley Village's main street, lined with shops and businesses, while he ate an early lunch. At least the rabbit stew was good, something he couldn't say for his day so far. He'd come to town to 'accidentally' run into Genevra on her usual shopping day, but he'd had no luck after combing the stores.

If all had gone well, she would have been sharing lunch with him across the street at the inn instead of him eating alone at a lesser establishment with only its view of the street to recommend it. If she was in the village he'd see her.

Henry's spoon stopped halfway to his mouth. There she was, coming out of the inn, the basket on her arm full, indicating she was done with her shopping. Henry grimaced. She'd be unlikely to want to wander the shops if that was the case and, to all appearances, she'd already stopped for refreshment. His options were a bit limited. Still, he had to try. At the very least he could accompany her home. Henry hastily dug for some coins to leave on the table and hurried to follow her. But he didn't get far. Another all-too-familiar face emerged from the inn. Ashe.

Henry understood immediately what had happened. He'd not seen Genevra on her usual rounds because Ashe had beaten him to it. Henry stepped back inside the public house. There was no sense going after her now. He would merely be redundant if she'd already met with Ashe.

'Do you know that bloke over there?' A gruff presence established itself over Henry's right shoulder. A hulk of a man stood there.

'He was in here last night, playing billiards,' Henry's newfound companion said over mugs of ale. 'He cleaned me out. Suckered me, he did. He played false for a few games and then started to win and didn't stop. I left after I lost, but I hear he played all night, beating all comers. He's a sharp, that's what he is.' The man scowled into his mug.

Henry smiled. Hammond Gallagher was a poor loser. He could use that. 'That's Ashe Bedevere, the late earl's son. The Honourable Ashton Bedevere to us commoners.'

Hammond's eyebrows rose and Henry knew what he was thinking: he'd been beaten by an earl's son, there was some pride in that. Now it was time to disabuse him of the notion.

'Bedevere hasn't been around much, he's spent his time on the Continent whoring, drinking, gambling.' Henry shrugged in disapproval of such activities. 'He's only home now because of his father's death and here he is gambling when he should be in mourning and finding a way to support his dear old aunts.'

'Sounds like he might need a lesson.' Gallagher blew into his ale.

Henry hid his smile in his mug. This was what he'd been angling for and it hadn't been hard to get. Henry eyed Gallagher. Gallagher was built like a blacksmith: broad of shoulder, wide of chest. Ashe would have difficulty with the sheer mass of him if Gallagher took him by surprise.

'Bedevere is not well liked by some,' Henry began. It wasn't a complete lie. His cartel certainly didn't like him. 'I have friends who would pay if you had friends who would be interested in a little fun at Bedevere's expense. After all, he's already had fun at yours.'

Gallagher looked thoughtful for a moment and Henry knew he'd been right. Gallagher wanted a bit of revenge and the only thing holding him back was the thought of taking on a peer's son. Henry pushed some of Trent's coins across the table. 'There's more where that comes from once the job is done.'

Gallagher pocketed the coins with a nod and left. Henry thought his day was vastly improved. A good drubbing wouldn't remove his cousin from the estate, but it would certainly slow him down and right now Henry needed time—time to court Genevra, time to work out how to gain a majority control of the estate's management.

Ashe was proving more difficult to dislodge than previously imagined.

It was most disappointing. Henry'd had it all worked out. He would wait a decent interval, court Genevra, marry her and settle at Bedevere without her being any the wiser as to the real motives behind his courtship. After all the time they'd spent together over the winter, it would seem a natural course of events. Henry had hoped his uncle would have settled full custodianship of the estate on him. Coupled with Genevra's fortune through marriage, he'd have been indisputably in charge. But nothing had gone as planned.

The terms of the will made his courtship look obviously avaricious. But if it hurt his cause, it hurt Ashe's, too—perhaps even more so. Four per cent would not nearly be as threatening to Genevra as Ashe's forty-five.

Henry took a final swallow. He would not be

thwarted by the matchmaking efforts of old ladies. He'd come too far, waited too long. He'd coveted Bedevere and its hidden treasures for years. He'd spent countless hours currying favour over the last months with the old earl. He wasn't about to let it go now nor the opportunities that came with it. If he could win Genevra, he could have it all.

There was always a chance she'd say no, but he'd deal with that when it happened. There were ways to make a woman say yes.

Chapter Nine

'Yes, Melisande, I loved your new design for hand-kerchiefs with the Bedevere family crest. Thank you for sending it over.' Genevra looked up from her work-space in the Bedevere drawing room, her gaze return-ing again to the scene outside the wide French doors.

There was nothing particularly lovely about the view. The day was overcast and the gardens were nothing but churned-up mud. String and pegs outlined spaces where something more substantial would later replace the expanses of dirt. It wasn't the view that drew her eye, but the man who walked among the plots, stopping occasionally to clap a worker on the back and talk, his hands pointing and gesturing.

The day was not especially warm. There'd been some wind when she'd driven over, but Ashe didn't seem to notice the cold. Ashe worked only in shirt and riding breeches, the sleeves of his shirt rolled up, and he wore no waistcoat. The lack of a waistcoat left him surpris-ingly exposed, Genevra noted. There were no illusions about what might or might not be under that waistcoat. Nothing prevented her from taking in the leanness of his waist, or the muscled length of his thighs beneath the dirt-smudged breeches. The sight of him working was really quite intoxicating—probably because it was the last thing one would expect of an earl's son. Or because it was the last thing she'd expect from Ashe Bedevere.

'Genni, dear, you've stopped cutting,' Lavinia said from the easel where she sat painting a pot of early primroses.

How long had she been staring? Apparently long enough for everyone to notice. 'I've been wondering what your nephew is up to out there in the gardens.' She might as well admit to it. It didn't sound so voyeuristic when she said it like that.

'He says he wants to get the gardens closest to the house organised for spring.' Melisande's voice held a tinge of excitement, her approval of the plan evident. 'It will be lovely to have flowers again and a place to walk. It will be just like the old days. I would give anything for one last summer in a real garden.'

Lavinia shot her a sharp glance. 'Don't be so maudlin, Melly, we all have plenty of summers left in us.'

'Of course you do.' Genevra turned from the window. 'We've got so many plans for the markets and things are already better.' She gestured towards the window. 'In fact, if you don't mind, I think I'll go out and see if I can give your nephew some advice.' If he was going to go forwards with his plans for the estate without consulting her, then it was time to talk. He could not treat her as if she were an invisible partner.

Leticia brightened at the prospect. Genevra could see the wheels spinning behind her blue eyes, none of it having to do with the conditions of the estate. 'By all means, Genni. I'm sure Ashton will welcome any input you can give him.'

Genevra picked up her fur-lined pelisse from the chair where she'd draped it and headed out to the garden, careful not to look back for fear of what she'd see: smiles of matchmaking satisfaction on the faces of four old ladies. She had no intentions of satisfying them on that account, although that left her with no small amount of guilt.

It seemed deceptive not to tell the aunts about her new role in the estate, but she could only imagine how their matchmaking efforts would blossom if they knew, to say nothing of how Ashe would exploit those efforts. Ashe would throw in with the aunts and manipulate their influence to its maximum, a potentially lethal combination.

Genevra stepped around pockets of squishy mud, gingerly navigating the terrain, much like she'd have to navigate their upcoming conversation. Both she and Ashe each had time to assimilate the results and those results of the will had to be discussed. He had started this work in the garden without her permission. If this went unaddressed, who knew what other larger issues he'd attempt to supercede her authority on?

Genevra lifted her skirts, barely missing a puddle of

mud. It was definitely much easier to appreciate Ashe Bedevere at a distance where one could afford to be entranced by the masculine beauty of his physique. Up close, there was much more than a pretty face to contend with: that seductive drawl of his, those eyes, those hands that knew just how to touch a woman, to say nothing of the man who played the piano so expertly, or who carried so many mysteries behind his green eyes—why hadn't he come back sooner? Why had he ever left in the first place? What had happened between him and his father? What had he been doing all these years in London? How did all of that factor into the decision to leave him only forty-five per cent of the estate?

Perhaps it was the hope of discovering answers to those questions that kept propelling her into the gardens. Perhaps it was just the thrill that came with being in his presence. His conversation carried an edge, everything around him seemed to vibrate with an energy waiting to be unleashed. For all his roguish airs, Ashe Bedevere was turning out to be the most excitement she'd had in ages, his forty-five per cent nothwithstanding.

Ashe saw her coming and moved towards her, holding out a hand. 'Here, Neva, let me help you over that so you don't slip. We can't have you twisting your ankle again.'

'Aren't you freezing?' Genevra took his hand, shivering underneath the pelisse.

'You don't feel the cold once you get moving.' Ashe shrugged. 'What are you doing out here?'

They were three sentences in and Genevra was thinking it might be the nicest conversation they'd ever had. She hated to spoil it with business just yet. 'I came out to see why you changed your mind. The last time we'd talked, you'd thought the gardens were a waste of time.'

'I had a change of heart, that's all. I can't very well entertain with Bedevere in this condition.' He was noncommittal at best, a sure sign he was hedging. Before she could respond, he tucked her hand through the crook of his arm and began walking. 'Come see what I've laid out. It's all very simple compared to your plans at Seaton Hall, just colourful flowers and trees really, but it's what can be managed this year with spring nearly upon us. Next year, I'll do more. Right now, I want to focus on the front drive and this space off the drawing room since that's what people are likely to see most.'

'We,' Genevra put in, stopping the conversation. 'You mean "we" should focus on the front drive.' She paused, letting him digest the import of that two-letter word. 'I am the majority shareholder in the estate, whether or not either of us likes that arrangement.'

Ashe turned to face her squarely, arms crossed over his chest. 'What exactly do you mean to imply by that reminder?'

Genevra met him firmly. 'You cannot randomly make unilateral decisions about the estate, to say nothing of the finances. I need to approve of any expenditures. You must know by now the estate's monetary resources are limited. We must make judicious decisions with the funds we have, *together*.'

'This is my home.' Ashe's tic began to work. His

short sentence said it all. He wouldn't tolerate being reined in like a recalcitrant schoolboy. Neither would he tolerate an outsider asserting her authority.

Genevra softened, laying a hand on his sleeve. 'I did not ask for this, Ashe. But we are in this together for the time being.'

'What do you want, Neva?' Ashe said in silky tones.

'I want to help you with the gardens.' If she could get a partnership out of this, she would be making progress. 'Tell me your plans. Your aunts are already talking about how good it will be to walk in the garden again.'

They turned a corner and the wind lessened. 'I want to make the aunts an outdoor room of sorts here, with roses and stone benches and comfortable places to sit where they can bring their work.'

Genevra stared hard at the man beside her. Where had *he* come from? This was *not* the Ashe Bedevere who sparred so seductively with words, who challenged her at every turn with his cynicism.

'What do you think, Neva? Will they like it?'

'Yes, I think they will.'

'And will you? Will you come and sit with them in the summer and do whatever it is you do?' There was a glimmer of his seductive self stirring to life in those green eyes. It was a softer version than she was used to, but seductive all the same.

'Of course you can help me with the gardens, Neva.' She was acutely aware of Ashe's other hand covering hers now where it lay on his arm. 'I meant to ask you the other day at the inn, but you were so set on refusing my proposition, I thought it best to wait.'

This had been his proposition? Genevra suddenly felt foolish beyond words. She'd given him quite a dressing down for a proposal she'd felt would be nothing short of scandalous and all he'd wanted was some help with his gardens.

She gave a short laugh and shook her head. She couldn't quite meet his eyes. 'You must think I'm a shrew.'

'I think you're a woman alone in the world. I think you've had to learn to protect yourself in the absence of anyone else to do it for you and I think you do an admirable job.' He spoke quietly, his finger tracing another of his circles on the back of her hand.

She looked up, able to meet his eyes this time. 'I think that's the nicest thing anyone has said to me for a long time.' She cocked her head and gave him a contemplative stare. 'Are we becoming friends, Ashe Bedevere?'

He laughed. 'I hope not. Women and men can't be friends, not for any long period of time.'

'Why ever not?'

'It's the sex, Neva.'

There was the Ashe she knew. Well, thank heavens, he wasn't gone entirely. 'That's too bad. I was hoping we'd be friends.'

'No, you're not,' Ashe replied in easy disagreement. 'Friendship is safe, Neva. It's a little interpersonal limbo you can live in somewhere between not acknowledging your attraction to someone and giving full vent to it. If I were you, I'd hope for something more. Now, before you cut up at me for that—I can see that you want to— come see the old fountain and tell me what you think.'

Just like that, the friendlier version of Ashe Bedevere was back, the *safer* version. There was a begrudging truth to what he said, Genevra thought as they trudged across the garden. The safe Ashe, the compassionate Ashe she'd seen today, talked of gardens and plans. The wicked Ashe talked of feelings and hard truths and things she didn't want to admit to herself.

The fountain was dirty and dry, the basin full of dead leaves from years of neglect. 'I know it's in bad shape, but I am hoping a good cleaning will help.' Ashe reached down and scooped out a handful of brown leaves.

Genevra nodded. 'If it's like the one at Seaton Hall, the hydraulics have been turned off. A good scrubbing and a look at the pipes will solve your problems.'

'I played a lot in this fountain as a boy.' The nostalgic quality of his tone caught her off guard. She turned to face him, trying to imagine this grown man as a small child.

'Did you have a boat?' She tried to picture him in a sailor suit.

'A ship actually, a four-masted schooner. It was my pride and joy. I spent hours sailing it. Sometimes, on warm days, I'd put my feet in the water.' Ashe bent down and scooped another handful of leaves out. 'I've not thought of that for years. Alex had a boat, too. Often times we'd play together and have glorious naval battles.' His voice trailed off, leaving his thought incomplete. But she could guess where his thoughts had gone, back to those happy days running around the estate with his brother and not a care in the world.

'Whatever happened to your boat, Ashe?'

Ashe looked away from her towards the fountain. 'Henry broke it.'

'On accident?'

'No, he broke it quite on purpose. Alex gave him a black eye for it.'

Genevra idly picked at dead leaves on the edge of the fountain. 'Is that why you dislike your cousin? Because he broke your boat?' She gave a quietly coy smile, but Ashe was in deadly earnest.

'There's not one event that made me dislike my cousin. It's a combination of many events. But Alex and I were always able to handle him.'

'You're a lot like your brother,' she murmured. 'He talked often of growing up here.' She hesitated at the last. Discussion of Ashe's brother was new ground and he'd been so touchy that night in the conservatory when she'd mentioned his father. But his reaction today was far different.

'My brother was here?' Ashe's eyebrows drew together in confusion.

Genevra nodded. 'Didn't you know? Your father kept Alex here after the breakdown. He was here when I arrived in the area last June. I gathered from the aunts that he wasn't physically incapacitated in any way, his mind had just gone somewhere else and not came back.'

She could see the pain in his eyes at the thought and rushed on to alleviate it. 'Alex was always telling stories about the two of you when you were younger.' She paused, her gaze going to an invisible point over his shoulder so she wouldn't have to look at Ashe.

He had to be told. If no one had told him, she had to. 'I think that's where his mind lives now, back there in his childhood with you. He liked the story about the time you climbed the apple tree and sat up there all day eating apples until your stomachs hurt.'

A brief grin flashed across Ashe's face. 'We'd been told to go pick the apples and we didn't want to, so we decided to eat them. We thought doing it that way would make it look like we'd picked them since there wouldn't be any apples in the tree for proof. We didn't count on the stomach aches afterwards. We were so sick.'

He drew a deep breath. 'Where is Alex now?'

'He's been moved to a private institution outside Bury St Edmunds. It's a nice place where they care for people like him. Henry thought it would be best,' Genevra said. 'I'm sorry you didn't know.' She could see it was an enormous surprise to him.

Her heart went out to him in that moment. For all his audacious behaviour and flirtatious ways, he wasn't without redemption. He loved his brother. Impulsively, Genevra put a hand on his sleeve. 'I could take you to see him, if you'd like.'

He nodded without words. 'Was Alex brought home for the funeral?'

Genevra shook her head. 'No, I offered to drive over for him, but there were so many other arrangements to make and Henry thought—'

Ashe exploded at that. His quiet reserve had become a storm. 'I do not want to hear the words "Henry thought." one more time.' Alex should have been here. He should have been here to say goodbye to his father. He should have been here always, he should not have been shuffled off to strangers or put out of the way as if he doesn't exist. This was his home. He was safe here.'

He bowed his head, his eyes shut tight. She could see the tic in his cheek jumping with a ferocious effort to hold on to his control.

'Mrs Ralston, please excuse me.' He did not wait for a response. He turned on his heel and walked away from her with a rapid stride that suggested he might not reach his destination before he broke. It took all of her will-power to not run after him. She'd had two glimpses into his depths and it was rapidly becoming clear to her that Ashe Bedevere was not all he seemed. Heaven help her, such a revelation only served to make him that much more irresistible. A rake with a soul was a rare thing indeed.

Chapter Ten

How had it come to this? It wasn't the first time he'd asked himself the same question since his return. Ashe wanted to kick something, punch something, do *some* violence, so great was his anger, his outrage, his grief. But there was nothing to hit, nothing to break in the vast openness of the Bedevere parklands. All he could do was run and he did, just as soon as he was out of Genevra's sight. Boots weren't the best shoes for running, but Ashe shoved the discomfort aside and ran, letting the wind take his hair and bathe his face, letting his legs pump up and down in rapid motion in the fleeting hope that the activity would keep his emotions at bay for just a little longer.

Everything he'd kept so carefully tamped down inside him since his arrival was threatening to break loose. Hell, it wasn't threatening, it *had* broken loose after all this time. He'd held on to his control long enough to get out of Lady Hargrove's bedroom, long enough to get home, long enough to take stock of the situation. But his time was up.

His feelings, those things most of London believed he did not possess, would have their day. He hadn't had them the day he'd faced Lord Longfield at twenty paces over an accusation made at cards. He hadn't had them when he'd cut off Lord Hadley's curricle coming around a sharp curve in a dangerously mad race that could have seen him dead. But, by God, he was having them now.

Ashe had no conscious idea of where he was headed, only that he was headed away: away from Genevra Ralston and her grey eyes that saw too much; away from his gentle aunts who looked to him for support; away from Henry and his treacherous coveting; away from Bedevere and the responsibilities it posed.

Aimless as his mad journey was, he wasn't surprised when his feet stopped running to see he'd arrived at the one place on Bedevere property he hadn't been yet— the domed mausoleum. Ashe braced himself with an arm against the stone sides of the structure and bent over, trying to gather his breath. The intensity and the distance of the run had left him winded. He hadn't run out here since he'd been in his teens. He and Alex used to play out here when they'd been younger, and later they'd raced out here in friendly competition.

His breath gathered, Ashe sat down on a stone bench placed at an angle for better viewing of the mausoleum. It was a handsome building with its dome and Palladian columns. A regal resting place for generations of Bedevere males, generations that went back long before the Bedeveres were earls.

Ashe supposed that might be why he was so attached to being 'Mr Bedevere'. It had always been the family's name, just as this house had always been the family's house, although other properties had presented themselves with the earldom. In the great scheme of history, the title of Audley was relatively new come to the family, the earldom only four generations old. But Bedevere had been around nearly as long as England. Growing up, he and Alex used to fancy they were related to Sir Bedevere, who'd sat at King Arthur's fabled table. *That* probably wasn't true. But who knew? The remembrance began to calm his roiling emotions.

He wasn't ready to go inside yet. Ashe reached for a small piece of wood on the ground and pulled out his knife. He whittled while he sat, letting his thoughts wonder along whatever paths they preferred to take. Pride had done this. The real Bedevere legacy was the stubborn Bedevere pride. The same pride which had driven his great-grandfather to build an earldom was the pride which had driven Ashe from home at the age of twenty.

No doubt it was the same pride which had perhaps persuaded his father at the last to gamble with Bedevere's future. Unwilling to admit his prodigal son had not returned in time to make amends and unwilling to admit defeat in the face of economic disaster, his father had found a way to defy traditional law and push

Bedevere towards the future, uncertain as it was. It had been an enormous gamble.

His right hand began to ache from the knife work and Ashe flexed it out of old habit. The cold weather and the rough work outdoors this week, even with gloves, had aggravated it. He hadn't done his hand any favors these past few days with letter writing and gardening and playing the piano. Usually, regular activity didn't bother it, but regular activity in London was something of a subdued nature compared to the 'rigours' he'd encountered out here.

Ashe held out his hand and slowly turned it over, palm side up. A thin, pale-white line bisected the palm, a mark nearly invisible after eight years, but not forgotten. Pride had done that too.

Ashe huffed a sigh, his breath swirling like a mist in the cool air of late afternoon. His body was cooling, too. He shouldn't stay out much longer in only a shirt. He brushed his hands against the thighs of his breeches and stood up. It was time to do what he'd put off doing since the moment he'd arrived. It was time to go inside and pay his respects.

There was a certain finality to seeing a life etched in stone, chiselled into a three-line biography for descendents to linger over: name, title, date of lifespan. That finality was not lost on Ashe as he entered the marble-floored mausoleum and followed the dates to the most recent row. His father was there, of course, marked by a polished marble plaque containing the dates; February 7th, 1775–January 25th, 1834. Ashe raised his hand and traced the chiselled numbers, emotions rising. This was why he hadn't come out earlier—not because he hadn't cared, not even because he'd been busy with other important things to do for the estate and for the living. The dead could wait after all. They weren't going anywhere—but because he knew once he got here, he'd break down.

He was right.

Ashe backed to the wall where a slab for sitting had been cut in marble blocks. He sat hard, feeling the hot sting of tears behind his eyes and then he gave himself permission to do what he hadn't done in a decade.

He wept.

He wept for being too late to say goodbye. He wept for Alex, for a neglected home, for a ruined hand and a ruined dream, for all the things that might have been in a more perfect world where dreams and sons and fathers could co-exist. And when he was done, he would be ready to face again the imperfect world that was.

It was dusky-dark when Ashe stepped outside, one of his favourite times where night met day. Daylight hovered on the hem of the horizon while early stars poked their brilliant heads through the night fabric of the sky. He looked up at that sky and drew a revitalising breath and stiffened before he could exhale. Someone was here.

With reflexes honed from too many years spent in the alleyways of gaming hells, Ashe bent swiftly to retrieve the knife in his boot. He palmed it and called out.

'It's me.' A dark figure rose from the bench and stepped forwards, the clear shape of a woman becoming evident.

'Neva.' Ashe sighed and replaced the knife. 'You startled me. I wasn't expecting anyone to be here.'

'Obviously.' She shot a wry glance towards his boot where the knife was sheathed. 'I brought you this.' She held up his coat. 'When you didn't come back, I got to thinking you might be cold if you stayed out too much longer.'

Ashe shrugged into the jacket, appreciating its warmth. 'Thank you. How did you know where I'd be?'

'It wasn't hard to figure out,' Genevra said softly, those grey eyes once again seeing more than he wanted to reveal.

'Your father would have liked to have seen you again,' Genevra offered quietly as they began the long walk back. Her arm was tucked through his for balance so she wouldn't trip over the uneven ground in the growing dark.

'I'm not sure I agree. I might have hastened his decline,' Ashe said truthfully. 'I think sometimes the living require absolution more than the dying.'

'Absolution comes in many forms.'

The words brought Ashe to a halt. It occurred to him in those moments that loss and forgiveness were things she would understand. The conflict fuelled by his father's will had obscured her humanity. She was more than the physical embodiment of 'fifty-one per cent', more than someone to be manipulated.

'Is that why you're here? Is Staffordshire your absolution, Genevra?' She was a young widow, a woman who had lost a husband not long after their marriage and most likely in sudden circumstances, so goodbyes had not been possible. He thought of her comment earlier about his need for atonement. Had she guessed because of her own?

She turned away from him. 'I suppose it is,' she said quietly. 'Seaton Hall is more than absolution, it is a redemption of sorts, a redemption for other women.' She paused here and Ashe waited for her to go on. 'I haven't told anyone yet, but I plan to make it a business *and* a home for women who have no place to go and no means to support themselves. Once the place is renovated, I'll look for women to come. They can give tours, tend the garden, put on teas. I think it's the perfect genteel business opportunity.'

'Like my aunts selling handicrafts at the local fairs?' Ashe murmured with a smile.

'Yes,' Genevra replied staunchly. 'Everyone needs to have a purpose, to feel useful. No one wants to be a thing. No one wants to be helpless.'

The statement spoke volumes, Ashe thought, although he could not imagine Genevra tolerating being minimised. 'Did you love him? Your husband?'

Her husband. Philip Ralston. A handsome bounder who'd convinced a young girl he was desperately in love with her.

Genevra looked down at the ground, studying her

feet as they began walking again. She seldom spoke of Philip to anyone but perhaps Ashe would see now the kind of resistance he was up against. Philip had ruined her for marriage. She would not risk walking that path again. She was not that naïve. 'I suppose I did in the beginning before I saw him for what he was.'

'What was that?' Ashe prompted softly.

'A man who loved my money far more than he loved me, only I was too young to know it.' Even after the distance of time, it was still hard to admit that awful truth. 'My father tried to warn me, but I was too stubborn to listen.' Genevra shrugged and gave a half-hearted laugh. 'It sounds like a Gothic romance, doesn't it? Rich girl falls victim to a fortune hunter. It's hardly original.' There was more to it, of course, but she wasn't ready to share the sordid details. She didn't want Ashe's pity. It was time to move the conversation on to a different track. She'd reached the limit of what she wanted to disclose.

'I have to confess there's another reason I came out looking for you. Henry is staying for dinner. I thought you'd want to know in advance.'

Just like that, the brief magic of the evening faded.

Chapter Eleven

It could have been worse; not the most stunning accolade to attach to a dinner, Genevra thought. But at least Ashe hadn't thrown anything at Henry beyond words and vice versa. She'd been more than glad to make a hasty retreat to one of Bedevere's quiet sitting rooms and spend the remainder of her evening with a book.

She'd not planned to stay overnight, not after having so recently made a return to Seaton Hall, but the weather had conspired against her. The moderate breeze that had accompanied her drive over this afternoon had become something rather more by nightfall. Why not stay? the aunts had argued. There was no one expecting her at Seaton, and no plans that demanded her immediate attention, so here she was, tucked away with a book and hoping for some peace, something that had been in short supply since the earl's death and Mr Bedevere's arrival.

Genevra tucked her legs beneath her and opened the

book, a posthumously published edition of Ann Radcliffe's *Gaston de Blondeville*.

'Genni, there you are. I've been looking all over for you.' Henry's convivial tones broke her concentration on page five. Genevra fought the urge to let her shoulders sag in disappointment.

'Hello, Henry.' She looked up and smiled, pushing back her more uncharitable thoughts. It wasn't Henry's fault, not specifically anyway. She'd come to Staffordshire to avoid male attention and here she was with a fifty-one per cent share in an estate and two cousins circling like vultures, waiting for her to decide what her role would be in all this.

'I'm not interrupting, am I?' Henry pushed off from the door jamb and sauntered over. She wondered what he'd do if she actually answered the question.

'Of course not.'

Henry took the chair next to the sofa and pulled it forwards. 'I've been wanting to talk with you for ages, but I haven't been able to catch you alone.' He smiled boyishly, his golden hair falling across one eye. He brushed it back. 'I even went into the village on your shopping day in the hope of catching you, but…' his voice trailed off and he shrugged. 'Seems my cousin had beaten me to it.' He furrowed his brow. 'Has my cousin beaten me to your affections, Genni? Have I erred by playing the gentleman too long?'

She feared where this conversation was headed, but she'd known it would happen since the will had been read. 'Your cousin has had more important matters on his mind than flirting with a neighbour,' Genevra said lightly. It was almost true, except for that kiss in the conservatory, or the incident in Audley Village.

Henry leaned forwards in a pose of earnest. 'I must warn you about him, Genni. You don't know him like I do.' He paused. 'I know you were with him that day in Audley Village. I saw you come out of the inn and he came out a few moments later.'

'People can have tea together in a public setting, Henry,' Genevra laughed it off.

'It's never just tea with him, Genni. Do you know what he'd spent the night doing? He spent it gambling on billiards.'

That explained the stale smell of smoke and ale on him. Well, she shouldn't be surprised. She'd thought as much, but the confirmation was still disappointing.

'Genni, he's been home for a handful of days, supposedly to mourn his father and take up some form of an active role in the estate. Instead he was gambling. He's a rotter through and through, Genni.' Henry sounded genuinely aghast, perhaps a bit too much. Genevra had the fleeting notion he would do well on Drury Lane with that expressive face of his.

'Henry, I think you make too much of it,' Genevra said softly, but she wasn't convinced of that, or of Ashe being entirely a 'rotter'. She'd had glimpses of a far nobler man beneath the roguish exterior. 'I think, too, that you misjudge him. He's beside himself over his father.'

Henry snorted at this. 'Don't be misled, Genni. He could have come home sooner and maybe none of this would have happened. Now, he wants to waltz in here and claim *all* of the estate after the rest of us have propped it up in his absence.'

Genevra heard the vehemence, the envy in Henry's words. 'What of you, Henry? What do you want to claim? I don't believe Ashe is the only one with an agenda. You were upset the day the will was read. You expected more?'

'I want you, Genni.' Henry fixed her with a strong look. 'I don't care about estates. I want you and if I sound angry it is because I see you slipping away from me, slipping towards Ashe. I know I should wait a decent period before I ask, but I find I cannot risk it. If I wait any longer, I fear Ashe will steal you from me.' There was another of his dramatic pauses. She was starting to become truly annoyed by them.

'He's stolen a girl from me before, you see. There was a girl, the daughter of gentry. They're no longer in the area. I was seventeen and I was in love. We walked out a few times together, did all the things that typify young love: strolled the summer fairs, sat together at local socials. But Ashe was home from Oxford, older, richer and he took a fancy to her.' Henry shook his head. 'How could I compete with an earl's son, even a second son? I was just the nephew, visiting for the summer with a modest inheritance.

'I would protect you, Genni, from being his next victim. I would not see you thrown aside when he was done with you.'

'I don't need protecting, Henry. I can take care of

myself. But thank you for the concern.' Genevra picked up her book, signalling she'd like to start reading again, a sure dismissal. But Henry would not be daunted by the subtle manoeuvre.

'I am not asking to protect you, Genni. I am asking you to marry me. I meant it when I said I wanted you, only you. I've grown fond of you in our months together and I find that none other can compare. I'm twenty-seven and it's time to be looking to my future. I want you in that future.'

It was a pretty speech with all the requisite elements of a decent proposal—an expression of affection, of sincerity and an allusion to the acceptability of his prospects—although both of them knew she was the one with the prospects if they wanted to live beyond his mid-sized manor farm.

'Forgive my surprise, Henry,' Genevra began delicately while she searched for the right words. 'I had not realised your affections had transmuted from those of friendship.'

'I could make you happy, Genni. You're far too young to be alone in this world for the rest of your life. Surely you cannot mean to remain a widow for ever.'

'I am flattered, Henry, truly I am. But now is not the time for me to be thinking of marriage. I have Seaton Hall to finish at the very least,' Genevra hedged.

Henry smiled good-naturedly. 'You sound like you're not sure?' He reached for her hand. 'We can take things slowly. We can always announce our engagement and wait until you're ready. We should wait, anyway, with the funeral having been so recent, so you needn't feel awkward about it.'

If she'd been a different kind of woman, a woman who craved the respectability and security marriage brought with it, she would have taken Henry's offer. He was good looking, possessed of a certain charm. Some woman, somewhere, would be thrilled to marry Henry Bennington, but that woman wasn't her, not at the present at least, although she doubted that would change.

'Your offer is generous, I just can't accept at present,' Genevra said. Something stirred at the door and she looked past Henry to see Ashe in the doorway. He'd only just arrived, unlikely to have overheard the conversation, but the look on his face was thunderous. She could imagine how the situation appeared to him— Henry sitting close, her hand in his grasp, Henry looking earnest.

'I was on my way to read some post.' Ashe fixed her with a piercing stare. 'Gardener informed me a letter of some importance arrived late this afternoon from London.'

Was she supposed to have known about the letter? His look suggested he suspected she did. She had no energy left to play 'divine the secret message in my gaze'. She'd had to work too hard with Henry. Genevra rose with her book. 'I think I'll retire. Goodnight, gentlemen.' She felt Ashe's hot eyes follow her out the room. As exits went it was of the same calibre as dinner—it could have been worse.

* * *

But that didn't mean sleep came easily. The wind howled at her window and her thoughts rambled around in her head, conspiring to keep her awake well after midnight.

What had the old earl meant by leaving her such a controlling influence in the estate? She was happy enough to offer her ideas on boosting the estate's productivity and happy enough to even offer a loan. She didn't need fifty-one per cent to do that. Surely the earl had known she would have done all that anyway? But he'd given it to her none the less and now she had to honour that position by not letting Ashe Bedevere exclude her from estate business.

Only it just wasn't about the estate. She was drawn to Ashe Bedevere against her better instincts. It had been easy to refuse Henry. He had been a companion, but nothing more. He didn't stir feelings to life in her that were hot and dangerous. She didn't want his kisses, didn't want to probe the depths of his mind. But Ashe had merely to enter into a room and all of her attentions were riveted on him, as he'd so aptly demonstrated tonight.

She knew all too well how such a reaction could cloud her judgement. Ashe was most assuredly a rake, a character trait that would normally not earn him any points with her. But then there had been glimpses of a far deeper, far more decent man beneath that roguish exterior and the combination was potently compelling: the noble rogue. The woman in her wanted him unabashedly, but the business side counselled caution against such rash behaviour.

Genevra threw aside her covers. This was the second sleepless night she could lay at Ashe Bedevere's feet. She grabbed a dressing robe and belted it with determination. Mrs Radcliffe's novel had not accomplished its purpose. Perhaps there was something more suited to her temperament in the library. She grabbed a candle and headed downstairs.

The library was dark and she set the candle down to light a lamp, letting the larger lamp throw its glow on the walls. She trailed her hands over the book spines, pulling out one book after another, none of them satisfactory. Even the novels held little appeal. She decided on *Waverly* and turned to go, only to discover she wasn't alone.

A little shriek of surprise died on her lips as she recognised the broad-shouldered frame standing in the door. 'You scared me, Ashe.' An odd thought occurred. 'How long have you been standing there?'

'Long enough to know you had difficulty making up your mind.'

Genevra was glad for the protection of her robe. No doubt he'd been standing there long enough to know she was indecently clad for such an encounter too.

He advanced. 'Having difficulty sleeping?'

'Yes.' She swallowed hard, glad her voice hadn't cracked. He was a decadent wolf by lamplight, his green eyes glittering. He took the book from her hand and studied the cover. '*Waverly?* He marries the baron's daughter, the coward.' Ashe set the book on a nearby table.

'I've read it before.'

'Then you know what motivates our hero's choice. He chooses the safe course with Rose instead of the passionate way with Flora.'

Genevra was about to respond with a defence of Waverly's solid choice but Ashe silenced her with a finger pressed to her lips. 'I did not come down here to debate Waverly's notion of good choices. And we both know it's not the reason you're here searching for a book after midnight.' Challenge flared in his eyes daring her to gainsay him.

'Exactly what would that reason be?' Genevra answered in haughty tones.

'Henry's proposal has unnerved you,' Ashe asserted boldly, his eyes watching her intently for any tell-tale sign of remorse or happiness.

So Henry had told Ashe. 'I wish he had not mentioned it.' Genevra idly fingered the spine of the book where it lay on the table. 'Nothing will come of it.'

'He meant it as a warning for you and me both. Did Henry tell you how despicable I was? Did he fill your head with tales of my decadence?' Ashe had stepped closer to her during the conversation. He laughed now in the darkness, a deep, sensual chuckle.

'He did mention your reputation was less than pristine in that regard.' She was aware of his closeness, of the smell of him, clean and appealing even after a long day. Her body was starting to stir.

'I will not respond in kind by slinging arrows at Henry's reputation. It can prove itself on its own merits, which I am sure it will do given enough time.' There was an edge to Ashe's voice that implied one should be sceptical of Henry's golden-boy charm.

'I am not looking to make a marriage, not to Henry or to anyone else.' She might as well be clear on that matter with Ashe from the beginning.

'Not tonight anyway.' Ashe laughed at her defiance. 'That doesn't mean we can't explore other interesting avenues of association. Unless, of course, you are indeed committed to Henry? Are you, Neva? Are you and Henry secret lovers? Secret conspirators?'

Ashe had not liked seeing them together and he'd drawn his own conclusions. He was daring her to prove it was otherwise. 'I decide for myself. Neither Henry nor you have any claim on me,' Genevra asserted, although her body knew the latter statement to be something of a lie. Ashe did claim her attentions in a way that transcended their connection through the estate.

Ashe's long fingers reached out to stroke a cheek. 'And what have you decided, Neva? Have you decided to allow yourself the pleasure of a night? It is too late to deny it. I see the desire in your eyes, and not only tonight. I've seen it before, in the conservatory. I intrigue you and you intrigue me. I would gladly give you the one night your body is asking you for.'

Genevra whetted her lips, weighing the invitation against the challenge. Already, in the midst of this little quarrel, her body was rousing for him, her mind excited by the possibilities he promised, her curiosity provoked by Henry's insinuations about Ashe's reputation as a lover.

What would it be like to be with a man such as Ashe Bedevere, who would give pleasure without extracting a price? He was promising a moment out of time, a moment outside of the life she'd so carefully cobbled together after Philip. Maybe if she leapt, the nobler Ashe Bedevere would be waiting on the other side. That would be a man worth leaping for.

Ashe tipped her chin upwards, taking her mouth in a most decadent inducement of a kiss and she accepted, *Waverly* forgotten. Who needed a paper hero, when she had Ashe Bedevere very much in the flesh and blood and a chance for just one night to throw caution to the wind?

Chapter Twelve

Ashe released her long enough to shut the library door, the snick of the lock bringing with it a finality in the silence. Decisions had been made, consent had been given. Genevra gave the ribbon that held her hair a swift tug, letting it fall loose about her shoulders.

'Lady Godiva.' Ashe's voice was hoarse with anticipation. He crossed the room in a slow approach, giving her time to drink in the enormity of what she was about to do. His own hair was loose, creating the impression of a dark mane, framing the sculpted planes of his face, highlighting his eyes.

He did not stop beside her, but went on to kneel in front of the fireplace giving her a glimpse of his backside as he laid a quick fire. He was still dressed in his shirt and trousers from dinner, enough to be considered in dishabille, but wearing entirely too many clothes for Genevra's preferences at the moment. Then he turned and faced her, his hands at the waistband of his trousers as if he'd read her mind. In a fluid, cross-armed motion,

Ashe pulled his shirt over his head. Genevra sat down hard, suddenly aware of the chair that met the back of her knees. He was not a man to appreciate standing up. In the firelight the contours of his torso were like a map leading downwards to that most obviously male region of him. Her hands itched to trace those lines to their logical conclusion.

His hands drew her gaze once again to the waistband of those damnable trousers. He pushed his trousers down lean hips, past muscled thighs that spoke of years in a saddle.

She clutched the arms of the chair, vaguely aware that her mouth had gone dry as all this glorious English manhood was revealed slow inch by slow inch. He gave a quick flick of his foot and his trousers were off. Completely. It occurred to her briefly that such a skilfully effortless undressing was not accomplished without practice—lots of practice. But tonight she didn't care. Tonight, he would be hers and in the morning there would be no complications because they both understood there couldn't be, not with the estate between them.

'Come, Neva,' he coaxed from the fireplace, hands on his hips, his index fingers pointing ever so subtly to the jut of his phallus. 'It's your turn—I want to see you naked.'

She rose, suddenly shy, her fingers fumbling with the sash of her dressing gown, acutely aware she'd never disrobed quite so deliberately for a man before, or stood naked before one. To undress deliberately was erotic and powerful. Ashe's eyes were hungry for her. It had not been like this with Philip. She pushed the thought away. There was no place in this interlude for his intrusion. This was her moment of pleasure. She was due this.

'No, wait. Not yet, I've changed my mind.' Ashe moved towards her, closing the small distance, enviously comfortable in his own nakedness and clearly unabashed by the noticeable proof of his arousal. Ashe placed a finger on her lips when she would protest and drew it down the base of her neck.

At his touch, heat pooled low in the cradle between her legs. He could excite her so easily. His hands found the belt of her robe, letting the halves of it fall away before he pushed it back from her shoulders.

He turned her gently, putting her back to the fire, his breath catching. 'Firelight and lawn becomes you, madam.' He did not take her gown immediately, instead he traced her against the flame, making her aware she might as well be naked already for all the covering the fine material of her nightgown afforded. He cupped her breasts, drawing the material taut against her nipples, the light friction of the fabric beneath his thumbs eliciting a tender ache that sought fulfilment. But she knew instinctively fulfilment would not come yet and that knowledge in itself fuelled her arousal.

Genevra arched against him and he knelt before her, his hands framing her hips, his thumbs massaging the low bones of her pelvis in deliciously tantalising circles not unlike the ones he'd drawn on her hands. He looked up at her, green eyes blazing, and she felt her power. She was Venus in that moment, her supplicant worshipping at her feet, seeking only her pleasure. It was heady ambrosia indeed, but nothing compared for what Ashe did next. He kissed her through the thin fabric of her gown with all the reverence due a goddess. A sharp arrow of heat sang through her, a moan of want escaping her lips.

'Sit down in the chair, Neva and spread your legs for me,' Ashe commanded, no longer the supplicant, but the wolf. There was an undeniable thrill in what he asked, in being vulnerable and exposed before him. He knelt again and pushed up the material of her gown until it bunched at her waist. His hands gently skimmed the soft skin of her thighs, his thumbs stroking the softer folds of her womanly places.

She trembled, her body begging. Then he lowered his head to her, no longer the supplicant or the wolf, but something in between: the seducer, the lover, the pleasure-giver. His breath was warm and welcome at her juncture and she sighed from the sheer delight of it. Then his tongue flicked across the tiny secret nub of her and all delight fled, replaced by something more intense, more overwhelming than anything she'd known and she was drowning in it. Her hands were in his hair as if, by holding on, she could drive him deeper into her and resolve the search for fulfilment. She was vaguely aware of thrashing now as the ecstasy began to take her, his hands strong and firm at her hips, steadying her until at last she broke against him with a sob that sounded more like a scream.

Ashe rose and gathered her to him, his arms about her, his hands stroking her back in a gentle rhythm while she recovered. He took her down to the floor after she'd quieted and they lay in stillness, her head on his chest, his arm about her, tracing shapes on her back. But he was by no means done with his seduction. His own need had not yet been slaked. His phallus rose firm and insistent in the firelight, the flames dancing on the crystal bead of moisture at its tip.

Genevra sat up and pulled her nightgown over her head, arms extended, ready at last to be naked, to have nothing between them. This was heady new ground. But if the night had taught her anything, it was that she'd known nothing of passion until now. What had passed between her and Philip had not been this. It had been fumbling and harsh. It had lacked all the beauty and release that Ashe had shown her and she was hungry for more.

Ashe's eyes were on her, as hot as any flame, watching her discard the gown. 'You're beautiful,' he whispered. 'I could look at you all night.' His hands mirrored his words, reaching up to push her hair over her shoulders so that no curtain hid her breasts. He rose up on his knees to meet her, taking her breasts in his hands, kneading them ever so gently, his thumbs circling the aureoles. His mouth found hers in a kiss that spoke of slow sensuality.

'We are like Adam and Eve in the garden,' she whispered.

'Discovering each other,' Ashe replied. The desire

in his eyes had changed from a primal smoulder to a deeper flame. They were getting to the core of the fire, the place where the flame of passion burned more fiercely now that the initial wildfire had been subdued. There was time now for exploration.

Genevra pushed lightly at his shoulders, signalling she wanted him to lie down. 'It's my turn.'

Ashe gave her a lazy wolf's grin. 'For a while.'

She started with his chest, tracing his aureoles, watching his flat nipples pucker in response. 'Is it the same for you, I wonder?' She'd hardly been aware she'd spoken out loud until she heard Ashe give a throaty laugh. His hand came up to capture hers.

'It's not nearly as stimulating. I don't mind it, of course, it's nice, but it's not as arousing for men.'

Genevra gave a little pout. 'I feel sorry for you then. You're missing out.'

'Men have other spots, my dear.' He guided her hand lower, mischief in his eyes. 'If you're willing, there are those who believe a man's sac is his sensual equivalent to a woman's breasts. I happen to be among their number.'

Genevra complied, marvelling at the weight of them in her hands. She gave them a gentle, experimental squeeze and was rewarded with a moan. There was joy here. She'd never taken a man in her hand before, never known he could be so open to pleasure, that this love-making could be a congress of equals.

His phallus beckoned and she moved her hand to

cover the sparkling tip and began a slow journey up and down its length.

He bucked hard against her once. 'I think it's time, Neva. I won't last much longer. Rise up over me, take me inside you.'

Her eyes widened at the exotic nature of the challenge. How amazing. She had not guessed. She hesitated for the briefest of moments, but Ashe was there, taking himself in hand and guiding her on to him, a wondrous 'ohhh' escaping her as he slid home. This was incredible indeed, to be able to look at him, to watch him as need took them both. His hands were at her hips, guiding her into a rhythm, her body aware of the pressure building in her once more as it had done in the chair. Release would come. She wanted to hurry it along, wanted to feel that blissful emancipation one more time.

In a sudden remarkable move, Ashe gathered her to him and rolled, taking her beneath him, their bodies not parting. Above her, the same pleasure captured him. It wouldn't be long until they were both there together. Once, twice more, she shattered and somewhere in the prism of fractured sensations, he shattered with her.

Ashe waited for the sensation to pass, waited for the momentary physical peace to fade all too soon as it always did. Tonight, it was being gloriously stubborn. It was lingering and he was happy to bask in its unlooked-for afterglow.

Beside him, nestled against his body, Genevra dozed, naked and satiated beneath a throw he'd managed to pull down from the chair without rising up and disturbing her rest. She'd been a sensual marvel, an intoxicating mixture of bold experience and shy reserve. It was a combination even the most practised of courtesans could not replicate. It was insightful, too. Her husband had failed her.

There was no issue of virginity between them, but virgin or not, she had been untutored. He would wager his last pound she was not trailing a string of sundry lovers behind her. Her knowledge had not been as fully formed as her willingness. Yet she'd taken his instruction eagerly. He knew a particular manly thrill in having been the one to instruct her on finding her pleasure. Whatever experiences had preceded him, none had equalled him, of that he was certain. He was counting on that now to override her misgivings about marriage. Tonight didn't have to exist in isolation.

Bedding an heiress was a tricky business when one was a poor man. They were not impressed by baubles and trinkets. They could buy enough of those on their own. The only currency he had here that carried any value was the pleasure he could give.

Ashe pushed such sordid thoughts aside. Yes, he had to think about winning her, but, no, tonight had not been entirely about that. He'd found pleasure aplenty with her that far superseded plans and calculations or any of the physical enjoyments he'd found in the arms of London's more adventurous ladies.

Tonight had been about acting on an attraction that had sizzled since the moment he'd seen her. It was a balm to his post-coital conscience that, Bedevere aside, he would still have wanted to bed her and most definitely would still have tried. He was not in this alone either. Even without the complications of Bedevere, she would still have wanted him, would still have chosen to be with him.

But Bedevere *was* involved. Ashe knew he was betting heavily on the pleasure they'd found to count for quite a lot in the morning light, not the least being the contents of the envelope that had arrived from London.

Ashe hated himself immediately for the thought. Had he really fallen so far as to use sex as a tool to coerce a woman into a marriage of convenience? If so, what did that make him?

Genevra stirred in his arms, her body warm against his as she dozed, so very unsuspecting of the turmoil in his mind. He reminded himself it was all for a good cause. But when would the ends stop justifying the means?

Chapter Thirteen

'Genevra, would you like to tour the estate with me, this morning? The weather has turned out to be fairer than expected after last night.'

Genevra's fork stopped halfway to her mouth, shirred eggs dangling dangerously in mid-air. Had any man in the history of the world used those words to follow up a mad night of passion? *Would you like to tour the estate?*

'I need to get out and see the tenant farmers and assess their needs before spring planting gets underway,' Ashe continued from the sideboard, piling a plate high with eggs and sausage.

He was doing so much better than she at pretending last night hadn't happened. Then again, he hadn't been the one to wake up on the library sofa. He'd been gone when she'd woken. But she couldn't argue with that. It was the right thing to do. The English had protocol for everything. He couldn't very well be discovered sleeping on the floor with her. It would be far easier for her to explain having fallen asleep on the sofa should an early-morning maid walk in to build up the fire.

'Genni is just the right person, Ashton,' Leticia put in from her place at the table. 'She knows everyone. She'll see to it that you're introduced. Everyone will be glad to know it's business as usual at Bedevere.'

'I would be glad to go,' Genevra said because there was nothing else to say without looking querulous. Leticia was right. She would be the best person for it, she'd ridden out several times during the old earl's illness, but she didn't relish spending the better part of the day riding around on a bench seat next to Ashe.

There would be too many reminders of the previous night. Even now it was hard to look at him and not remember the decadent things he'd awoken in her. It was probably no less than she deserved. There was a reason curiosity killed the cat. She'd satisfied her curiosities and now she knew exactly what it was like to be with Ashe Bedevere. Those exquisite moments would be for ever etched in her mind, on her body, for the rest of her life, for better or worse.

'What are you going to do today, Henry?' Genevra asked, turning the conversation a different direction in hopes of distracting her thoughts.

'I have a meeting,' Henry offered vaguely. He made a great show of taking out his pocket watch and checking the time. 'In fact, I am nearly late. If you'll all excuse me, I need to go.'

Ashe put aside his napkin. 'We need to make an early

start as well. I'll call for the gig and have it brought around in twenty minutes.'

Genevra couldn't help but notice the aunts smiling at one another as she left to go change. No doubt this was a prime opportunity in their eyes for her and Ashe to spend time together. Perhaps they were already thinking Ashe was showing signs of interest by extending the invitation to join him. The poor dears would be shocked if they knew the truth.

'We should talk about last night.' They'd barely turned on to the road, Bedevere still visible behind them.

'We both know what last night was.' Genevra kept her eyes fixed on the road ahead.

'What was it?' Ashe said coolly.

'Two people satisfying their curiosity about each other, I think,' Genevra replied.

'A curiosity that could have resulted in a child. Surely you didn't overlook the fact that we took no precautions,' Ashe pressed.

'I very much doubt it. Before my husband died, we'd resigned ourselves to a childless marriage. It is unlikely I'll conceive.'

'I do love American bluntness.' Ashe's voice carried an edge to it. They went over a deep rut in the road and the gig lurched heavily. Genevra grabbed Ashe's arm to steady herself.

'Well, there's no sense mincing the truth and I won't lead you down a path I know to be a dead end.'

'Still, I think it must be considered. Infertility isn't always the woman's fault. Men don't like to admit it, of course. Should your hypothesis be proven wrong, Neva, I would want to know.'

It had been on the tip of her tongue to say something cutting such as, 'so you can trap both of us in a marriage neither wants'. But intuition struck and kept her silent. Is that what he wanted? Did he want control of Bedevere so badly he'd risk a child to force a marriage? Would he doom himself to a relationship he didn't want? Of course, it wouldn't be a hardship for him. He'd marry her, leave her at Bedevere and return to London for his mistresses and entertainments.

Genevra spoke in sober accusation. 'You promised last night didn't have to mean anything beyond pleasure.'

'So I did.'

But it occurred to Genevra as they pulled up to the first cottage, that this was a promise Ashe Bedevere might not be able to keep.

The day sped by, filled with faces and names. Ashe shook hands with farmers, toured their fields, met their wives and children. He made list upon list, overwhelmed at the need. There were roofs to repair, fences to mend, farming implements to replace. Everyone he met was polite, but Ashe had a growing sense that things had not been taken care of at Bedevere for a very long time. The guilt he'd fought since arriving flooded back. This was his fault.

He would have to make it right somehow. He was starting to suspect making it right would involve swallowing his pride. There weren't enough billiards games in the county to bankroll these improvements. He was going to need Genevra's money.

Meeting with the shopkeepers in the village went better. Ashe positioned himself outside the inn, setting up a hasty plank 'table' across barrels and ordering ale for those who wanted to sit and talk.

One theme emerged regularly in those conversations. Business had been slow since the farmers had less money to spend, merchants were worried about their revenues. The item on their minds was the annual St Bertram's festival. Some believed it would help bring additional revenue to the village while others thought they ought to forgo the festival out of respect for the old earl's passing.

Ashe smiled. The festival of St Bertram had been a regular occurrence in Audley Village since nearly time immemorial. He and Alex had enjoyed the festival as boys. 'Is it still the first week of June?' Ashe asked, quelling the growing discussion with his question.

'Yes, and it's still the largest local fair in these parts,' the owner of the tavern put in, bringing another round of ale.

Ashe looked over the heads of the men gathered at his makeshift table. He spied Genevra with a group of women, someone's toddler on her lap. She was never very far away. She looked up, having heard the talk of the festival. Ashe chuckled to himself. She was probably already calculating how many handkerchiefs and jars of jam she could sell, God bless her American sense of entrepreneurship.

'I think the festival should go on as planned,' Ashe declared. 'Summer is a time of renewal and Bedevere is ready for that. A new time has come.' Never mind at the moment he was responsible for only forty-five per cent of that new time. No one needed to know that except he and Genevra.

Over the seated crowd, Genevra's eyes met his and she smiled her approval. It was gratifying and surprising to feel pleased at having obtained her favour, but Ashe felt them both. It had been a long time since he'd allowed himself to care what anyone thought about him or what he did. But he was caring now, a definitely new sensation.

'You made a good choice today,' Genevra offered once they'd completed their visits and turned the gig towards Bedevere. 'The festival will mean a lot to them and it's well positioned right at the end of spring planting.'

Ashe nodded, his attention only partly on the conversation. The gig seemed to be listing slightly to one side or perhaps it was his imagination and too many ales this afternoon. Too many ales? Really, the thought was laughable. He'd been in the country too long. He was Ashe Bedevere. In London, he could drink all night and not feel the effects. He doubted four ales in the middle of the afternoon was responsible for this.

Perhaps it was the road. There were ruts aplenty, left-over from winter snows and rains. 'Alex and I used to love the festival, we played all the games. Alex was a crack shot with a pistol. I don't think he lost a shooting contest since he was fourteen. Our father was so proud.'

'What about you?' Genevra ventured. 'Were you a pistol man, too?'

'No, I was a knife man.' Ashe smiled as he bragged. For the first time since coming home, it felt good to talk about the past, about his family. All those years alone in London, he hadn't realised just how little he spoke of them. 'Whatever Alex could do with a gun, I could do with a throwing knife. I wouldn't be surprised if there isn't a box of ribbons still tucked away in the attics. Our mother saved everything.'

'Your mother?'

'Yes, I had one, you know.' Ashe joked.

'It's just that no one ever mentions her,' Genevra replied quietly.

'Well, she's been gone a long time.' They were back to more painful memories now. It was more fun to talk about the festival. 'She died in a boating accident when I was seventeen. Alex was nineteen. She had been visiting friends over in Trentham and they'd gone out on the lake.' Her death had marked the beginning of his troubles with his father. Without her to act as a buffer between them, he and his father had failed to manage their disagreements. Not even the presence of the aunts could mitigate those quarrels.

'I didn't mean to stir up sadness.' Suddenly the gig

lurched. Genevra grabbed for the side railing of the bench, barely keeping her balance. 'That must be some rut we hit,' she gasped, recovering her seat.

Ashe shook his head. 'We would have seen a rut that big. Do you think the gig is riding lopsided?' The words were barely out of his mouth when there was a final lurch and the little cart crashed, turning on its side and taking them both to the ground.

Ashe's first and only thought in the time it took for the accident to happen was Genevra. She would take the brunt of the fall. Whatever had happened, happened on her side of the vehicle. He grabbed for her, trying to break her fall, trying to roll with her out of harm's way. Only the weight of the horse still in the traces prevented the gig from rolling once more on top of them.

'Are you hurt?' Ashe asked briskly, staggering to his feet.

'Nothing mortal, I'm sure.' Genevra replied in shaky tones, but Ashe noted she was slow to rise.

'Stay here, I'll see to the horse,' Ashe ordered. The sooner the situation was stabilised, the safer they'd be. Fortunately, the horse had had the good sense to remain still after the initial excitement of the accident passed.

'Steady there, old girl,' Ashe called out softly, taking the horse by the harness. From the horse's head he could survey the ruin. The back wheel had come off. It lay shattered in the road not far from the remains of the gig. They wouldn't be using the gig again. Ashe quickly freed the horse from the traces and led the mare away from the wreckage.

'I've got transportation!' he called down to Genevra, trying to make light of the situation. She smiled up at him and managed to get to her feet. 'Can you take the horse while I look at the gig?'

There was no reason the wheel should have come off and he wanted a better look at the hub and axle before it got dark. Ashe bent down for a closer look. He found the culprit immediately. The wheel had been loosened. It had simply rolled right off the axle itself.

'Neva,' he called out, 'did you ever take the gig out or my aunts?' It would be interesting to know when the gig was last driven and what kind of regular maintenance it was given.

She nodded. 'We used the gig for the summer and autumn fairs. We drove it quite a lot. But we haven't had it out since December.'

'No troubles with it?' Ashe stepped back from the wreck.

'None. What is it?'

'The wheel came off.' In itself that wasn't uncommon. But it was a rather bizarre occurrence for a vehicle that had been driven regularly without mishap and then lain unused for only two months. It was hardly long enough for the equipage to go to rack and ruin. Wheels simply didn't come off carriages without a little help.

It made one wonder what kind of help might have hastened the wheel's departure from its axle and Ashe didn't like the speculations he came up with or what they might mean.

Chapter Fourteen

Genevra didn't like the look in Ashe's eye one bit when they arrived back at Bedevere. The stare he gave her when she slid off the back of the horse and announced she'd be returning to Seaton Hall was proprietary and unyielding.

'I think you should stay,' Ashe said tersely. He'd been silent most of the way home, speaking only to enquire if she was all right. 'I want to speak with our groom and then you and I need to have an overdue discussion.' She didn't like the sound of that any more than she'd liked the look.

'I think I should go.' Staying would mean another night at Bedevere, which might lead to another night with Ashe. While there were appealing aspects to such a prospect, that had definitely not been part of the bargain she'd made with herself last night. Last night had been a moment's pleasure, a curiosity satisfied, but not to be repeated.

'Go inside and freshen up. I'll be along shortly. Try not to alarm my aunts.'

He was deliberately ignoring her request. Genevra's temper over the high-handed treatment rose. 'I will not be dismissed in such a manner,' she countered.

Ashe's eyes glinted dangerously, green coals waiting to ignite, his voice a low growl of authority. 'Yes, you will, temporarily. If you want to cut up at me, you can do so in the estate office in a half-hour.'

There would be no winning this. Genevra drew a deep breath to still her temper. She would temporarily cede the field. But she'd be waiting.

Ashe was prompt, early even. He was the one waiting for her in the office. Sitting behind the big polished desk, he looked every inch the peer's son. Even though time had been short, Genevra noticed he'd managed to change into clean attire. Looking at him, one would not guess he'd been in a carriage accident a scant two hours ago. She hoped she looked as well put together. There'd been time only to change her dress and re-pin her hair.

'Was your talk with the groom satisfactory?' Genevra took the seat on the visitor's side of the desk, feeling very much the supplicant come to beg crumbs from his lordship's largesse. She would not be intimidated by the big desk and the handsome man sitting behind it. For heaven's sake, she was a businesswoman. But all her mental protestations could not deny the flutter in her stomach when she looked at Ashe Bedevere.

'Somewhat,' he replied enigmatically. His tones were cool, exuding authority. He was going to be stubborn, she just knew it.

'I don't think the wheel was an accident, Genevra.' Oh, this was serious. He wasn't calling her Neva. She braced for the storm that was sure to come.

'The groom said the gig was in good shape when he harnessed the horse. The groom confirmed what you'd told me, that you had used the gig quite regularly and it had not been sitting idle. The groom also said no one had been near it this morning except himself. Which makes sense...' here Ashe paused with a chuckle of derisive laughter '...since we no longer employ a full complement of grooms.'

Genevra furrowed her brow. 'All that seems to support the wheel *was* an accident, which, I might remind you, is the exact opposite of what you postulated moments ago.'

'You Americans are too impatient. Let me finish.' Ashe waved a long, elegant hand. 'What it means is that someone tampered with the wheel while we were in the village. The gig was out of view during part of our visit. It would have been easy enough to do. There would have been no one around, everyone was gathered with us.'

'All right.' Genevra folded her hands in her lap. 'If that's true, why would someone do it?' She thought Ashe was seeing villains where there weren't any. His conclusion was somewhat extreme.

Ashe fixed her with one of his hard stares. 'You're the one with a jilted suitor and fifty-one per cent controlling interest in an estate. Why don't you tell me?'

'Henry? You think Henry did this?' Genevra said in disbelief. 'He was at a business meeting all day. I doubt he knows the mechanics of a carriage wheel to begin with. Your cousin's a book man. He's hardly the type to get his hands dirty.'

'He's the type to pay someone to do it for him,' Ashe said succinctly. 'I don't think Henry did it himself, but I think he is likely behind it.'

Genevra shook her head. 'You're seeing the worst because you don't like him.' It was absurd really.

'Sometimes our eyes deceive us.' Ashe's long fingers fiddled with a paperweight, tracing the lines of cut glass. 'Forget about Henry's golden good looks and that boyish smile of his. Think about the facts, Genevra. You saw how angry he was when Marsbury read the will. He'd clearly expected more. He's tried to get more by proposing marriage to you. You've refused him and effectively scotched his last avenue to gaining nominal control of the estate—'

'You're spinning out of whole cloth, now, Ashe,' Genevra interrupted. This was silly. 'Why would he go to all that trouble for an estate that will not be his once Alex dies? Whatever he gains will only be temporary. You'll be the earl eventually.'

'Unless I die first,' Ashe drawled. 'Henry needs Alex alive. Whether Alex lives or dies, Henry can still wield control. Right now, it's better if Alex lives. As long as I'm alive, Alex is safe. Henry doesn't want to risk me inheriting because his control of the estate, meagre as it is, goes away.'

Genevra's quick mind grasped the implications. 'But if you're dead, Alex isn't as useful to Henry.'

'No, then Alex becomes expendable. He becomes more of an obstacle, the only obstacle that prevents Henry from having complete control and the title, too.' Ashe got up and pulled open a drawer in one of the glass-fronted bookcases lining the wall. He pulled out rolled paper and spread it on the desktop, holding it down on each end with paperweights.

'Come have a look, Genevra, and get your first lesson in English inheritance law.' Genevra rose and stood next to him, studying the lines he traced with his long finger.

'Here's my father, Richard Thomas. He has two sisters, Lavinia and Mary. Lavinia never had any children. Mary, Henry's mother, made a disappointing marriage to local gentry, Steven Bennington. They both died several years ago, leaving Henry a small property. That leaves my father's line. He's the earl. He marries, he has two sons, all seems well.' Ashe's hand traced the lines leading to his name and Alex's. 'But now Alex is mentally incapable and there's just me. Henry is next in line as the next male of the family line as the only nephew of my father.' Ashe shot her a wry look. 'As you can see, it's a fabulous game of live and let die.'

'It doesn't convince me Henry's a murderer. It just convinces me that primogeniture is complicated,' Genevra argued.

'A man's life hinges on its protocols from the moment he's born.' Ashe rolled the parchment up and put it away. 'What a man can and can't be is tied up with his birth order.' There was great hurt, a gaping chasm behind Ashe's comment. For a moment, the authoritative aristocrat gave way to the enigmatic man she'd glimpsed beneath his urbane surface.

Genevra smiled softly. 'In America, we believe a man can be anything he wants.'

'And yet you left such a land of promise.' The harder side of Ashe had returned. He motioned for her to take her seat. 'I think the point of this conversation has escaped you. Allow me to spell it out. I am in danger because I stand in Henry's way. You have refused his proposal and, by doing so, have effectively shut down his last avenue of legitimate recourse for gaining control of the estate. You are now in danger as well. If we're both eliminated, Henry gains control of our shares. What he can't accomplish through marriage, he can now accomplish only through death.'

Genevra scoffed at the notion. 'I am thankful I don't have your imagination for the morbid. Do all Englishmen sit around and daydream up myriad ways of how their families could dispatch them? What a paranoid lot you must secretly be.' She rose to go. She'd had enough of the ridiculous.

Ashe stood too and reached for her arm across the desk. 'We're not finished, Genevra. Sit down.'

'I want to get home before dark,' she protested.

With his free hand Ashe pulled an envelope from the desk drawer and tossed it on to the polished surface. 'You might feel differently after you read this.'

Genevra sat down, sceptically eyeing the letter. It was the one that had arrived from London yesterday.

A cold knot started to form in her stomach. 'Your office has the most interesting things in its drawers,' she remarked, unfolding the letter. 'Family trees, letters from London.'

'We're very thorough,' Ashe said drily.

'I can see that,' Genevra replied with equal coolness, her eyes scanning the crisp white paper. The opening sentence boded ill—'the woman in question…' which no doubt was her. He'd had her investigated.

She read the letter in quiet rage. 'I have nothing to fear from this letter. My husband is dead and that has been settled for quite some time.'

'Nothing except quite a lot of scandal should all the details be unearthed. His death was not quite as simple as stepping out in front of a dray and being run over by a twelve-hundred-pound draught horse.'

No it wasn't. He'd come home the night before in a drunken rage, blaming her for another failed business venture. He'd smashed stained glass and china. He'd come after her, too, until she'd feared for her safety. She'd spent the night at her father's. But in the morning he'd come for her, hungover and dishevelled and begging for money again. That was when she'd threatened the divorce and two of her father's men had to physically remove him from the house. She'd stood on the front steps, watching it all happen. They'd been rough, throwing him on to the street, and he'd cursed her and stumbled to his feet, only to step out backwards into a busy Monday-morning street full of delivery carts.

His family blamed her of course. They said she might

as well have pushed him herself. She'd provoked his distraught mentality. He hadn't been in his right mind, they said. She'd wanted to scream he hadn't been in his right mind for some time.

'Now you know the truth.' Her tone was icy as she laid the letter on the desk. 'You wanted to know what I was doing here—now you know. Is the truth gratifying to you?'

Ashe was unfazed by her quiet anger, which was most unsatisfying. He just sat there, looking at her with those green eyes. 'You're right, you have nothing to fear from that letter. There is nothing criminal there. But there is scandal. That scandal could be potentially embarrassing should it come out.'

Genevra clenched her fists. 'If you mean to blackmail me with this, you are a far worse rogue than I first believed.'

Ashe shook his head. 'No, I don't mean to do anything with it. I want you to realise that if I can get this information, Henry can too. I don't promise his motives will be as pure.'

Genevra's eyebrows raised. 'Pure? Perhaps you'd like to outline your motives so that I might better understand your application of pure?'

'Leave it alone, Genevra. It's enough I didn't mean any dishonour by it,' Ashe cautioned.

'No, I will not leave it alone. You had me investigated, behind my back. You will tell me why.'

'I wanted to know if Bedevere was in any danger from you,' Ashe said shortly. 'I wanted to know if you had misled my father in any way, hoping for a piece of the Bedevere pie.'

Genevra paled. 'You thought I was a fortune hunter.' She covered her mouth with a hand in abject horror. He'd implied as much in the conservatory that first evening. But hearing the words spoken so blatantly was different. It was the worst thing he could ever accuse her of being.

'I did not mean to distress you,' Ashe said. He might as well have said, 'I told you so, I told you to let it be.'

'You don't understand, Ashe,' Genevra said quietly, mastering her temper. 'You just accused me of being the very thing I abhorred in my husband.'

Well, that had gone poorly. Ashe raked his hands through his hair. No doubt Genevra was upstairs right now, packing her things and preparing a retreat back to Seaton Hall and all its dropcloths and new-paint smell. He couldn't blame her. For a man skilled in seduction, he'd certainly bumbled this. Ashe folded the letter up and put it back in his drawer.

He'd only meant to show her the danger of secrets. If Henry knew this, he could easily use it to blackmail her into marriage. This would be a scandal she'd want repressed. It could hurt business with her shipping line and it would certainly hurt her socially if she decided to enter London society at some point. Henry would not hesitate to use it as leverage.

But Genevra hadn't believed him about Henry. She

didn't think him dangerous. That was the problem. No one ever did until it was too late.

Gravel crunched on the front drive and Ashe looked out the long windows. Genevra's carriage was ready. She hurried down the front steps and the carriage pulled away. She was gone. For now. His body protested her leaving. There wouldn't be a chance now of coaxing a night of passion from her. Last night had been extraordinary, far more than a physical seduction. He'd thought of little else all day. Even while he'd listened to tenants and shopkeepers, part of his mind had been on her.

The women of the village admired her. Their approval had been evident in the way they'd gathered around her, showing her their babies and taking her into their circle. Ashe didn't think Genevra had been without a baby in her arms or a toddler on her hip all afternoon. Whenever he'd looked over at her, she'd had a child with her.

Babies raised a whole other issue. Ashe was convinced his father meant for them to marry. Had he known Genevra believed she couldn't have children? Marrying Genevra meant the end of the Bedevere line. Assuming she was right, of course. There was no question of Alex siring an heir. Any heirs would have to come from him. It would be something of an irony to sacrifice himself in marriage to save Bedevere only to have no one to save it for. But perhaps the present was more important than the future.

Marrying Genevra was fast becoming the only solution available, not only for Bedevere's well-being but for her own well-being, even if she wasn't willing to see it. He hoped it wasn't a lesson she had to learn the hard way. Marriage to him would put her out of Henry's way. She would no longer be an obstacle to the estate, all the authority would now lie solely with him. If Henry wanted Bedevere, he'd have to go through him to get it, and him alone. That meant he had to protect Alex, his aunts and perhaps most of all Genevra, whether she wanted his protection or not.

Chapter Fifteen

His week was up. Genevra had refused him and Henry thought Marcus Trent was taking the bad news rather well. Henry shifted in the deep leather armchair across from Trent's desk, trying not to prematurely breathe a sigh of relief. It was just he and Marcus today. The others were blessedly absent.

Marcus leaned forwards, elbows on the cherrywood desk. 'Then it's time to not play nice, Henry. Everything is in place for our venture. We're merely waiting for permission from the estate to start the mining process. Either we get that permission through marriage, or through some other means.'

'Some other means', Henry very well knew, meant fatal accidents. Trent's cartel had been involved with other ventures that had got off to difficult beginnings until certain 'coincidences' had marginalised or eliminated those who had been difficult. Here was a chance to impress Trent with his forward thinking.

'My cousin has offended a few men in Audley. He

won money from them at billiards. One of those men was more than glad to arrange a carriage accident when Ashe was in town this week.'

Trent's reaction wasn't quite what Henry had expected.

Trent raised bushy black eyebrows. 'And by doing so, you may have tipped your hand prematurely, Mr Bennington. In fact, it may have been downright foolish of you at this stage of the game.'

'But you just said it was time to stop being nice,' Henry sputtered in argument before Trent silenced him with a look. One did not argue with Marcus Trent.

'Violence isn't the only way to coerce,' Trent said with a pointed look. 'While you've been failing to secure our heiress, I've been researching. Mrs Ralston was of little interest to me before your uncle's death, but circumstances have demanded I pay attention to her.' He touched his temple with his index finger. 'Lesson one, Mr Bennington, is to always know one's opponent. What are their weaknesses, what are their strengths? Mrs Ralston's weakness is her past, as is most people's. Have you ever asked yourself why a rich American would come to Staffordshire and bury herself in the country when she has enough money to go anywhere and do anything?'

No, he'd never wondered. Genevra had simply presented herself as a widow looking to make a new start away from America. Up until this week, he'd assumed a new start would include a new husband. But apparently she had no proclivity to marry again. That had been a surprise. Didn't all women want to marry? Even rich ones? He felt foolish now. Even when she'd refused him, Henry hadn't thought about the reasons why.

Henry's silence was answer enough. 'I can see the thought didn't cross your mind. Thankfully, for all of us, it did cross mine.' Trent gave him a patronising smile. 'My sources in London tell me her first marriage was nasty and her husband's death nastier. She stood on the front steps and watched two footman all but shove the poor blighter into the path of an oncoming delivery dray. He was killed instantly.' Trent shook his head as if in disapproval. 'I'm certain it wasn't *exactly* like that. But still, if such aspersions were to get around, it would be damaging for her.' He slid a brown paper envelope to Henry. 'It's all in there. I think Mrs Ralston might find marriage more palatable, especially if it ensured permanent protection from such rumours.' Trent cocked his head. 'She's not indifferent to you, is she, Bennington? I thought you'd said the two of you were good friends.'

'No, she's not indifferent,' Henry lied. His pride could not bear to admit otherwise.

'Good. She might be amenable to such an overture coming from a friend. But I wouldn't wait too long, Mr Bennington. I hear your cousin was seen with her in town.' Trent leaned back in his chair, studying his nails.

'This is your chance, Mr Bennington, for revenge. Steal his woman, steal his estate. It's what you've been waiting for all your life and I am serving the opportunity up to you on a very nice platter.'

Henry nodded his thanks and rose to leave. Trent was indeed providing him an invaluable service. He was well aware that Trent's plans, Trent's consortium, Trent's money had greased the way this far in the plan to mine the wealth of Bedevere. He was also aware Trent wasn't a man who gave such favours for free. Trent would receive a fair share from the mining venture, but Henry couldn't help but wonder if Trent was after something more. Henry pushed such deep thoughts aside. Perhaps it didn't matter. Trent was entitled to play whatever games he liked as long as Henry got what he wanted and that started with an afternoon call to Genevra.

Bad news was supposed to travel in threes, but the post proved it could travel in twos just as effectively. Genevra's hand shook as she set down the two letters. Neither was good. Henry had sent a note asking permission to call that afternoon.

In light of the note's tenor and his recent behaviour, she was beginning to rethink the reasons for Henry's sudden desperation. Lately, Henry had been far too keen on pressing a friendship into something more even after she'd tried to scotch those efforts as politely as she could. Henry was a changed man since the earl's death and she worried what he might intend by requesting this meeting.

The second note was from Ashe and it had arrived only hours after her return on stiff cream-coloured paper bearing the Audley seal. The wording was formal; Mr Ashton Bedevere wished to call tomorrow afternoon on Mrs Genevra Ralston at her convenience to discuss a proposal of mutual benefit to them both.

If the note had come from a different man, or under different circumstances, she would not be worried. It would be perfectly understandable that he'd want to speak of business and the estate, maybe even to discuss the use of a loan. After a week of assessing the situation, the usual man would be ready to embrace the realities of their partnership. But she did not fool herself into thinking Ashe was the 'usual man' and that meant she had no idea what he wanted with this request to call. They'd parted in anger over an issue that had been part business in its origins, but had quickly become personal in its outcomes.

Genevra looked at the hands of the clock. It was barely eleven. She had two hours. All she could do now was wait and perhaps change her dress, a small but useful distraction.

Genevra had dressed carefully in a dark-blue receiving gown trimmed in white lace. Her maid had arranged her hair in a sophisticated twist, creating the image Genevra was looking for: a respectable woman, confident in her own abilities. She had just put on her tiny pearl earrings when Henry was announced. She smoothed her skirts and drew a deep breath. So it began.

Henry waited for her in the drawing room, looking polished and well groomed in buff breeches and a coat of blue superfine. His gold hair was brushed to a fine sheen and he'd brought her flowers, a rare treat in the last weeks of winter.

Genevra took the flowers, wary of what they might be a prelude to. 'They're lovely, Henry. I'll have them arranged in a vase and set them in here. They'll look beautiful in this room. Wherever did you find daffodils so early?'

'A friend of mine has a hothouse,' he supplied with a glib smile. 'The house is coming along splendidly, Genni. Are there other rooms that are done as well?'

'My bedroom and the kitchen. But the downstairs is scheduled to be completed within the month.' Genevra sat and smoothed her skirts. The conversation felt stunted.

Henry must have agreed. He cleared his throat. 'Thank you for agreeing to see me. Might we sit?' He looked eagerly towards the chairs, his nerves apparent in his stiff manners. He was playing the anxious suitor once more to perfection. The realisation hit her again as it had her last evening at Bedevere—Henry was quite a role player. What other roles had he played over the course of their association? The friend? The loyal nephew rushing to the side of his ailing uncle?

Genevra marvelled that she hadn't seen it before. Henry was a consummate actor. She'd seen his many faces, but she hadn't yet really seen him. The realisation stung with the tang of betrayal. If it was true, he'd willingly duped her and duped the aunts. The only one not taken in had been Ashe. Genevra knew a moment's alarm. If Ashe hadn't been taken in, did that mean Ashe was right in his less savoury conclusions about Henry as well?

'Genni, this is more difficult than I thought,' Henry began and her sense of alarm ratcheted up a notch. 'I know that you refused my initial offer of marriage, but I have hopes you'll reconsider in light of new information that might change your circumstances.' He said the last gently with the tones of the friend, but his eyes held a hard glint that belied the tenor of his voice. She was learning to read him, to see the little chinks in his façades she should have seen before, but for which she had no cause to suspect.

'What new information, Henry?' She fought the urge to clench her hands in her lap. This revelation worried her greatly, but she dare not show it. Ashe's warning came back to her: if Ashe could discover her secret, what was there to stop Henry from doing the same?

Henry lowered his eyes, seeming to debate with himself over the words to use. He began slowly as if he still grappled for words. 'It has come to my attention that your husband's death is surrounded with unsavoury details.'

It was Genevra's turn to assume a role. She looked down at her hands. 'His life was unsavoury, it is no surprise his death was, too.' Henry would have to make his accusations more blatant than that if he wanted to scare her. How brave would Henry be?

'The unsavoury details are about you, however.' Henry pushed in a spurt of boldness. 'I am sure you would not want to fall victim to such rumours even if they were unfounded. Through marriage to a respected family, you would be protected from such nasty repercussions. No one would dare to gainsay the Bedeveres.'

So Henry knew. It was quite enterprising of him really, and highly out of character for the man she'd thought she'd come to know over the winter. Genevra gave him a sharp stare. 'Are you trying to blackmail me into marriage, Henry?'

'Genni! How can you think such a thing?' His shock appeared genuine, or perhaps it was embarrassment over having been called out on his improper game.

'Well?' Genevra pressed. 'Let's call it what it is. You were politely refused and now you think to regain your position through less palatable means.'

Henry rose, his face suffused with anger, his jaw stiff. 'I came here to make you an honourable proposal of marriage and you treat me like a dog.' He slapped his gloves against his thigh in a gesture of agitation. 'Has my cousin already poisoned you against me? I warned you he would, but that warning, like my offer, has fallen on deaf ears,' Henry sneered. 'Maybe you think to wait on an offer from Ashe, the great Mr Bedevere himself. You'll probably get one. He's that desperate to hold Bedevere against me. He didn't care a jot for the estate until he discovered I had a toehold in it. He'll marry you, for Bedevere, for money, but not for love. He'll never be faithful. He's a tomcat if ever there was one. I don't think you're the kind of woman who could tolerate that, yet when I offer you a decent marriage, you scoff at it.'

Genevra rose. This angry Henry thought to intimidate her with his height. She would not scare so easily. She kept the low table separating the chairs and the sofa between them. 'I'd like you to leave now,' she said in even tones.

This Henry-chameleon who stood before her disturbed her with his ability to switch in and out of roles so adroitly. This Henry was a stranger to her and one she did not trust. He'd come here the suitor, but had abruptly become an angry man.

Henry advanced on her, the table proving to be a useless barrier. There was no place to go. Genevra squared her shoulders. She reminded herself there were servants about.

Henry's hand reached out to caress her cheek. 'You're the answer to Ashe's prayers. He wants to marry you for the money and the estate. He'll bed you and leave you. But I would protect you from that and whatever else, my sweet.'

Genevra slapped his hand away and repeated, 'I'd like you to leave now.'

'You can't make me, though.' Henry's blue eyes glittered with a hard cruelty as he dragged her to him with a fierce grip about her waist. Genevra struggled.

He gave a cold smile and held her fast. 'Perhaps if you had a taste of what you'll be missing you might change your mind about marriage. I can make it good for you. Ashe isn't the only lover in the world.'

Genevra shoved at him hard, fists pummelling his

chest, but she gained little ground against him. She'd not realised how strong Henry was.

'Leave the lady alone, Henry. She's made her intentions clear, as have you,' came a dangerously cold voice.

Ashe.

Henry let her go so swiftly she nearly fell to the sofa. 'This is none of your business.'

'A woman in distress is always my business. We seem to have done this before, Henry.' Ashe moved from the doorway to the centre of the room, his eyes locked on Henry although his words were for her. 'Are you all right, Neva?'

'Yes.' She was breathless, watching the two men circle one another. Her drawing room was too small for the both of them. She had visions of her newly redone room being smashed to bits.

'You do remember the squire's daughter, don't you, Henry?' Ashe said in cool, mocking tones.

A knife appeared out of nowhere in Henry's hand. Genevra stifled a scream, but Ashe was fast. In the same fluid move she'd seen at the mausoleum, Ashe retrieved his boot knife. It stalled Henry momentarily.

'Quite the equaliser, Coz.' Ashe was all cold focus as he palmed his knife. 'I'm not afraid of a fight. I believe I won the last one.'

Oh, lord. They were going to fight over her, with knives, in her drawing room. She did not want this, but she was powerless to stop it. She was no coward, but only a fool would come between two men with knives. Genevra stifled a gasp and retreated as far back on the sofa as she could lest she become a casualty of the cousins' war.

Henry's gaze shifted a fraction. 'This is unseemly conduct for a gentleman and I will not engage in it.' It was a coward's strategy, taking refuge in the high road.

Genevra breathed a bit easier. If Ashe had any sense, he would give Henry this polite *congé*. Ashe sheathed the knife back in his boot and gave Henry a hard look that chased him from the room without even a goodbye.

It was only then that Genevra realised Ashe had come to call looking resplendent. White breeches were tucked into high black boots polished to a gloss. His greatcoat was brushed with buttons polished, and, beneath it, a blue coat trimmed in heavy gold braiding graced his broad shoulders. A ruby stick pin was stuck in the snowy cravat that peeped elegantly over the vee of a silk waistcoat. The sight was breathtaking even under these circumstances.

Ashe noted her lingering gaze. 'Wearing my station, as the expression goes.'

Ah, and setting the tone of the meeting as well. From the formal note to the formal attire, he meant for this to be an official visit, which worried her even more. What could he mean by this?

'My apologies, Neva.' Ashe made her a short bow. 'A beautiful woman often brings out the worst in men.'

'As does money,' Genevra said with a certain sang-froid now that she'd recovered her wits. 'I'm not naïve enough to believe you and Henry were fighting over me.' No, they'd been fighting over her money with the knowledge that whoever controlled her controlled Bedevere. It was something they'd all known, now it was out in the open.

Ashe remained undisturbed by her declaration. He settled himself in a chair and fixed her with his mossy eyes. 'Good, then you will understand why it is now absolutely imperative that you and I marry with haste for our mutual benefit.'

Chapter Sixteen

'Do you believe me now about Henry?' Ashe asked once the shock had left her face. 'Henry will blackmail you down the aisle, all for his own avarice.'

'Then that makes two of you,' Genevra said coldly.

'I will not be classified with the likes of him.' Ashe's tic began to twitch at her words. 'I come to you with honesty. He came with protestations of love and the trappings of romance, both of which are a lie. A man in love does not importune a lady the way he did today. I am hiding nothing from you, Neva. I am not masking my proposal as anything more than what it is, a business venture. Once I am legally in control of Bedevere's trusteeship, Henry will have no reason to bother you. You will be safe. You will be a countess-in-waiting for your efforts.'

Painted like that, it sounded like a very tempting offer indeed until one remembered all that Ashe gained in exchange: money and control of his estate and control over her. She was in England now. Their marriage laws when it came to property rights for women were very different. Marriage to an Englishman would demand some compromise on her part.

'Such an offer demands the surrender of my freedom,' Genevra challenged.

'It secures your protection,' Ashe countered.

He was crazy to think she'd give up her freedom to a man she'd known barely a week. Then again, she'd kissed him on the acquaintance of a few hours and had done much more on an association of days.

'I hardly know you,' Genevra stalled.

Ashe gave her a wry smile, his eyes half-lidded. It was a sensual look that said he knew her secrets. 'You know enough, I think, to know marriage to me would hardly be an onerous chore.' Genevra felt her face burn at the reference to their one night, a night that wasn't supposed to matter.

'Think about it, Neva. How will you thwart Henry on your own? Even if you manage to escape the repercussion of his nasty rumours, he will come again, next time with violence perhaps. Actually, there is no perhaps. He came with violence today, you saw that. What he cannot take by subtle manoeuvres, he will attempt to take by force. Henry is a predictable creature.'

'That is no reason to trap ourselves in marriage.'

'It's only a trap if you don't see it. There is no trap for us, Neva. We know exactly what we're doing and exactly what we'll get.' Lord, he was silky toned and his arguments as slick as an eel. It all seemed so probable, so sane when he laid it out like this. But in the end, it all came down to one thing—did she need protection from Henry's threats badly enough to risk her freedom? No, that wasn't fair. There was more than protection at stake, there was an estate to consider as well. It had been given into her care. What would serve it best? Uniting with Ashe or remaining his adversary?

'You and Henry seem to think I have only two options: him or you. There is a third option, however. I could turn over my shares to you, leave Seaton Hall unfinished and go live somewhere else. I could wash my hands of the entire mess your father left behind.'

It was an empty threat. Even as she spoke the words, she knew it would be leaving too much: leaving her dream of helping other women become independent, leaving the aunts and walking out on her promise to the old earl. In sum, leaving would make a hypocrisy of all she thought she'd stood for. She could not make others independent if she could not do that for herself.

'I think you torture yourself unnecessarily, Neva. You'd never have been with me if you hadn't trusted me.' Ashe reached for her hand, pressing a kiss to her knuckles and then turning it over to press a slow kiss to her palm. The fires started to stir, challenging her objectivity, her reasons.

Henry's warnings rang in her head—Ashe was a tomcat, he'd never be faithful. Most certainly he'd not pledged to be any of those things today. He'd pledged only to be a source of pleasure and protection. Yet when he kissed her hand like that, she wanted him to be so much more even while she knew he saw this marriage as nothing but an expedient means to an end.

There was a wicked gleam in his eye as Ashe relinquished her hand as if he knew he was gaining ground.

Genevra rose and began to pace, trying to re-establish her objectivity. Henry had tried to force her compliance today—he might even have been behind the carriage accident. She had to admit that sawed spokes weren't accidental. Henry was a desperate man. Could she really expect to stay in Audley and remain unscathed from his efforts? 'It's not exactly the kind of marriage proposal a girl expects to hear.'

'Can I take that as a yes?'

There was no choice. If she meant to stay in Audley and see her plans to fruition, if she meant to stop running, she would need help. Ashe had proven most willing and able to offer protection today without protestations of love. That had to count for something. So, for the sake of her dreams, for the sake of a promise to a dying earl, Genevra said, 'Yes, I suppose you could.'

'I am well honoured by your acceptance,' Ashe said with a stiff formality required of the occasion. Inwardly, he breathed a little easier, but only a little. He would truly celebrate once the marriage was done and Henry was no longer a threat to her or to Bedevere. It had angered him beyond measure to see Henry's hands on her when he'd arrived and the anger had been surprising.

Ashe recognised it would have infuriated him no matter who the woman was. He might be a profligate rake, but he only dallied where he was welcome. Henry, on the other hand, knew no such restraint. But the anger that had rocketed through him today had been different, it had been deeper, more possessive, and it had shocked him with its ferocity. Henry had been accosting *his* wife-to-be. Ashe had known relief when Henry had drawn a blade, it had given him an excuse to draw his own and let go some of the feral energy coursing through him.

'Neva, there is a last thing I'd ask of you. I'd like you to accompany me back to Bedevere so we may tell the aunts our good news. They will want to make plans— it will be best if you're there to guide them.' He gave her a conspiratorial wink.

Genevra answered with a smile that softened her whole face, 'They don't know about the will, do they? They will think this is a love match.'

He leaned back in his chair, stretching his long legs, ready to do some teasing now that his initial anxieties had passed. 'Yes and yes. But I think we can offer a reasonable facsimile of their expectations, don't you, Neva?'

She favoured him with a blush. For all her sharp wit and shrewd insights, he could still get to her. Ashe was finding he liked that quality about her. She wasn't as worldly wise as she often pretended, but she was not beyond a little humour of her own. 'When shall the wedding be, Ashe? Shall we play the romantic lovers to the hilt and marry in haste or shall we wait a decent period because of the funeral?'

'I think in haste would suit best given the circumstances. Even the king will understand the need to secure the succession. The potential of a babe in the Audley cradle within the year will forgive a multitude of sins.' The sooner she was under his protection, the better.

'I have told you there is little possibility of children—' Genevra began, but Ashe cut her off with a sharp shake of his head.

'You don't know that for certain. There's no sense in bringing it up. It does not help our cause,' Ashe cautioned. 'We can marry within the week, I think. I need to procure the special licence and I want my brother here for my wedding, if it's possible. With your permission, we will leave in the morning to get Alex.'

'You want me to come?' Genevra was clearly surprised by the request.

'Four hours in the carriage will give us time to become better acquainted,' Ashe said with a levity he didn't feel. It would give them time to talk but, in truth, Ashe was worried about what he'd find when he saw Alex. He'd never fully understood what had happened to Alex. He'd been too horrified over the news to properly pursue it. It would be a help to have Genevra with him if the situation was worse than he imagined. She'd been here a short while with Alex. She would be familiar to him, perhaps even a comfort.

They departed promptly at eight in the morning, taking the travelling coach, hitched with the four horses remaining at Bedevere for just that purpose. Bury St Edmunds was too far to risk going unprepared for the weather, which promised only to be inconsistent despite the blue skies that oversaw their departure.

The journey would take two days if nothing went wrong. Genevra had done the calculations in her head. With luck and good roads, they'd arrive around one in the afternoon, perhaps earlier. Ashe would be able to go straight to see Alex. They'd spend the night at an inn, visit Alex one more time in the morning and make the return trip home with or without Ashe's brother. The schedule would be grueling, but Ashe had been clear he didn't want to spend more time away from Bedevere than he needed to.

Genevra tried to keep herself busy with reading. But sitting across from Ashe Bedevere and remaining entirely aloof was a nearly impossible feat. She'd already lost her place five times for sneaking a look at her handsome husband-to-be. He was dressed today in tight buff breeches and high boots that showed off his legs to perfection in the confines of the coach. She couldn't help but notice his long legs, stretched as they were between the two opposing seats. Long, strong legs, with well-defined thighs, giving way to the coat of blue superfine and turquoise waistcoat beneath. He was always immaculately turned out, even for travelling.

The sixth time she looked, she got caught. 'What are you staring at so intently and so often while you pretend to read your pamphlet?' Ashe drawled, that teasing, arrogant smile of his on his lips.

'I'm merely contemplating some of the material I've been reading. It provokes much thought.'

'Well, while you've been contemplating the wonders of—what is it?—' Ashe leaned forwards and tipped her pamphlet up '—Ah, the wonders of knot gardens by Mr Hayman—I've been staring at you. I think I have the better of it, frankly. Agricultural tracts have never held any allure for me.' His tone made it clear, however, what did indeed hold an 'allure'.

This was the Ashe Bedevere she'd come to know, perhaps the Ashe Bedevere that would make up the bulk of their convenient marriage. It made her wonder if the Ashe who'd spoken of reminiscences in the garden or so fondly of shooting contests at a country fair had been a figment of her overactive imagination.

'Is everything a seduction to you?' Genevra countered.

'When it comes to you,' Ashe said boldly. 'Do you want to know what I was doing in my mind while I stared at you?' It was a rhetorical question. She didn't get to answer. 'I was playing this decadent game with your hair. I was wondering how many pins I could pull out before all that glorious hair came tumbling down.'

The temperature in the coach seemed to skyrocket. He was wreaking havoc with her senses, with her body. His voice, his touch, his presence, all commanded her attention. She couldn't simply ignore him and it disturbed her. Deep down, she didn't want to ignore him. She liked his naughty banter with its witty innuendos. Ashe kept her on edge, kept her looking forward to his next outrageous suggestion. Life with Ashe around had been more, well, more exciting.

That frightened her. She hadn't come to England looking to fall in love. She'd been looking for precisely the opposite. She'd wanted to get away. She didn't want to fall for anyone. But falling for Ashe Bedevere would somehow be worse.

'What are you afraid of, Neva?' came the seductive whisper. 'We are to be married. Lust won't be a sin any more.'

'You, Ashe. I'm afraid of you. I think you can turn a girl's head without her even realising it and that's a frightening thing indeed.' Genevra stiffened her resolve. 'Our marriage is based on convenience, not on romance. You're too dangerous to a decent woman's heart. I've told you before I'm not interested in what you're offering.'

'Yes, but we were talking about gardens then, Neva.' Ashe's green eyes sparked with mischief. He was enjoying this far too much.

'Most of the world's problems came from a garden.'

'Only Man's. Man is the only part of creation to have fallen, Neva, and some of us have fallen further than most.'

There it was again, that glimpse. Just when she was convinced he was one-hundred-per-cent pure rogue, he gave her a glimpse into the very human depths of himself and created chaos out of her preconceived notions. Genevra picked up her agricultural tract and focused on it with exaggerated attention. If she wasn't careful she'd be falling right along with him. Marriage might protect her from Henry, but what would protect her from Ashe?

They made good time, pulling into Bury St Edmunds an hour ahead of schedule. Ashe settled them at the Fox, an inn at the east entrance to town and closer to the place where Alex was housed. The Fox was a nice inn with heavy oak timbers and panelling in true Jacobean style. Plain and unassuming, what it lacked in luxuries it made up for in cleanliness. Ashe secured two rooms upstairs and gave instructions for the horses to be stabled. He would rent a small gig from the livery for the short trip to see Alex.

'You've checked your watch three times in the last minute. It won't make the horses come faster,' Genevra scolded playfully while they waited in the courtyard for the borrowed gig to arrive.

Good lord, he was nervous, Ashe admitted to himself. He had no idea what he'd find. Where had Henry housed Alex? Was it some raving-lunatic asylum? What was Alex like now? Would Alex even know who he was? That probably scared him the most. He supposed he harboured hopes that Alex could give him answers to all his questions. It was hard to imagine Alex's mind being gone.

The gig had arrived and they made the short drive to the home a few miles outside the city. Ashe's worries eased slightly as they approached. The home was an old estate, well kept with a neatly trimmed yard. The house itself seemed to be in good repair.

Inside, they were welcomed. Ashe gave the man at the door his card and they were ushered into an old library converted into an office by a matron dressed in a clean grey-and-white uniform. Then they waited. But not for long.

The door opened and a bearded man in an austere dark coat and simply tied cravat entered. 'I'm Dr Lawrence, Mr Bedevere, what a pleasant surprise to see you. Audley doesn't have many visitors.'

'I must apologise for the abruptness of my visit,' Ashe said. 'I've recently returned home and I did not want to delay in seeing my brother.' He was glad to note that the hospital had shown Alex the proper reverence and adopted the use of his official title when referring to him. He wondered if it meant anything to Alex, though.

'Does he understand our father has died?' Ashe asked, taking a seat opposite Dr Lawrence.

Dr Lawrence shrugged. 'At times. But not always. What can I help you with today?'

'I want to see him and I want to hear about his condition. It has not been fully explained to me. I would also like to discuss the possibility of having Alex come home with me.' At the last comment, the doctor stiffened ever so slightly. He covered it hastily with a condescending smile, but Ashe had noticed.

'I think those are laudable sentiments, Mr Bedevere. However, I think once you understand the nature of his condition, you will realise it is best to leave him here where he can be under professional supervision. We have others like him, others from families not unlike your own. He is in good hands.'

Ashe studied the man. Dr Lawrence had been good natured and open, but the mention of taking Alex home had changed him into a man of great wariness. Ashe could see it in his eyes. He chose to let it go for the moment. He would not help his cause by alienating Dr Lawrence too soon.

'Tell me about my brother.'

'Lord Audley has been with us since November. It is a shame we didn't have him right away after the breakdown. We might have been able to do more for him. But, as you know, nearly three years had elapsed and there is little hope for any further recovery. Instead, it has become apparent that he is prone to recurring breakdowns.'

'Breakdown? Define that for me,' Ashe prodded. He was interested in causes right now.

'Nervous breakdowns are triggered by a stressful event in a person's life. From what Mr Bennington shared with us, it is likely the trigger was the Forsythe scandal or perhaps the family's failing financial situation in general. Unable to face up to his financial responsibilities, Lord Audley's brain simply stopped functioning. He was despondent, he didn't answer when spoken to, he stopped eating. He lost all time orientation.'

Dr Lawrence paused, his voice lowering. 'Mr Bennington shared with me that one night he found Lord Audley with a gun. His intentions were quite clear.

'I must be straightforward with you, Mr Bedevere. Your family did an admirable job caring for him as best they were able even after that incident. But when your father began to fail last autumn, there simply wasn't the time or ability to look after them both and your brother's condition appeared to worsen. He would have periods where he wouldn't know who he was or what his circumstances were and this created an intense paranoia on his part. He'd begun taking long walks and not know how long he'd been gone. There were occasions when he'd become lost and had to be searched for. Mr Bennington and four ageing aunts couldn't manage the dual responsibility. Mr Bennington put your brother here, because he has become a danger to himself.' '

'I would like to see him.'

Dr Lawrence nodded and rose. 'Please follow me. You must understand he lives mainly in the past now.'

Ashe asked Genevra to wait in the foyer. He wanted to meet Alex alone. Dr Lawrence led him upstairs and down a hall. 'Your brother has access to the entire house and grounds, but we have a companion assigned to him so that he goes nowhere alone.' He stopped at a big, bright room at the end of the corridor. 'I'll leave you for a few minutes.'

Ashe stepped into the room. It was white and clean and stark in its features except for a little vase of yellow flowers on a small table, but Ashe's gaze spared little consideration for those details. His attention was focused on the lanky figure standing in the big bay of the window looking out over the lawns, his back to Ashe.

Alex was much as Ashe remembered him: a thinner rendition of himself. Even growing up, Alex had sported a more slender physique, a poet's build. It wasn't a weak man's build, but he'd never had Ashe's powerful shoulders or muscled thighs. Alex had been strong in other ways. He was an astute thinker and a compassionate human being. He would have made a good earl.

Alex turned from the window and saw him. Ashe's breath caught. He looked so *normal*. Ashe wasn't sure what he'd expected. Shouldn't a crazy man look a certain way? He supposed he thought one should. But Alex was dressed in a patterned-blue waistcoat and trousers, polished boots and a pristine white shirt. He looked no crazier than the next man and Alex hadn't known he was coming. It gave him hope.

'Alex,' Ashe said simply.

Alex's brown eyes registered recognition. 'Ashe. I knew you'd come.' In a moment Alex's long legs had covered the distance of the room, Alex's arms enveloping him in an embrace. 'Thank God, you've come at last,' he said in quiet but firm tones. 'You have to get me out of here.'

Chapter Seventeen

'Get me out of here.' It was what insane people said all the time. Alex was prone to periods of extreme paranoia. Dr Lawrence had told him it was customary. Still, Ashe couldn't bring himself to share that bit of information when the doctor had come back for him. He'd said simply it had been a good visit and that he'd come back tomorrow. Other than that bit of paranoia, Alex hadn't demonstrated any more outwards signs of mental debility.

He told Genevra as much over dinner at the Fox that evening. 'Of course, we didn't talk of anything upsetting other than Father's death.' He poured her another glass of the excellent red wine. They had a private parlour and dinner was proving to be a delicious meal of venison stew and freshly baked bread. A mincemeat pie waited on the sideboard for dessert. 'Perhaps he can handle little things without becoming overwrought.' There was a pathetic amount of hope in his voice. There were no cures for these kinds of ailments. He didn't do himself any favours in pretending there was.

'I'm glad the visit went well.' Genevra took a bite of the stew, the candlelight limning the delicate curve of her jaw. She looked like a veritable angel in the flickering lights.

His angel.

Or his devil.

He had won her, for better or worse, for Bedevere, for his aunts, for Alex. He needed her money for all of them. For them, he'd bought her the only way he knew how—binding her to him with passion and seduction, even if he feared it would cost him the last of his pride and the last of his soul. He could talk about protection all he wanted, but once the concern over Henry was retired, he would be left with only the pleasure he could give her in bed to keep her bound to him. He'd have to look that man in the mirror every morning, knowing he'd found his price.

'I will go back and see him tomorrow.' Ashe rose to fetch the pie. He'd given explicit instructions that they be left alone while they dined. 'Will you be all right on your own for a few hours?'

'I'll be fine. I'd like to explore the market and see if there's a merchant who would be willing to take some of your aunts' designs for the summer.' Genevra reached to take the pie and knife from him with a laugh. 'Let me do that. It's a pie, not a pig. You're butchering it, Ashe.'

Genevra passed him a slice of pie and he was struck by the domesticity of the moment. Little things like that had not mattered much to him before. This idea of someone doing something for him who wasn't a servant was quite novel. He wondered if this was how it was like for his friend Merrick and Alixe. Of course it would never really be that way for him and Genevra. They *had* to marry. Merrick and Alixe had married for love.

It occurred to him, as he finished his pie, that he wished it could be different. If he had seen her across a ballroom in London, if he had been able to marry anyone he chose, he might have been tempted by her beauty, her grace and her wit to fall headlong into a decent romance. It was a shame he'd not find out what it would be like to come to her honestly as a man in love.

This was a new revelation to him that perhaps a heretofore unacknowledged part of him had secretly wished to marry for love, in spite of the realities he'd long ago accepted. Even second sons, *especially* second sons, had to marry where the money was.

'You look deep in thought. Are you thinking about Alex?' Genevra rose to clear the dishes, another intimate, domestic act.

'No.' Ashe sighed and pushed back from the table. It would do no good to tell her he wished it could be different. Instead he said, 'Thank you for coming. Alex seemed quite well today. I've changed my mind about tomorrow, I think he'd like to see you. We can tell him together about the wedding.' He smiled mischievously. 'It would mean giving up your tour of the market and franchising my aunts' handiwork.'

Genevra gave a light laugh. 'Ah, I see you're start-ing to accept the idea.'

'Tolerating the idea.' Ashe chuckled. 'Since there's no dissuading you from it, I've decided to tolerate it.' This was a good moment, a hopeful moment. In time, their marriage might be full of more moments like this where they weren't merely two strangers thrown to-gether by circumstance.

'It's late, I should go up.' Genevra gathered the last of their dinner things and set them on the sideboard next to the remaining pie.

'I'll walk you up.' Ashe rose. He smiled at her wari-ness. He could see she wanted to protest his offer. Going up alone would preclude any seduction. She'd be safely ensconced behind a locked door before he mounted the stairs. And that would not do tonight for either the rake in him or the husband-to-be.

The rake in him argued this was a perfect opportu-nity. They were here, alone, at an inn with no one but Genevra's maid and the coachman for chaperons. Who would know if he went to her bed or if she came to his? And with nuptials pending, who would care? The soon-to-be bridegroom in him saw it as another chance to remind her that she could trust him. They might marry without the benefit of romance or common knowledge but he would not be a cruel husband, he would not be another Philip.

'It is not necessary. Stay here and enjoy your brandy,' Genevra offered generously.

It was on his lips to answer, 'When I could be up-

stairs enjoying you? Never.' But tonight was not an evening for glib words. 'Tonight is not for being alone, I
think, Neva,' he said in quiet tones. The last two days
had been full of strain for them in separate ways. She'd
witnessed Henry's duplicity firsthand and faced the reality of her options. For himself, he'd reunited with his
brother and secured a marriage, neither event without
its own turmoil of emotions. It was time to seek solace
for those emotions.

'Very well, you may see me up.' Genevra's voice was
as quiet as his as they exited the private parlor, a sure
sign she understood.

Ashe kept his hand at the small of her back up the
stairs. At her door they stopped. She fumbled for her
key. 'Allow me.' Ashe deftly took the key from her and
fitted it to the lock, swinging the door open. The room
inside was lit by a carefully laid fire. One of the inn's
maids had been here recently.

'Do you have everything you need?'

'I think so.' She looked up at him, her grey eyes lu-
minous, her thoughts transparent behind them, her pulse
racing at her neck. She was not unaffected either by the
domestic intimacy of their dinner or their companion-
ship on the long carriage ride.

She wanted him. Ah, Ashe understood her reticence
downstairs immediately. She wanted him, not as a result
of any flirtatious games he'd invoked at dinner, because
he'd invoked none, nor did she want him as a means to
satisfy a growing curiosity like she had in the library
at Bedevere. She wanted him simply because she did

and that was very gratifying indeed. For him. For her, Ashe thought, such a realisation would be frightening, a clarion call to caution. She would worry he would use such knowledge against her as Philip had. She would worry such a wanting would make her weak in this fledgling partnership of theirs.

He understood those feelings all too well. They were not that different than his own. God help him, tonight he wanted her for reasons that had less to do with securing his inheritance and more to do with a being a man desiring a lovely woman. He tilted his head to capture her mouth in a slow, lingering kiss at the door.

'Neva, I'd like to come in,' he said in hushed tones against her ear. Tonight, he would show her with his body what he could not tell her in words. He could feel her body tremble against him as she made her brief contemplation and decided.

'Yes,' she whispered.

There was no going back now, perhaps there never had been. Perhaps she'd been fooling herself all along about the one night in the library. It had never really existed as a moment out of time. Genevra stepped into her chamber, feeling Ashe's body move behind her, hearing his elegant hands shut the door. Tonight he would be her lover. She had no illusions about what he'd requested. He wasn't coming in to check for rats. He was coming in to share her bed and she could not pretend she'd not thought about it throughout the day.

It might possibly be the most audacious thing she'd

ever done. This would not be like the library, rash and unplanned. She'd not gone downstairs that night thinking she'd encounter Ashe and let him seduce her. Tonight was premeditated. There could be no excuses for rash behaviour afterwards.

Genevra turned and faced him, her hand reaching for the hairpins. She tugged once, twice and her hair fell. 'Two, the answer is two.'

Ashe gave a low growl, all manly appreciation. His eyes glowed with the intensity of coals. 'Allow me to do the rest. Let me undress you, let me worship you.'

Genevra gave a throaty laugh. 'Shall you play lady's maid?'

'Oh, no, I shall play the supplicant. No lady's maid has ever undressed you like I shall.' He managed the tiny buttons down the back of her dress with alarming efficiency, pushing the sleeves of the gown down her arms with a gentle thrust that sent goose bumps of pleasure coursing through her. His lips skimmed her bare shoulders, his hands holding her firm at the waist, his thumbs deliciously close to the undersides of her breasts.

She moaned in frustration. She'd become greedy for his touch in such a very short time. He kissed her neck, nipped at her ear. His hands moved up at last to cup her breasts, caressing and teasing through the fabric of her chemise until they felt heavy with desire in his hands. Only then did he reach to gather up the cloth of chemise and tug it over her head. Genevra wiggled her hips and let the gown slide to the floor. At last she was bare and free. She turned in his arms and his mouth met hers in a fierce, possessive kiss.

It was her turn now to undress him. She reached for the cravat and tugged, laying waste to his efforts at an intricate knot. She drew him out of his coat, then his waistcoat, her hands fumbling at the buttons in her haste.

'I thought it was only women who dressed in layers,' she teased. She had not imagined undressing him to be frustrating, but she had not imagined her need being so great. She was well aware her body thrummed for him, that his caresses had driven her to a perfect state of readiness.

Genevra tugged on the tails of his shirt, pulling the length of fabric from the waistband of his trousers. Ashe stepped back and finished the shirt himself. 'Look at me, Neva.'

Again, he was magnificent in the firelight, his torso limned by flame, his musculature defined by shadow and light. Genevra's fingers itched to trace the lines of those muscles and the tantalising path they drew leading to the waistband of those trousers. She swallowed hard as his hands followed her eyes down. He boldly cupped himself through the tight trousers, making her fully cognisant of his arousal.

He pulled at his boots and pushed at his trousers, his eyes never leaving her. It was the most erotic undressing Genevra could imagine. He was displaying himself for her, letting the disrobing heighten her own desire until she was nearly overcome with it and he missed not a moment of it. He was entirely conscious of the effect.

He came to her, gloriously naked and brazen. He drew her into his arms, the hard length of his phallus pressing against her unabashedly. There was no pretence or modesty between them. The bed was at her back, she could feel it against her knees. He urged her on to it and straddled her, his haunches taking his weight. He looked like an American native in the firelight as he rose above her with his dark hair framing his face.

'You're beautiful, Neva,' he whispered hoarsely and she revelled in the power of knowing she could trigger this depth of desire in a man who could have any woman. She was Eve in that moment, or perhaps Lilith.

His mouth found her bare breast, sucking and coaxing her nipple into erect hardness. She arched against him, her body begging for more, begging for the intuitive release that lay beyond even this pleasure.

He moved his mouth to her navel and feathered it with a breath. 'If we had wine, I could show you a trick,' he murmured, his breath warm and arousing on the surface of her skin. She shuddered delightfully. Just the mere decadence of the suggestion was enough to set her on desire's edge.

Her hands stroked the muscled length of his back, cupping his buttocks, urging him to that most private place between her legs. At last he came, the moist tip of his phallus nudging at her entrance, his knee spreading her legs wider still for him and she welcomed him.

There was more they might have done, more play they might have had, but they were ready for each other and the dance had gone on long enough for tonight.

He rose and thrust and she took him in with a cry that bordered on joyous. He thrust again and again and she joined him in the rhythm his body created within her. Her hips rose to match him, her legs wrapped about him, holding him, her hands raking his back in abandon. He was fierce in his possession, their desire riding him hard, and she met it equally. They were in the throes of a magnificent madness. Suddenly the madness crested and then it broke all around her, shattering into a million fragments of desire achieved and passion spent.

Ashe lay beside her, unquestionably as depleted as she. His breathing was ragged and his skin held the sheen of sweat in the firelight. She rested her head against the strength of his shoulder, their breathing slowing at last. And then, without words, she slept.

Chapter Eighteen

As a rule, Ashe hated mornings. They were bright and littered with realities. This morning was no different. He stretched and waited for the regrets to flood with the sunlight, but none came. He waited for his mind to chastise; he'd allowed himself to get caught up in sentiment last night. Beside him, Genevra slept soundly, no doubt exhausted by the evening activities. He'd taken her again twice more in the night, the last right before dawn.

He should feel something, but he felt nothing of the usual recriminations, only an alien sense of deep contentment such as he had felt in the library. Only this time, it was far more intense. He also felt a sense of resolve. It was the sense of resolve that propelled him out of bed. Alex was waiting, counting on him to return. Ashe made a quick *toilette* and dressed before waking Genevra. He would slip downstairs and arrange for the carriage, giving her the privacy of the room to make her morning ablutions.

Ashe sat on the side of the bed, pushing back her tousled hair to wake her. Even in sleep, she was a beauty beyond compare. 'Neva, we must get up.' She moaned a little at the intrusion. He was tempted to let her sleep, but decided against it. He wanted her with him. If Dr Lawrence tried to forcibly prevent Alex from leaving, Ashe wouldn't have time to stop by the inn and pick Genevra up.

Genevra stretched and rolled on to her back, the sheet slipping to reveal the swell of a breast. His body hardened. If there hadn't been the business with Alex this morning, he'd gladly have slid back into bed. But the sooner he dealt with Alex's situation, the better. What else might Alex tell him if put to the question? How much of it would be driven by the paranoia of his condition and how much of it was real? He kissed Genevra's brow with a final admonition to get up and went downstairs before his body could launch an effective counter-argument.

Alex was dressed for the day and having breakfast when they arrived. Dr Lawrence had not been pleased to see them, nor had he been pleased with Ashe's request for a private meeting after the visit. But Alex had been ecstatic over his return and that he'd brought Genevra. They pulled up chairs to the table and the three of them sat down to a breakfast of tea and pastries.

'We have something to tell you,' Genevra began after they'd all fixed their plates. Alex looked up from his food with interest and wariness.

'I hope it's not more bad news. The aunts are all fine, aren't they?'

Ashe was pleased by the response. Alex remembered everyone, was able to be concerned about them. Alex had always been alert to the needs of those around him. Such a quality would have made him a grand earl.

Genevra reached out a comforting hand. 'It's nothing like that. They're fine. It's good news, actually. Ashe and I are getting married just as soon as we can and we'd like you to be with us for the wedding.'

'You're taking me home.' The emotion of the simple statement nearly broke Ashe. He'd come as soon as he could. There'd been so much to do right away at the estate. But he wished he'd come sooner—the books, the will, the bills, the garden, even courting Genevra, be damned.

Ashe stood up and walked to the window to gather himself. He let Genevra chat with Alex about the aunts and Bedevere and the plans for the garden. When his emotions were under control he returned to the table.

'Congratulations, brother.' Alex's eyes sparkled with genuine affection. 'Finally, there's a woman who can settle you down.' He winked at Genevra. 'Has he told you all about his wild escapades in Italy or how he held Vienna in thrall with his piano playing? He even performed at Schonbrunn Palace.'

Genevra shook her head in mock seriousness. 'He has neglected to mention much of that to me. But he has played for me at Seaton Hall. He is magnificent.'

'I'm standing right here, you know,' Ashe put in.

Alex meant well with his stories, but Ashe didn't want him to tell too many. That was all in the past and not all of it was as rosy as Alex painted it.

Genevra tossed him a smile and moved towards the window. 'I'll give the two of you a moment to talk.'

'Alex, do you know why you're here?' Ashe asked, taking his seat again.

Alex set down his cup and sighed, hanging his head. 'I am not well, Ashe. They tell me on occasion I am given to bouts of paranoia and despondency where I don't talk to anyone and I think everyone is conspiring against me.'

Ashe leaned forwards. 'Is now one of those occasions? Do you think you're in your right mind?'

Alex held his gaze with solemn dark eyes. 'Yes, I am absolutely in my right mind for the time being. But I never know when an episode of madness might come upon me. That's why I must stay here.'

Ashe's heart cracked at the admission. His brother had always been so confident, so certain of himself. Now, he was shadow of that former self. 'Henry says you are a danger to yourself and to others.'

'Ha! Henry. What does he know? He says and does whatever is best for Henry. You know that.' For a moment Ashe glimpsed the old fire.

'Henry said there was an incident with a firearm.'

Alex snorted at this, very much like his former self when Henry would challenge him with absurd untruths in their youth. 'It was hardly an incident. If I'd known what he'd make of it, I'd have shot him then and there and saved all of us the trouble. Next time I will.'

The fire of his statement riveted Ashe. 'What trouble would that be?' Was this paranoia speaking or a genuine plot being uncovered?

Alex leaned towards him across the table. 'The trouble over Bedevere. Who is to rule Bedevere if I am unable? They call me the earl and I suppose nothing can change that except my death. That doesn't serve Henry. He can commandeer Bedevere as a trustee as long as I live. Heaven forbid I die, then you're the earl and Henry loses all claims.'

'Bedevere is broke—why does Henry want it at all?'

Alex lowered his voice. 'It's for the coal. He believes he'll mine Bedevere and make a fortune. I found out right before I got ill. He's spent two years amassing investors and biding his time.'

'And the Forsyth scandal?' Ashe's suspicions were on high alert. The coincidences were starting to mount. Very soon, he'd have another look at the books. Maybe with Alex's memories to fill in the gaps, the odd entries would start to make sense.

Alex shook his head. 'Dr Lawrence says that must have been my first fit, although no one realised it. I have no recollection of ever having authorised those investments. I had the running of the household. Father was unable to do much of anything. It's my signature on the receipts, but I don't recall having done it.' The eyes that held Ashe's were serious, earnest and entirely sane. How could he doubt his brother?

Suddenly Alex grabbed his forearm. 'Ashe, you do believe me? You are taking me home for good, not just for the wedding?' The gesture stank of desperation and Ashe's hopes fell. How was he to know if these were the ramblings of a man who needed care or a man who'd been marginalised and pushed out of the way by a scheming cousin who coveted his estate?

It didn't matter. Alex had never failed him. Ashe owed him this. Ill or not, Alex was coming home. Ashe covered Alex's hand with his own and bowed his head until their dark heads met across the little table. 'You're walking out of here with me today. I promise. The Earl of Audley belongs at Bedevere.' Then he called to Genevra, 'It's time to go. Take Alex straight to the carriage. I'll settle things with Dr Lawrence.'

The interview with Dr Lawrence did not go well. Lawrence was visibly upset by the decision to remove Alex. He made all the usual arguments: Alex needed care, he needed doctors, one never knew when a fit might take him, he was a danger to himself. Ashe met each of them with a sharp emerald gaze and crossed arms.

In the end, Ashe simply said, 'Who pays your bills? Mr Bennington?' Dr Lawrence paled at the mention of that particular fact. It had been a logical but lucky guess. Ashe pressed his advantage. 'If so, I doubt you'd want those monies scrutinised. If I looked too closely, I might discover something much akin to bribery in those payments.'

That silenced him. Ashe smiled coldly. 'I thought as much.' He also thought the terrified Dr Lawrence would have a letter posted to Henry within minutes of their departure. The other concern was whether or not Dr Lawrence would recover some modicum of courage such as it was and try to stop their departure from the city. For both those reasons, Ashe wanted to be well away with all haste.

He joined Genevra and Alex in the carriage and gave the signal to be off. If their leave-taking resembled a getaway more than a departure, so be it. Ashe didn't trust Dr Lawrence any further than he could throw his knife and that was about twenty feet.

The trip home was blessedly uneventful. Alex sat in relative silence, drawn carefully into conversation by Genevra. She chatted of the improvements being made at Bedevere, of Ashe's plans for the gardens and of the aunts' new designs for the summer fairs. Occasionally he would nod and smile, but for the most part he held himself rigid as if his good fortune would be shattered at any moment.

Ashe watched them both: the woman he'd marry and the brother who needed him. What an odd family he was assembling. After years without one, he now had a family of ageing aunts, an ailing brother and an American bride. A very odd assortment indeed. Each in their own way were counting on him. He wouldn't have it any other way. A primal desire to protect rose in him. With Alex coming home, everyone who was entitled to that protection would be under one roof: his. He would not let them down.

Henry was waiting for them when they arrived in the late afternoon. They'd no more than pulled into the drive than Henry was down the steps, livid with rage. Ashe grimaced as he stepped down from the carriage. He could guess the source of Henry's fury. Henry hadn't been there the night he'd announced his betrothal.

'What were you thinking to take Genni with you?' he thundered the moment Ashe's feet touched the gravelled drive. 'Have you no sense of decorum? People will talk. She will be ruined.'

'We are to be married, cousin. No one will mind if we travelled together for Genevra to pick up a few essentials for the wedding.' Ashe could not resist a cold smile as he delivered the news. He reached into the carriage to hand Genevra down. 'Do wish us well.'

'I cannot believe you left with nothing but a maid,' Henry charged Genevra.

'And my clothes,' Genevra said just to be perverse. The spirit of her made Ashe laugh, but he could feel her grip on his arm tighten under the furious look Henry gave her.

Henry was scandalised. 'Genni!'

'Oh, for heaven's sake, Henry, it was hardly a holiday,' she scolded lightly. Ashe knew what the brave front cost her. Just days ago, Henry had tried to force his attentions upon her. She would not soon forget or forgive the imposition. If Henry didn't voluntarily leave

Bedevere before supper, Ashe would 'suggest' it. His protection started now.

Ashe glared at Henry. He might have banished Henry right then if Alex hadn't intervened. 'It seems I am one of those wedding essentials,' Alex said congenially, stepping down on his own. 'It's good to see you, Henry.'

Henry's anger over Genevra was nothing compared to the pale rage on his face when Alex emerged. He'd not expected that, Ashe thought.

'What have you done?' Henry turned his anger back to Ashe.

'I have brought my brother home where he belongs,' Ashe said sternly. 'If I were you, I'd be more concerned about what you've done. Now, if you'll excuse me, I want to see my brother settled.'

Ashe was intoxicating like this, Genevra thought quietly, making her way to her borrowed chambers at Bedevere, all his authority unleashed as it had been the first day she'd seen him. She would let the family settle Alex. She had thoughts of her own to settle and she needed distance from Ashe's potent sensuality. Her room at Bedevere was the best she could manage. There was no question of going to Seaton Hall. Henry's gaze this afternoon had been venomous. She didn't want to be caught alone and Henry's recent behaviours suggested he wasn't beyond such tactics.

Whether she wanted it or not, Ashe's protection was becoming very necessary. But it came with risks of it own.

Up until last night she'd believed she could have her fantasy with Ashe and remain detached. She would satisfy her curiosity and nothing more. It was becoming more difficult to do that in practice.

She had not guessed they would share something so monumental between them not once, but twice. Nor had she guessed the depths of loyalty he carried. Bringing home his brother was not the action of a man who thought only of himself and his pleasure. It was not the first time she'd glimpsed this about him. But his choice with Alex had certainly solidified that such behaviour was not an anomaly. It would be easier if it was.

It would be far easier if Ashe Bedevere had turned out to be precisely the man she'd thought he was: a rake, a gambler, a seducer of women. Instead he'd turned out to be something far worse; he turned out to be a man she could love. That could make for a disastrous, lopsided marriage. Ashe had made it clear he would protect her and pleasure her, but he'd never promised he'd love her.

Still, there were small things to be thankful for. Ashe informed her as they went into supper that Henry had left the premises on a more permanent basis. Supper was a simple meal, but one full of celebration. Henry was gone, Alex had returned and a wedding loomed on the near-horizon.

By the end of dinner, the aunts and Ashe had decided it should take place on Friday, just two days away. Such haste was probably best, Genevra concurred. There was no need for lots of plans. The family was in mourning and she and Ashe knew what the wedding really was even if the rest of the family didn't: a convenient merger. Such an alliance didn't need to be heralded with ribbons and roses and other wedding fripperies. She would send to Seaton Hall for a good dress she had in mind for the occasion and that would be the extent of her preparations.

The happy little group adjourned to the music room where Ashe played for them on the old Broadwood piano while the aunts chattered excitedly about Bedevere weddings past. Genevra listened to their tales with half an ear. She was more interested in the man who played the piano. What was it that Alex had said today? Ashe had played at Schonbrunn? It occurred to her she could ask Alex for more of the story, but that seemed hypocritical. If she wanted to know, she should ask Ashe himself, especially after her tirade over Ashe's investigation of her background.

Alex rose and went to the piano. Genevra followed his movements with her eyes. He murmured something to Ashe. Ashe stopped playing and shuffled through the sheet music until he found what he was looking for. Genevra was aware of Leticia setting aside her needlework in expectation.

'The boys are going to sing like they used to,' she said in an excited whisper, nudging Melisande and the others to the attention. 'Alexander has a lovely tenor.'

What followed was grand fun. Ashe and Alex entertained the group with lively songs that made the aunts laugh and they closed with a sad rendition of 'Barbary Allen' that left a tear in the aunts' eyes. Even Genevra found herself wiping at wet eyes as the last notes faded. Ashe's gaze caught her out as they all rose for bed. Their eyes met and held and Genevra understood. He would come to her soon.

Chapter Nineteen

Ashe was coming. Her body thrilled to the idea even as Genevra's mind counselled against it. She should send him away, give him some nonsense about wanting to wait for the wedding before they were together again. But that was ridiculous. Her body didn't want to wait even two days.

She realised in retrospect that he'd been priming her for this all night in subtle ways. His hand had lingered at her back when he'd seated her for dinner. His eyes had held hers a bit longer than necessary during the meal. He'd been flirting all night in small ways, heightening the anticipation that they would continue what they'd started at the inn. Perhaps he was already setting the pattern for their marriage.

It had most definitely worked. Here she was, dressed in a satin nightgown in record time and all put pacing the floor when she knew he couldn't possibly venture to her room until the house was settled. Impending nuptials or not, it wouldn't do to be caught sneaking up to her room.

Genevra hoped the house would settle soon. Perhaps she should make a list of all the things that needed doing, all the plans she'd need to co-ordinate for her own estate from here. She went to the little writing desk and pulled out paper and ink. She'd just begun the task when the scratch came.

A slow smile crept across her lips. He was here. Genevra rose and smoothed her gown for good measure. 'Come in.' There was a small catch to her voice that belied her anticipation. If she sounded more eager than she preferred, she could be forgiven for that. Ashe in dishabille was a sensual sight designed to arouse the staunchest spinster.

He carried a small black canvas bag in one hand and was dressed for the night in a blue-paisley banyan and slippers, but not much else if the view of smooth skin at his neck and chest where the banyan vee'd was to be believed. A tremor of desire shot through her at the thought of him naked beneath the robe. How daring, too, it had been of him to take such a chance wandering the house dressed like that.

'I see we are of like minds.' Ashe's eyes slid over her form, hot appreciation evident in his gaze, her body responding instantly.

'Only I'm not wandering the house,' Genevra teased. 'Is Alex settled?'

'He is very glad to be back in his own rooms.' A faint

smile hovered on Ashe's lips. 'I stayed and talked with him a while. It's why I'm a bit later than I expected.'

'No apology needed. He is your brother—'

Ashe shook his head in interruption. 'It's been a long day, right now I want to set all that aside. I just want you.'

I just want you. Those words could atone for a variety of sins. But Genevra was careful to understand them for what they were. She was his escape. There was both compliment and insult in that. Was this the pattern he wanted established in their marriage? Would he come to her after a long day and lose himself in her body while keeping his thoughts locked away?

He came to her now, ready to be lost, his hands resting possessively on her hips, his mouth engaging hers in a light caress that aroused and promised, while still saying 'not yet' in the most tantalising of ways. 'Give me a moment to make everything ready,' he whispered against her neck.

He left her and strode purposefully to the delicate white table beside her bed. He placed the bag on it and began setting out items: small stoppered vials, a tiny shallow-bottomed pan and a small wire stand. He turned back to look at her with a wolfish smile. 'Sit. You're welcome to watch and to imagine what we might do with these things.'

Genevra watched intently, giving her mind permission to move her earlier misgivings to a far corner. Ashe's movements were too mesmerising to concentrate on much else. There would be time for those contemplations later. He removed the chimney from her lamp and set the stand over the open flame. With deft hands, he adjusted the flame and settled the shallow pan above it, creating a burner, carefully pouring in liquid from his bottles. With another man, the process might be merely scientific, but he had the uncanny ability to turn the act of warming liquid into something sinfully decadent. He put his nose over the little burner and inhaled deeply, his eyes shut, his dark lashes long and sensual against the sweep of his cheek.

He exhaled and she could smell it, too, the scent of lavender tinged with the spice of lemon slowly filling the room. He faced her and held out an inviting hand. 'I am ready for you, Neva. I've thought of nothing else a good part of the day.' *When he wasn't thinking of his brother, or ousting his cousin from the family seat, or dealing with recalcitrant doctors,* came the unbidden thought, quickly pushed aside but no less powerful for its brevity.

His eyes were on her and she rose, determined to make good use of his attention. If escape was where they started, she would accept that for the time being and move on from there. Genevra slid the thin straps of her nightgown down her shoulders and gave a graceful shrug that sent the satin garment slithering to a pool at her feet.

'Temptress,' Ashe growled his approval, his hands going to the belt at his waist and making quick work of the garment.

Her breath caught at the male beauty on display. She

had seem him naked before, but only in firelight. In brighter light, too, he did not disappoint. He smiled in comprehension. 'Tonight, there will be plenty of time to, ah, shall we say, "appreciate" one another. Come lie down, Neva.'

She felt sure those four words were uniquely designed to render her incapable of any sensible thought. She gladly complied. It was clear he had something planned for her although she could not guess what it was. She was well aware that she was entirely at his mercy while she was naked and sprawled on the bed, a realisation that made her more uncomfortable than she cared to admit. Last night she'd felt in control, a partner. She did not feel that way now. 'What are we doing?' She eyed him suspiciously as he retrieved the pan from the burner.

'Are you nervous?' The bed took Ashe's weight as he sat on the edge.

'Yes,' she said frankly.

He smiled, all traces of the wolf gone, but he made it clear he would not brook any balking. 'We won't do anything you don't like. We'll begin with a massage and I guarantee you'll like it very much. Let me start with your feet.'

Oh, she did like it! The warm oil on her skin was a wicked pleasure made even more so by the slide of his hands on her body, expertly rubbing and pressing as they moved up the length of her: feet, legs, thighs, buttocks. Was there anything as heavenly as this? As *decadent* as this? Lying naked with a man, his hands on her body, soothing and coaxing, readying—the ultimate foreplay. When he reached her back, he levered himself over her, careful to avoid giving her his full weight. She could feel the heavy brush of his sac as he massaged her back.

'Where did you learn to do this?' She was amazed she could form any words at this point.

'In Venice.' His hands were at her shoulders now, his thumbs at the base of her neck. 'It's quite an art, mostly an eastern one.' She could believe that. It was far too sinful for stuffy old England to embrace wholesale.

'Venice sounds wonderful, then,' she murmured, not wanting to think of who might have taught him the art or where precisely in Venice he'd acquired it.

'Venice *is* wonderful. East meets west—it's the gateway to the Adriatic, to Istanbul, to Egypt. Britain is just starting to see its potential, although others in the east have long recognised it.' He could make even a lecture in geography sound sinful.

He leaned over her, pushing her hair to one side, his voice low at her ear. 'Shall I take you now, Neva?' His phallus nudged at the place between her legs and her buttocks rose instinctively to meet the request. This was new and unfamiliar territory, but her body knew what to do and she'd abandoned her inhibitions at the first caress of his hands.

His arm was about her waist, holding her steady, lifting her to him and then he was in her, his entry swift and sure until she could feel him deep inside her, her body flowing around his intimate presence. This was the pleasure she'd waited the day for, the pleasure that kept her at Bedevere. Pleasure seemed far too bland a description for the sensations rocketing through her anew at each of his powerful thrusts. She gasped and moaned, reaching for the penultimate release. The thundering pulse of his phallus assured her it was not far off for either of them.

In a fleeting moment of clarity before the shattering liberation of climax took her, the thought swept her ever so briefly; this was not merely sex, a messy act of physical gratification, this was *art*.

Whoever had taught her had not thoroughly tutored her. There was a spark of pride in knowing that he was truly the first to awaken real passion in her. It wasn't perhaps the most refined of thoughts to have after such a critical moment, but it had popped into his head none the less, a random tangent that had resulted from contemplating the woman beside him.

Ashe propped himself up on one arm and traced lazy circles around the tip of her breast. 'Will a Friday wedding suit you, Neva? It occurred rather belatedly to me that you might have some friends to invite. We could wait a few days for their travel.' Now that Henry was physically off the property, Ashe could afford the luxury of a slight delay.

'No,' Genevra said simply, but the negation aroused Ashe's curiosity.

'I can hardly believe such a beautiful woman has sprung from wholecloth in the midst of Staffordshire.'

She laughed, the delightfully enticing smoky sound that promised a man a lot more than she knew. 'Hardly wholecloth. You know I'm American. It wouldn't be prudent to invite my family. We haven't the time.'

'Oh, so you do have a family,' Ashe said in teasing tones. His drawings moved to the other breast. It was hard to believe she was entirely alone.

'Did,' Genevra said slowly. 'There was my father and I for a long time. He passed away shortly after Philip's accident. Then there was no one to speak of. I have an uncle who grows hops outside Boston. We are not so close any more.' The scandal, Ashe guessed without asking.

'Is that why you came to England? Because there was no reason to stay?'

'Something like that. It seemed like a good challenge.'

'And you like a challenge? Apparently I do, too. Getting you to talk about yourself is becoming a Herculean feat,' Ashe joked.

'You're not the easiest either.' Genevra rolled to her side, dislodging his hand and propping herself up. 'Why did you leave Bedevere?'

Ashe groaned, but it was more playful than tortured. He flipped on to his back, hands behind his head. 'Second sons are supposed to leave, to get out of the heir's way so there's no dissension. I'd always understood that. In a way, I even welcomed that. After Oxford, I was ready to take my gentleman's education out into the world and see what I could become.' He sighed.

Genevra watched the rise and fall of his chest. 'It's not the leaving I regret, Neva, it's the not coming back.'

Genevra moved a finger in patterns on his chest, copying his earlier gesture. 'Why is that? Does it have to do with Vienna?'

Ashe shook his head and gave a short laugh. 'Alex talks too much. I'll tell you some time, but not tonight.' He offered an apologetic smile, but no answers, no absolution for her curiosity. Neva would have to wait to learn his darker secrets. Some things were harder to admit to when one cared what someone thought. It was a stunning revelation to make for a man who'd spent most of his adult life not giving a fig what others thought of his exploits.

He still didn't care what London thought of him, but he realised he cared what Genevra thought. What would she think if she knew what he'd been doing when his father died? About the quarrel? About Vienna? Would knowing those things affirm for her he was just as bad as she believed him to be? Or would she see the man he was starting to become since he'd arrived home—a man whose past did not necessarily predict his future. He did not regret his past entirely, but neither would he let it drag him down with its limits.

'I'll tell you something about me, one of my most shocking secrets.' Genevra's voice pulled him away from those thoughts. She was teasing, of course, he could hear it in her tone.

'I like to make money,' she announced. 'And I'm good at it.' The announcement carried its own shock value. She knew men in London who would be genuinely alarmed. In their world, gentlemen didn't make money and neither did well-bred ladies. 'Last year, I doubled the shipping company's profits with my investments overseas.'

She paused. Ashe could practically hear her gathering her thoughts. 'You could make money with Bedevere,' she began tentatively.

'I'll get the tenant farms back on their feet in time for spring planting.' He'd not planned to think about Bedevere while he was in bed with Genevra.

'No, not farming,' Genevra insisted. 'Although that's fine, too. I mean with the house and the garden. In the spring and summer you can open the house and garden up for tours. We can make scones and serve tea. We can advertise in the guidebooks. I'm doing it at Seaton Hall this summer, giving it a trial run.' She sounded so earnest, so enterprising.

'Where do I live while people are swarming my home?'

'You'll be in London at least part of the time, I suspect.' Was she fishing for something there? He heard the hedge in her tone. Did she think he'd go up to town and leave his American wife in the country? He'd not thought of that. It would be one more thing to work out. Genevra would need to be introduced to society eventually. He didn't relish the prospect, not because he didn't believe in her capability to pull it off, but because he didn't necessarily want her encountering the more sordid elements of his life.

'Maybe I'll choose to stay in the country,' Ashe said for the sake of argument just to see what she'd say.

'Or you can lease the Audley town house if you decide to stay here. There are families visiting London for the Season that wouldn't mind renting. Either way, you should consider it. You cannot be in both places at once and there's no sense in one residence remaining idle.'

Ashe laughed. 'Neva, did anyone ever tell you it's not sexy to talk about money after making love?' He was rewarded with a warm hand on his stirring phallus.

'You don't seem to particularly mind,' she whispered coyly.

'You're the one who does that to me, not the money, I assure you.'

She straddled him, leaning forwards to let her breasts brush his chest. She kissed him full on the mouth, her hair falling about him like a curtain. His body was rousing, ready for the next bout.

'It's better not to know too much all at once, don't you think?' He reached for her ear lobe, sucking hard on the tender flesh. 'I like it this way—pleasure without expectations, without complications.' She moved a hand between his legs again and he gave up the fight. It wasn't a hard fight to lose. She liked it this way, too—being enjoyed for simply being a woman, not an heiress. The problem was it couldn't stay that way. In time, Ashe feared she'd want more than his body. She was that kind of woman; the kind who chose to love fully and would expect that fullness to be reciprocated. Could he be that kind of man? He'd known from the outset this marriage would involve setting aside his pride. He had not expected it to involve love, even one-sided love, but that was fast becoming a consideration and a complication all rolled into one.

Chapter Twenty

It was fast becoming the time to not play nice. Henry hoped the cartel would see recent developments as Ashe's fault and not his. If there was any nastiness, Henry preferred it be directed at Ashe. Trent, Samuels, Bardsworth, Ellingson and Cunningham were all assembled and anxious. He eyed the group of investors with great trepidation. For the second time in a span of weeks he had to face them with bad news.

'Your Mrs Ralston is set to marry your cousin in the morning,' Trent began. 'It's not what we talked about.'

He made it sound as if a minor mistake had occurred, like a tailor producing a waistcoat in a slightly different shade than what had been agreed upon, but Henry was not fooled into believing his complacency. There was a very real danger to himself here if he did not deflect it.

Henry opted for the high road of righteous indignation. 'My cousin is worse than ever. He's thrown me out of the house.'

It wasn't the strongest course of action. He'd hoped

to paint Ashe in a malicious light, but the complaint only weakened his position.

Cunningham looked up. 'Now you have no direct access to him and no way to keep an eye on things.'

By things, Henry knew Cunningham meant the books. The last disaster would be for Ashe to discover the errors in the ledgers and his perfidy there. It would be enough to get him locked up or transported, neither of which option suited him. It would also be enough to expose the cartel's interference in the dealings.

'Bennington hasn't mentioned the other piece of news,' Marcus Trent drawled from the head of the table. 'Tell them, Bennington, how Bedevere brought his brother home.'

'Damn it!' Ellingson exploded from the other end of the table. 'Can you do nothing right, Bennington? First you lose the heiress, now this. The crazy loon might tell Bedevere something of use and Bedevere might believe him, whether he's crazy or not.'

Henry forced himself to remain outwardly calm. Inside, however, he shared Ellingson's explosive feelings. Here at the last it was all falling apart. If it did, he would pay dearly with his freedom and quite possibly his life. Newgate or a prison hulk would be the least of his worries if Trent and company got to him first.

Henry tried a desperate deflection. 'We must act quickly. It's not too late to salvage this. We need to shift our plans from minimising the players to eliminating the players.' It would all be easier if Ashe were simply removed from the situation. The time had come for him and his investment partners to revisit more drastic means of minimising Ashe's role in the estate's future. The future of Bedevere lay below ground, not above it. That just might be where Ashe's future lay, too.

'Perhaps a kidnapping,' Samuels spoke up, his narrow eyes thoughtful and malevolent. 'We could use your fellow in the village, Bennington, the one that did the carriage wheel. Perhaps we could exchange someone for mining rights. The earl? The bride? I've always fancied doing a bridal kidnapping.'

Trent shook his head. 'Bedevere knows we can't harm his brother without ruining Henry's claim. Our threat would have no bite. As for the bride, who knows what Bedevere would or wouldn't do for her? He's marrying her for money, not love. Why would he exchange her for his estate? It's counter-intuitive to his plans.'

'Death, then,' said Cunningham. 'Bedevere simply has to die. Soon.'

Trent gave a casual shrug as if he planned executions every day. 'Both of them. With the brother out of the way, Bennington's the earl. It makes sense. It takes away the chance that Henry's crimes in the ledger might be discovered.' He winked at Henry and Henry felt cold. 'Forgery is still a nasty crime to be convicted of, isn't it, old chap?' Trent said it as if it were a lark. To him it might be. It wasn't his head on the chopping block if he was discovered.

The whole investment wasn't supposed to be this complicated. It was supposed to have been a simple matter of taking over Bedevere, of taking advantage of circumstances. Henry had never guessed it would lead to a discussion of murder or him becoming the earl in quick succession. But he was powerless to stop it—why should he when it came with a title? That was a powerful carrot to dangle in front of him indeed.

Henry was a selfish creature. If he had to choose between Ashe and himself, he'd choose himself, but he'd be damned if he was going to pull the actual trigger. 'I think we need to have a professional do it,' Henry put in. He was done taking risks for the moment.

'Cunningham'll do it.' Trent nodded towards the thickset man with small eyes. Cunningham grinned. 'Yeah, I'll do it.' He cracked his knuckles with no small amount of glee. 'If we can't kidnap a bride, we can at least shoot a groom.'

Trent smiled. 'And you, Henry, will be the bait to draw Ashe out.'

Henry felt cold fingers walk down his spine. 'Oh, don't worry, Henry,' Trent drawled with impatience. 'Confession is good for the soul.'

'Any last confessions, little brother? You're about to be a married man,' Alex joked in a little antechamber at the side of the chapel.

'I don't think we have that much time. Genevra should be here any minute.' Ashe looked past his brother's shoulder one more time, distractedly watching the door at the chapel's entrance. It wasn't quite ten o'clock.

Technically, Genevra still had another ten minutes. What was she doing right now? Was she coming downstairs at Bedevere? Climbing in the carriage? Was she already on her way? Was she having doubts and wondering what she'd done? Perhaps she was thinking she could manage Henry and his threats on her own, that her freedom was too high a price to pay for protection.

Alex's hand gripped his shoulder. 'Don't worry, she'll be here. Everything will be all right.' Alex smiled. 'She likes you, you know. More than likes you. She wants to know you, Ashe.'

'She knows what must be done.'

Alex nodded. 'Still, she's not a woman who does things against her will. She would not marry you if it didn't suit her.'

That was what worried Ashe the most. What did he know of marriage and having a wife? He'd hardly kept a woman over two weeks, let alone a lifetime. Failing was not an enjoyable prospect, but neither was the alternative. What if he did fall in love with his wife? Then the risk of disappointing her would be far greater than disappointing someone who didn't hold his affections.

Vicar Browne motioned for them to take their places. Ashe drew in a deep breath. The carriage must have been sighted. Salvation was in sight. Genevra hadn't run, although he had no reason to think she would have.

Alex embraced him one last time. 'The next time I do that, you'll be a husband and within time a father.' The wistfulness in his voice could not be completely hidden.

'It should be you, Alex,' Ashe whispered. But it would never be Alex. Alex would never marry.

'I will be a doting uncle and very happy. Let yourself be the same, Ashe. You carry too much guilt with you. Don't think I don't see it. I am your brother and I know you better than anyone. Let yourself be happy.' Alex stepped back from their embrace and smoothed the shoulders of Ashe's morning coat. 'There. You're ready.'

Ashe squared his shoulders and took up his place, Alex beside him, at the front of the little chapel. The chapel had played witness to generations of Bedeveres; his own parents had married here, he and Alex had been baptised here. His father's last service had been here. Leticia's own wedding had been here. He was cognisant as he stood at the front of the church, with his covey of aunts looking on, how auspicious the place and occasion was to them. Life passed through this little stone chapel.

His aunts might be the only guests in attendance, but they had not let the event go unmarked. A pristine cloth covered the altar. Silver candlesticks burning new wax candles sat on that altar, bracketed by two vases of hothouse flowers. Genevra would not look back on her wedding day and say it had been devoid of any decoration, even if it had been devoid of guests and the great pomp that would have, *should* have, accompanied the wedding of a lord under other circumstances.

The door to the church opened. Genevra stood there, looking for something, looking for him. She found him, smiled and began the short walk down the aisle, composed and elegant in pearly-grey satin. The satin of her gown hugged the contours of her form, emphasising the slimness of her waist, the gentle curve of her hip as she moved towards him.

'She's beautiful—you're a lucky man, Ashe,' Alex whispered, following up with a surreptitious poke to his ribs. But more notable than her loveliness, she walked the short aisle alone.

Ashe thought she might well be one of the bravest people he'd ever known. She was alone in the world except for nominal family in America. Yet she'd thrown her lot in with his and chosen to march towards a very uncertain future.

Ashe reached for her hand and drew her to him. She was pale despite her composure and her hand trembled within his. He hoped she wasn't having regrets already. There would undoubtedly be some. English society would not look upon this marriage with kindness and it would be difficult for her initially. She was an outsider, married only for her money. London would not let her forget it, although he would do his best to smooth the way when the time came.

For now it was enough to know that she was out of Henry's reach. The papers had been signed yesterday in Marsbury's tiny office. Genevra was as legally safe as he could make her. She was no longer an official shareholder in the regency of the estate. Henry had not been seen since he'd left, but that didn't mean he was undefeated.

A jolt of pain shot up Ashe's leg momentarily and he barely bit back an 'ow!' Genevra had squashed his instep with her slippers. He speared her with a disbelieving look. What bride stepped on her groom's foot doing the service?

'I believe this is your part,' she whispered, an en-quiring smile on her very kissable mouth.

'Do you, Ashton Malvern Bedevere, take this woman to be your lawfully wedded wife?'

Genevra stifled a nervous laugh. His middle name was Malvern? She hadn't known. This was sheer mad-ness, marrying a man whose full name she didn't know. Then his green eyes held hers as he repeated the vows and the craziness seemed well justified, rational even.

This wedding was very different than the one she'd had with Philip. The comparison came unbidden and unwelcome—she didn't want to think of that earlier occasion on today of all days, except that the contrast was so glaring. That wedding had borne all the trap-pings a wedding should have, and borne them in ex-treme. There'd been fifteen urns of flowers lining the church in Boston, pews full of the city's finest, and her dress had been imported from France. The prepa-rations had taken months. In the end, it had been for naught. Philip hadn't loved her. Had never loved her, only feigned deep affection, and she'd been too naïve to know the difference.

Today was a simpler, more honest occasion. Ashe hadn't pretended to love her, hadn't whispered non-sensical flattery in her ear, but she knew from the start what she was getting: a man who would protect her from scandal, a man who was not entirely without feeling for her, a man who took his responsibility to his family with seriousness. That would have to be enough.

Ashe slid a ring on her finger and bent to kiss her. It was done now, enough or not. Marry in haste, repent at leisure, came the unbidden thought as his lips found hers. With Ashe Bedevere as a husband, that could be fun indeed.

But that would have to wait a few hours at least.

There had still been some wedding traditions to perform. They'd spent the day at Bedevere, lingering with Alex and the aunts over a delicious wedding breakfast before delivering tokens of the wedding to the few servants on hand. More would be hired within the week, of course. Now that she was the ostensible mistress, Genevra would see the place fully staffed as quickly as possible. It would be her first official task.

Afterwards, Genevra had changed into a walking gown and she and Ashe strolled through Audley to celebrate with the villagers and farmers. Ashe tossed pennies to the children in the village square and Genevra laughed at their delighted scrambling.

The shadows lengthened and at last it was time to turn for home and their wedding night. There'd be no wedding trip, but it was understandable. With Alex newly home, the funeral still lingering, and Henry out there somewhere licking his wounds, a trip seemed poorly timed.

But, Genevra discovered, Ashe was not without his resources. 'Where are we going?' she queried as they turned away from the house and headed down towards the little lake.

Ashe winked. 'The summerhouse. My aunts tell me

you've not been there yet.' But that was all he'd say on the subject.

Dusk and lanterns showed the structure to advantage and Genevra gasped softly when she saw it. 'Oh, Ashe, it's beautiful.'

She had not ventured out here before. It was not a place for winter visits and Ashe's father had been too ill to walk so far in any case. Ashe held the door for her and she slipped inside. The building was a three-walled structure with a bank of windows looking out on to the lake. In the summer the windows opened completely. Filmy white lengths of curtains hung at the windows and the room was comfortably furnished with *chaises*, chairs, small tables and, most importantly, a box bed. An armoire stood along one wall full of supplies: blankets, clean sheets and drawers for clothes.

'I might not want to leave,' Genevra confided.

Ashe was behind her, his hands settling at her waist, firm and possessive. An undeniable thrill ran through her at the thought: *I am his.*

'Perhaps we should try it out, though, before you decide,' Ashe suggested. 'There's bread and cheese and a bottle of wine on the sideboard.'

She turned in his arms, eyeing him with teasing scepticism. 'What shall it be first, Mr Bedevere, bread and wine or bed?' She warmed to his playful teasing.

'Why do we have to choose?' Ashe replied naughtily. 'Bed and wine are a delightful combination if one knows what they're doing.'

'And I suppose you do?'

'Oh, yes, I most certainly do.' Ashe stepped back, a seductive smile on his lips. 'May I be so bold as to say you might find yourself overdressed for the occasion? I think you'll find something more comfortable behind the screen.'

Genevra ducked around the screen that shielded the box bed from the rest of the room. There was a trunk at the bed's foot and she found it well stocked. Genevra pulled out a satiny dressing robe in white, trimmed with elegantly embroidered green flowers. Melisande's work, she thought with a sentimental tear. The old dear had outdone herself on the robe. She took out a second robe, a man's banyan, and laid it out for Ashe. She changed quickly, listening for Ashe beyond the screen.

It didn't take him long to appear, tray in hand, his green eyes burning with approval at the sight of her. 'Now it seems I'm the one who is overdressed.' She heard the desire in his voice. He set the tray down, his hand going slowly, deliberately, to the cravat tied at his neck.

He pulled it loose and drew it off. Then came the coat, the waistcoat and the shirt, leaving his chest bare to her scrutiny. 'You're doing that on purpose,' she accused playfully.

He looked at her with hot eyes. 'Maybe. Is it working?'

'You know it is.' Her husband was a fine specimen of male virility. Muscles defined his arms and his torso right down to the long lean length of his hip and thigh.

He sat for a moment to pull off his boots and shrug out of his trousers.

Genevra sucked in her breath. The strong planes of his back and the curve of his buttock as he bent to retrieve the bottle from the tray were positively enticing. 'Wine, my dear?' He held up the bottle, divinely unbothered by his nakedness.

'What about the bread and cheese?' This was shaping up to be unlike any picnic she'd ever experienced.

'There'll be time for that later. Now, take off your robe and lie back for me.' She did as she was told, carefully setting the robe aside.

He came to her, straddling her hips, his phallus teasing her where it brushed against her skin with promises of what was to come. 'Allow me to pour the wine.' With elegant grace he pulled the cork and trickled a few drops into her navel, running a trail up to her breasts. She gasped at the audacity of it, the absolute eroticism of it.

'Shh, be still or it will spill,' Ashe cautioned with a wicked smile. Then he bent his head and drank, and licked and sucked until she thought she'd go mad from the sensations he roused in her.

She thrashed a bit as he sucked the last of the wine from her breast, the sensation too much to contain. 'Remind me to tie your hands to the bed next time, my restless one,' Ashe murmured against her skin. 'Do you think you'd like that?' He sat up and shifted his position, moving lower until she had no illusions about what he intended next. Surely he didn't mean to… 'Ashe?' The one word carried her hesitation.

'Don't worry, Neva, you'll like this, I promise.' He'd been right on that account before. His head bent to that most private part of her, his tongue making good on the promise until she cried out her pleasure. Only after that did he cover her with his length and sheathe himself inside her and create pleasure for them both.

As wedding nights went, they were off to a good start and the sun hadn't quite set yet.

They managed to get to the bread and cheese an hour later, curled up on a double-sized *chaise* by the windows. Ashe poured a glass of wine for her. 'A toast is in order. To my wife, who has made me a happy man on this day and shall make me happier in the years to come.'

The toast was short but perfect, the words thoughtful. Emotion stirred. It would be easy to love this man, easy and dangerous. He couldn't hurt her if she didn't love him. But the chasm between 'just sex' and love didn't seem as broad as it use to be. If she wasn't careful, she could fall. The wicked rake was also a very good man at heart. She wondered if she'd be able to trust him with hers or whether she'd have any choice in the matter when the time came. She rather suspected she'd wake up one day and find it had simply become his without her consent.

Ashe reached for the bottle of wine and sloshed it a bit. 'There's half a glass left.' He made to pour it into her glass.

'No, I have a better idea.' Genevra gently took the bottle from him and came around to his side of the *chaise.* She knelt before him, untying the banyan and spreading the halves wide so that he was revealed in all of his male splendour. He was already half-aroused and she gave a seductive laugh, running her thumb lightly over the head of his phallus in preparation. 'I have it on good authority wine is good for other things besides drinking.'

She spilled wine along the ridge of his member and very slowly lowered her head to him and took him in her mouth with deliberate intimacy, tongue licking and coaxing. Her hands, braced on the insides of his thighs could feel his muscles tighten as his pleasure heightened. She heard a groan, deep and guttural, in his throat and then it was over, his hands tangled in her hair as he sought his release.

'Neva, you'll be the death of me,' Ashe whispered hoarsely.

'There are probably worse ways to die.' She smiled, revelling in her power for a moment. Whatever else might plague their marriage, the bedroom would not be part of it. This would be the one place where they'd have equal ground and equal pleasure of one another. Surely that counted for something. Marriages had started with less.

Chapter Twenty-One

Ashe leaned against the stone balustrade of the back veranda, savouring the surprising warmth of the day and taking in the rarity of the scene spread before him. The sun was out, teasing about the possibility of an early summer, and Genevra was home early from the village, a rare occurrence indeed. She sat with his aunts on the newly finished stone patio, reading while they were busy with needlework. It was a peaceful scene, much as he'd envisioned it when he'd planned the patio.

Ashe would liked to have said marriage was just as bad as he'd ever imagined it would be; that he'd knowingly traded his freedom for financial security and was now feeling the sting of being yoked to a harpy for the rest of his life.

The truth was, marriage to Genevra was working out just fine in its early weeks. Genevra was already vastly familiar with the workings of the household and Ashe realised for the first time how indispensable she must have been for the aunts during the past winter.

She had known few servants were left and had set about hiring more. Within a week, Bedevere was staffed as it had been in the years of Ashe's childhood. There were footmen running errands, maids polishing banisters, grooms in the stable and gardeners, well, in the gardens.

She'd been unstinting with funds, too. As soon as she could she had turned over a large sum of money to him for the welfare of Bedevere. He'd paid the outstanding debts and bought farming supplies for his tenants. He had commissioned more work on the gardens and set about buying horses for his newly staffed stables.

After the string of bad luck that had plagued Bedevere over the years, this was a heady time for the struggling estate and for him. He'd been without regular funds for years, living on his reputation. It had been something of a struggle to keep his rooms on Jermyn Street and to keep up appearances with his wardrobe. Now, money was no object, thanks to Genevra, whose generosity he saw everywhere he turned at Bedevere, but whose actual presence was much absent.

Without a wedding trip to intervene between the wedding and taking up the reins of the household, they'd settled into a schedule almost immediately. He saw his wife in the mornings over breakfast and the newspapers. They would adjourn to the estate office to discuss business, which Genevra would cover in a brisk manner, running through her itemised lists of things she was doing and things that needed doing in the near future: the attic needed cleaning out, several pieces of furniture needed bringing down, there were new window treatments and furniture to order, a decorator was coming from London with a store of silk wallhangings for the public rooms.

Three days a week, she was off to Seaton Hall to oversee the last of the interior renovations and some of the energy that radiated throughout Bedevere was gone. The other two days, she spent in the village helping Vicar Browne with those in need. She'd become the perfect lord's wife: busy and efficient, running his home, supporting her charities, and acting as his liaison in the village so that he could carry out his other responsibilities.

There were plenty of those. She wasn't the only one with a filled schedule. He spent time with the farmers learning how best to maximise Bedevere's crops. He'd thought he'd hear about how bad the harvests had been the last few years.

Poor harvests seemed to suggest themselves as a reason for Bedevere's failing fortunes. But harvests had been adequate. Many he talked to blamed the lack of proper equipment and poor maintenance of the land itself; a fence that had crumbled and not been repaired had let livestock in to trample cornfields; a dike had collapsed, leaving flooded crops in its wake. Someone had quietly sabotaged Bedevere in subtle ways. Ashe's first thought was Henry, but he could not prove it. Not yet.

But for all he'd learned, he wasn't making any progress in solving the financial mystery that haunted Bedevere. Crops had been set up to fail, the coffers had been emptied. By whom and why? If it was Henry, why? How had he done it? Ashe was sure the answer was in the ledgers somewhere, but he didn't know where to start or what to look for. Ashe came home each evening, tired and frustrated, wanting his wife and the few hours of peace she brought. He had her in the nights. But in the mornings, she was gone again.

He knew many men who wouldn't complain of such an arrangement. Three months ago, he would have been one of them. Three months ago, he'd been a different man.

That man had spent his nights carousing in all manner of establishments, perhaps going weeks without bedding the same woman two nights in a row, his fortunes dependent on the turn of a card, the roll of a billiard ball, or the right invitation. This man, the new Ashe, was more concerned about spring planting, about restoring the gardens outside his home, and about his absent wife. His old crowd in London would not know this new man. He wasn't even sure he did.

Genevra looked up from her book and saw him. She was lovely today in a sky-blue gown trimmed in white lace, a straw hat to match. She waved and motioned for him to join them. Ashe started down the shallow stairs towards the patio. The only complaint he had about his wife was that he was slowly but surely falling in love with her. He'd promised himself he wouldn't allow it to get that far. He could respect her, he could admire her, he could find her lovely, that was all. But he was failing at it. By now his initial passion for her should have bottled its edge as it had done with so many other

women before her. Instead, he found himself counting the hours until nightfall when she'd be his, not the
village's Lady Bountiful, not the aunts' companion or
Alex's. Just his. Perhaps he could persuade her to take
a walk and he could steal a march on evening.

He had eyes only for her and the knowledge of it sent
a thrill down Genevra's spine as Ashe approached. He
bent to kiss her on the cheek, so very chaste and hus-
bandly compared to the passionate lover she encountered in the night.

'Do you like the patio, Aunts?' Ashe settled himself
next to her on one of the benches, his thigh brushing
her leg. 'The roses will bloom before long and it will
smell wonderful out here in the summer.'

After a decent interval of small talk, Ashe reached
for her hand. 'Aunts will you excuse us? I want to take
Genevra for a walk in our glorious afternoon. Perhaps
we'll walk down by the stream.'

The aunts smiled at one another and Genevra knew
they didn't believe him. She blushed. The old dears
were romantics at heart and she guessed the directions
of their thoughts.

'Your aunts think you're stealing me away for an
afternoon tryst,' Genevra said once they were out of
earshot.

'They're good guessers.' Ashe laughed, not the least
bit ashamed of his transparency. She liked that about
him. He made no apologies for what he did or what he
wanted. For the time being, that was her.

He wanted her. How long that would last was anyone's guess. It was almost too good to be true. When she wasn't careful, it was too easy to forget it was her money rejuvenating the estate. Of course he wanted her—she held his welfare in her hands. Without her, he would be nothing. No, not quite nothing. Ashe Bedevere would never be nothing and, for a little while, he was hers.

She had to protect herself against the time that would come when he'd need her money a little less, or when he grew tired of her and sought someone else. A rake like Ashe wasn't used to monogamy. It had only taken Philip two months before he'd acquired a mistress. Out here in the countryside, Ashe might take longer, but it was still just a matter of time. She kept herself busy so that when that time came she might notice it a bit less.

'What is it, Neva? You look like a cloud passed over your sun,' Ashe scolded, helping her over some stones in the path.

Genevra shook her head. 'Nothing.' She'd been caught thinking. She needed deflection. 'How are things going with the ledgers? Have you made any progress?' She knew the estate's finances were an agony to him. He wanted to know what had happened, but that was one area in which she had no knowledge to offer him. When she'd first made the aunts' acquaintance last summer, much of the damage had already been done and of course no one ever showed people their ledgers.

Ashe pushed a hand through his dark hair. 'I don't want to think about it on such a nice day. It's a very dark topic. If I discover what happened and who did it, I am obligated to bring them to justice.'

Genevra shot him a querying look. 'Do you think the culprit is other than Henry?'

'There's always the possibility that it was Alex. Certainly, no one expects me to prosecute my brother in his condition.'

'Have you asked Alex? Surely he'd tell you? He knows you wouldn't harm him.'

Ashe shook his head. 'I haven't. I'm a coward, Neva. I haven't wanted to trigger a fit. I've enjoyed having my brother, having him here with me healthy. I can almost pretend he's going to be all right.'

Genevra smiled softly. This was the first time they'd talked of something personal since the wedding. Perhaps they were making progress of a different sort. 'Maybe I can help. I would be glad to look over the books with you if Alex can't. Who knows, there might be something I remember.'

'You have so many other activities right now. I don't want to bother you.' He was slipping away from her again. Genevra could feel it. The vulnerability of a moment earlier was vanishing.

'I'm your wife. You can let me help. I want to help,' she protested.

'I'll manage it, Genevra,' Ashe snapped, making clear the conversation was finished.

She walked in silence beside him, fuming over his behaviour. How dare he shut her out? 'Has there been any news of Henry?' Genevra ventured once she had her temper under control. Perhaps some of the walk could be salvaged.

Ashe shook his head. 'He's most likely at his farm.'

'Will he stay there?' Genevra queried.

'If you're asking are our worries over, the answer is maybe. You don't have to worry. You're safe now. If he wants anyone, it's me.'

That was the last straw. Really, the man's arrogance knew no bounds. 'That makes you happy, doesn't it? It's all on your shoulders. The rest of us can't interfere,' Genevra ground out. The man was infuriating.

'No one else need be placed at risk,' Ashe said simply. 'Ah, we're here. The stream. Alex and I spent countless summers sneaking away down here.'

He was about to launch into a story of boyhood adventure, but Genevra wasn't satisfied. 'We're not done with the previous conversation. I don't want you to shoulder all the troubles alone. I want to be more than your banker, Ashe.'

Ashe stiffened as if slapped, his gaze fixed straight ahead on the far bank of the stream. 'I've never treated you as just my banker.'

'You just did.' Genevra turned to go. Tears threatened. She would not let him see her cry, not over this. He'd never professed to love her. Whatever hurt she'd incurred was her own fault. She'd let herself believe so many things when she'd known better.

Ashe's hand seized her arm. 'Genevra, be fair. I never once—'

Genevra wrenched her arm away. 'No, not once, *al-*

ways, Ashe. You have consistently shut me out. You're bothered by the ledgers, but you won't let me help. You won't tell me what's on your mind half the time. I don't know why you fought with your father, I don't know why you stayed away for so many years. I don't know anything. You make love to me at night and I write you banker's drafts during the day and you expect that to be enough. It's not.'

Ashe sat down on a large rock, looking weary, all the teasing from minutes ago gone. She'd said too much. 'I'm sorry,' she began, but Ashe waved her away.

'Sorry for what? Sorry for the truth? It is the truth, you know, Neva. But I can't give you any more. Not right now.'

Maybe not ever, Genevra thought. She should have contented herself with her fantasies and make-believe. He didn't love her and she'd pushed him to say as much which only served to make things awkward, not better. Whoever thought honesty was the best policy had never been in love with a man who didn't quite love you back.

Genevra sat down beside him, trying to forget the ugly conversation. 'So, you and Alex used to come here as boys?' She looked overhead at the wide tree limb. 'Too bad there isn't a swing. This would be a perfect place for one.'

Ashe shot her a wry look. 'It is the perfect place and there used to be one. If you look closely, you can still see the remnants of the rope up there.'

Genevra squinted and followed Ashe's finger up into the leafy boughs. 'What happened?'

'Henry. He was always pulling pranks on Alex and me. Pranks was his word, not ours. At first, they were just malicious jokes, but as we got older the pranks got more serious. I think this one was the worst. The rope was sliced so that whoever was on the swing would fall when they swung out over the water. In the summer, you had to swing out to the middle of the stream before you dropped. The water was too shallow closer to the bank. If you dropped too soon, you could hit rocks, which was what Henry wanted.'

Genevra peered down into the water, trying to make out the rocks. 'You can't see them in the winter or spring when the stream is full,' Ashe explained.

Genevra stiffened visibly in shock over the revelation. 'Was anyone hurt?'

'A distant cousin. He broke his leg and has not walked properly since. The accident kept him out of the military, out of a livelihood. The cousin was a second son with hopes of a commission in the cavalry.'

'That's a terrible story. What happened to Henry? Was he punished?'

Ashe leaned closed, his voice quiet and intimate. 'We couldn't prove it. Ropes fray, especially ropes outdoors in the weather. Henry's very good at not getting caught, Neva.'

'Maybe you'll never discover what happened in those ledgers. Maybe it would be best to just move forwards.'

'And maybe if I do that, history will repeat itself. I can't take that risk, Neva. I have to know. If it's Henry, he has to be caught this time or he won't stop until he has it all. Don't you see, Genevra? The less you know, the safer you are. If it is Henry, and if he suspected you knew something that could ruin whatever scheme he's planning…'

He had shut her out to protect her, she could see that now, misguided though his plan was. Such a plan would have to be rectified. It wasn't love, but it was a start.

Genevra didn't let him finish. She placed a finger on his lips. 'If you brought me out here to seduce me, you'd better get on with it or risk disappointing your aunts.'

Chapter Twenty-Two

It rained the next day, just to prove it wasn't quite spring yet. The weather kept everyone inside, which suited Ashe perfectly. It was high time to tackle the ledgers, with help. Genevra's sharp words at the stream yesterday had given him pause for thought. On his own, he was no closer to resolving the mystery of where the money had gone than he was when he'd first arrived. It was also becoming clear that this was the last and perhaps most critical piece to resolve before his home-coming could truly be complete.

Ashe announced his intentions for the day at break-fast, earning an approving nod from Genevra, and the three of them sequestered themselves in the estate office, prepared for a long day. Ashe took up residence behind the big desk while Alex and Genevra stationed themselves near the fireplace with a low table between them, perfect for sorting papers.

'Are you sure you're up to this, Alex?' Ashe asked one more time before they started.

'I will be fine. It will be good to know if I am to blame or if someone else took advantage of the situation and used me as a scapegoat,' Alex said staunchly. Ashe admired his brother's courage in that moment. Alex had never been one to shirk his responsibilities and he wasn't avoiding them now.

Ashe spread his hands on the desk's surface. 'All we know is that it is likely someone behaved irresponsibly with the estate's finances. According to the ledgers, items were sold for far less than their actual worth. We want to look through the receipts for those bills of sale. The receipts will tell us who the items were sold to and perhaps even the actual sale amount.' Although, if it was Henry, and if Henry was smart, he'd keep the two prices consistent, perhaps issuing a receipt to the man he charged and making a separate receipt for the Bedevere records. Still, a receipt would have a name and they could always contact the new owner.

Sorting through the receipts was a daunting task. There were boxes of them and progress was slow. It was something of a needle-in-a-haystack-style search. Amid the receipts for daily living expenses and regular estate bills, they were looking for the odd sale.

Halfway through the pile, Ashe was beginning to despair. Maybe there was no receipt. Perhaps his assumption had been erroneous from the start. Then his hand stilled on a bill of sale. He read it twice to be sure. They'd had a few false alarms already. It was the receipt for the horses. His gaze dropped to the bottom of the page, searching for a signature. But the name he found wasn't either of the names he'd been expecting. The signature scrawled at the bottom was his father's.

'Alex, look at this.' Ashe handed the paper to his brother.

'In November.' Alex checked the date. 'It's likely I was gone by then. Father took a turn for the worse in November and Henry was eager to have me out of the way. It was a very difficult time.' Alex paused. 'I wasn't well in November, not that I remember any of it.' Ashe could see how difficult the confession was for Alex to make. He turned to Genevra, hoping to spare Alex.

Genevra picked up the receipt and shook her head after a moment's study. 'Your father could not have signed it. He was very ill and wouldn't have been interested in doing any business in the first place. But even if he'd wanted to sell the horses, he couldn't have physically signed a bill of sale. By that point, he'd lost the ability to use his right hand. He could not have written his name with that amount of precision.'

She checked the date again. 'You were not here, Alex. At least on account of the horses, you can rest assured they were not your doing.' There would be record of that, Ashe thought. The place where Alex had been kept would have a note of his arrival. That only left Henry. But it raised another question.

'How did Henry pay Dr Lawrence?' Ashe asked. 'There's no mention of payments in the ledgers and I haven't seen any receipts to that extent, yet Dr Lawrence gave quite the affirmative response when I asked if Mr

Bennington paid his bills.' He hoped Genevra would know. Henry had been living here full time by then.

'It was never discussed.'

Ashe drummed his fingers on the desk top, thinking out loud. 'Henry doesn't have that kind of money. His income is comfortable, but he's not that charitable. I can't see him depriving himself of his worldly pleasures to pay Dr Lawrence.' In fact, too much of this didn't fit Henry at all. It was all too carefully planned. The receipt for the horses matched, confirming either that separate receipts had been made or the items in question had been sold for far less than their worth. The only chink was that his father could not possibly have signed the receipt.

A devastating thought occurred to him: the will.

The date had been much later than November. Marsbury had the original, but Ashe had a copy of it for his records. Ashe dug in the desk drawer. 'Here, look at this.' He spread the papers out for Alex and Genevra to see. 'Father's signature is barely legible here, it's hardly more than a scribbled line.'

They found other receipts, all signed with his father's name in legible, impossible precision, but no sign of any monies having been sent to Dr Lawrence. Ashe drafted letters to the buyers, politely asking to verify the amounts paid for their items, but their answers weren't mandatory. The big question still remained unanswered: why would someone deliberately bankrupt the estate? Especially if that someone was Henry and had hopes of taking it over.

* * *

Ashe pushed back from the desk well into the afternoon. He'd come back to one thought time and time again throughout the morning. 'I think it's time to consider the possibility that Henry isn't operating alone.'

Alex looked thoughtful. 'Who?'

Ashe shrugged. 'I don't know and I don't know why. But they could be the ones who paid Dr Lawrence, which is why we have no record.'

'We also have to consider more than the receipts,' Genevra put in. 'These receipts are just the tip of the proverbial iceberg. Household items were being sold, but that alone wouldn't bankrupt a healthy estate. Whatever has been done here, has been going on for a few years. This doesn't explain where the usual income went from rents and crops.'

Ashe nodded in agreement. What they'd done today was merely pick the low hanging fruit. It was a start, but there was so much more they didn't have. They didn't even have Henry's name on a document to prove he'd been skimming money from the sales. If he'd actually sold the items for the recorded prices, then he was guilty of nothing except bad judgement in the eyes of the law.

Ashe rose. 'We're done for the day. Keep thinking of anything you might recall.'

He needed some time alone. It was still raining outside. A walk was out of the question, so he headed to the music room and took refuge in his piano. Today had been more emotional than he'd expected. He'd not thought looking over receipts and bills would affect him so strongly. But he'd been wrong. Seeing his father's signature on the will again, and hearing Genevra mention how his faculties had failed him, were potent reminders of mortality. If a man like his father could deteriorate, so could they all.

Ashe ran his hands over the keys, letting physical memory take over as he played so his thoughts could wander. He'd come to grips with his father's death that night at the mausoleum, but he'd not come to terms with the dying. He was starting to realise they were two different things.

He felt a presence rustle behind him, soft hands at his shoulders and the smell of lemongrass.

'He was alone. Both of his sons had left him.' Ashe spoke his thoughts out loud.

'Not entirely alone.' Genevra spoke quietly. 'He had his sister and his wife's sisters with him.'

'And you,' Ashe said.

'And me.' She was humble, but his father must have come to care for her a great deal. He'd pinned his estate's hopes on her and his father had not been misguided in that. Ashe had seldom known his father to make mistakes, as hard as that was to admit growing up. His father had been right about practically everything. His father had not been wrong now choosing Genevra, not just for Bedevere, but for him.

'Thank you for letting Alex and I help today.' She moved away from him and he turned to follow her progress to the window.

'Was it bad at the end?' Ashe went to join her at

the window. This was the conversation she'd wanted to have in the conservatory that first night, but he'd not been ready for it.

'He'd been failing for months.' Genevra sighed and leaned back against him. 'His doctor said he'd had a series of strokes over the past three years. Each one left him a bit more debilitated. He'd recover a little and there would be good days, but in the end it was just too much. He couldn't walk, couldn't write, speech was difficult.'

'I cannot imagine him that way.'

'Then don't. Keep him in your mind the way you remember him most.'

'I remember the last day I saw him. It was in this room. My bags were packed for Italy and the carriage was ready, even though we'd fought over my going. Father wouldn't have his son leaving in an old gig, disagreement or not.' Ashe caught himself smiling at the remembrance. His father had been duly proud of his station in life and had encouraged his sons to never forget what they'd been born to.

'He walked into the room and I thought, "Oh, no, here we go again." But all he said was, "Don't let yourself become less than you are." At the time, I only saw his words as another way of voicing his disapproval over what I intended to do.'

'What was that?' Genevra's body was warm and comforting against him and he tightened his grip about her waist. He'd not talked of this with anyone for years but it felt right talking with her now. He wanted to tell her.

'I wanted to be a pianist. I wanted to study in Vienna, I wanted to go to Italy and study piano-making. I wanted to make the grandest pianos of them all.' Ashe shook his head, remembering the numerous quarrels he'd had with his father over it. 'But that wasn't a dignified calling for a son of my father. The son of an earl, heir or not, did not put himself on stage performing, or dirty his hands in any form of carpentry. I'd been raised my whole life to understand that I would seek my career outside Bedevere. Bedevere was for Alex. But there were limits to what that career was supposed to be. Pianos weren't on the list. Unfortunately, I couldn't see myself in the military or behind a pulpit, God forbid.'

Genevra laughed softly with him. 'I don't know, you might have been a very popular vicar to say the least. The pews would have been full of women every Sunday. You might have done the Church of England a great service.

'But, you went anyway?' Genevra sobered and prompted him to return to the story.

'Yes, there were four of us that set off together on our Grand Tour. We went to Vienna first and took rooms on the Lanterngasse. I studied privately with a master there, but I was young and cocky and too talented for my own good. Suffice it to say, there were those who were jealous. One night, not long after I'd played at Schonbrunn, I found myself set upon by common street thugs after a performance. They'd been paid, of course, by those who thought I was rising too quickly.

It only took a sharp shard of glass to put paid to any future career hopes.'

Even now, years later, he could feel the pain of the slice that had ended his career, recalled the helplessness he'd felt in that alley, outnumbered five to one. Genevra was caressing his hand, turning it over before he could stop her.

'Is this it?' Her index finger traced the thin white line bisecting his palm. 'I'd never noticed it before. It healed well,' Genevra murmured.

'Thanks to a woman in Venice. We left Vienna immediately, but infection had set in and I took ill with a fever as we travelled. We got as far as Venice when we decided we needed professional help. She saved me.' Ashe winced. That part of the story was probably not suitable for a wife's ears. Genevra didn't want to hear about Signora de Luca. His friends had gone on after a while to other parts of Italy, but he'd stayed a long time with her, trying to piece together the remnants of his dream.

To her generous credit, Genevra did not pause on the mention of the good *signora*. 'Does it pain you? I think it must. I've noticed you flexing your hand on occasion. I thought nothing of it until now.'

'Only if it's overworked. I learned I couldn't build pianos, though.'

'What would you have built?' Genevra asked.

Ashe chuckled. 'I haven't thought of that for ages. I was going to build pianos with eight full octaves that thundered in a concert hall.' He sighed. 'It was too much strain every day. I also couldn't train or study with my former intensity. It was over. So, after a while, I rejoined my friends in Italy and I came back to England.'

'But not to Bedevere?'

'No.' This was the hard part of the story. He'd been too ashamed of his failure, too ashamed of the way he'd left to face his father. 'A twenty-three-year-old man's pride is a terrible obstacle, Neva.' It was also an obstacle that had grown more insurmountable as the years passed. He'd seen his brother occasionally when Alex had come up to town. But he'd not seen his father again.

'Your father would have forgiven you.'

'For leaving? Perhaps.' But for the rest? For deserting Bedevere, for deserting him? For becoming less than what he was? Ashe wasn't so sure. He wasn't certain he deserved it anyway.

He placed a kiss on the long column of Genevra's neck. 'I've never told anyone that story before. Not even Alex.'

She turned in his embrace to wrap her arms about his neck. 'I'm glad I'm the first,' she said, taking his mouth in a soft kiss, his body rousing at her touch.

'Do you know what else I've never done?' Ashe whispered.

'I can't imagine.' Her grey eyes were alight with teasing mischief. She boldly reached for him, finding the core of him and tracing its length through his trousers until he groaned.

'Careful, Neva, or I won't last until I get you to the piano.' His need was consuming him now as he lifted her to the piano. He needed to bury himself inside her, needed to feel her legs wrapped tightly around him. Her money had saved Bedevere, but *she* could save him.

Chapter Twenty-Three

'It has been a month and you've done nothing!' Henry's anger made him brave as the cartel sat at the long reading table adorning Marcus Trent's library.

'You are impatient, Bennington,' Trent scolded. 'How much bad luck do you think the Bedevere family can withstand before people start to question the reason for it?'

'The longer we wait, the better the chance becomes Bedevere will get a look at those ledgers and figure out something is wrong,' Henry argued. 'We already know he's started.' Thanks to Genevra's hiring flurry it had been relatively easy to place a man in the household who could monitor any interesting activity at Bedevere. He'd reported last week that Ashe had been combing the books and letters had gone out to names Henry recognised as purchasers of some of the goods he'd sold.

'If he's only looking at receipts, Henry, there's little to worry about. All he'll discover is your very poor sense of business.' Marcus waved away Henry's concerns.

Henry nodded, debating whether or not he dared to interrupt again. He'd sold the goods initially to continue breaking Bedevere. He'd not cared what price he got for them. It was all part of the plan to make the estate desperate, so desperate that whoever was in charge would welcome the opportunity to turn the parklands into a coal mine. But there was more to find in the ledgers if Ashe kept digging and Henry could not let it go unaccounted.

'If I might mention the other?' Henry began delicately. 'There's also the money "lost" on the "bad investments".' It wouldn't take Ashe long to start sniffing down that path. Most of the Bedevere funds had been drained that way. He'd signed Alex's name to most of them, most notably the Forsyth deal. The Forsyth deal had been real enough, but the other bad investments hadn't existed. They'd been fronts for Trent's cartel. The Bedevere coffers were now being used to fund the mining effort in part.

'Your name isn't on any of the deals,' Marcus said glibly. 'It's the young earl's name.'

'Signed by me,' Henry protested. 'Now that Alex is home—' The danger of discovery rose exponentially, but he didn't get to say that. Cunningham broke in.

'Now that the earl is home he can't be controlled by us any more. Dr Lawrence can't simply sedate him when he gets too assertive.' Cunningham glared.

That wasn't fair. It wasn't his fault Ashe had brought Alex home. Henry tried a different argument. 'We all have money tied up in this venture. The longer we drag it out, the longer we delay our profits. A month ago we'd agreed to take decisive action and we've done nothing.' A few heads nodded.

'All right, here's what I propose.' Marcus Trent rubbed his hands together and began to plan. 'We will try to buy him with his own money.'

'There are two gentlemen downstairs who wish to see you, sir,' Gardener announced in quiet tones.

Ashe looked up reluctantly from his game of chess with Alex. 'Do they have an appointment?' He didn't recall anything being scheduled on his calendar. 'Did they say what they wanted?'

'No, sir,' Gardener answered.

'Are they really gentleman, Gardener, or are you merely being polite?' Ashe gave a wry smile.

'They are businessmen, sir,' Gardener said without a trace of condescension, but the implication was there all the same. They weren't gentlemen and they were calling without a letter of introduction or an appointment. It was all very curious and out of the ordinary.

'I'd best go down and see them.' Ashe stood up, reaching for the jacket he'd discarded earlier. 'We'll finish when I get back. Don't touch anything, Alex. I know exactly where all my pieces are.'

'Maybe I should go with you.' Alex rose, too, but Ashe halted him.

'That's not necessary.'

Alex sat with a smile. 'It's probably not. Nobody

wants to do business with a crazy man.' He laughed it off, but the remark stung Ashe.

'It's not that. I was thinking of your safety. I didn't like the idea of you and I in a close room together with strangers.' Strangers who had no appointment.

'And the doctors say I'm paranoid,' Alex joked. 'It is possible, Ashe, that Henry has given up and is happy to remain on his farm. It's been a month and no news of anything nefarious.'

Ashe finished adjusting his jacket. 'I reserve the right to be sceptical on that account, Brother. Gardener, give me five minutes in the estate office and then show them up.'

Gardener had been right. The two visitors weren't gentlemen, although they tried very hard to be in their tailored clothes. But they lacked the accents that marked the upper class and that certain air of aristocratic hauteur. By the look of them, they were wealthy and that was the extent of their recommendation.

'Mr Bedevere, thank you for seeing us,' the larger, dark-haired man effused. 'I'm Marcus Trent and this is my associate Arthur Ellingson.'

Ellingson shot an eager look at the decanters lining the sideboard, but Ashe didn't take the hint. He'd offer them a seat and a few moments of his time, but that was all. 'Sirs, I haven't much time this afternoon so I'd appreciate it if we could get straight to your business,' Ashe said in aloof but polite tones.

'You might be in less of a hurry after you hear what

we have to say.' The one called Marcus chuckled. Ashe fixed him with a cold stare.

'It just so happens we know there is a significant deposit of coal on Bedevere land, a deposit, if mined correctly, that could keep the pockets of future earls lined for generations. We'd like to buy the rights to mine here for a significant fee of twenty thousand pounds and an offer of fifteen per cent of the profits once mining begins. It's a very generous offer.'

'I am sure it would be if I wanted to turn my estate into a mine.' Ashe's tone was glacial. 'But I assure you, I do not, never mind the fact that I have no idea how you've come by such information.'

Ellingson jumped in. 'I have charts, sir. You needn't worry about the authenticity of the information.'

'That's not what I'm worried about.' Ashe stood. 'Good day, gentlemen.'

'Don't be so hasty.' Trent met his gaze with a steely stare of his own. 'You'd hate to regret passing on this opportunity.'

'Is that a threat, Mr Trent?' Ashe did not mistake the intention of his words.

'Let's just say you can contact me if you change your mind.'

Or have it changed for him. Ashe understood this type of man all too well. 'I won't.' He called for Gardener to show the men out. He didn't want these two so-called businessmen lurking on Bedevere land any longer than needed.

* * *

'Where's Mrs Bedevere, Gardener? Is she home yet?' She'd gone down to the village to help a mother with a new baby.

'She hasn't returned yet, sir.'

'Send her to me at once,' Ashe said tersely. He'd breathe easier when she was home, safe. The pieces were starting to come together. It was supposition only, but what if Henry knew about the coal? It gave him a motive to see Bedevere penniless. A penniless estate would be tempted to take the offer and, if Henry were in charge of the estate, he'd take that offer. Twenty thousand pounds was a small fortune in exchange for simply walking away from Bedevere not to mention the eventual fifteen per cent. It would be a comfortable allowance.

That was where he was different than Henry. Henry saw only the profit. Ashe saw the legacy of preserving the estate. Even if it hadn't been for Genevra's money, Ashe knew he would not be tempted. Staffordshire was full of industry and mining and he knew well the sight of ugly industrialism. Staffordshire was also full of rural beauty. Not all of the county had been industrialised yet and he far preferred it to a factory landscape.

The door to his office opened and Genevra breezed in, her hair in slight disarray from her hat, her cheeks pink from her drive. 'You'll be glad to know they're all doing well—' Then she stopped suddenly, her exuberance fading. 'What is it, Ashe?'

'There's a cartel that wants the rights to mine Bedevere for coal.'

'Henry?' Genevra sat down quietly.

'It makes sense.' Ashe outlined his theory. 'I have refused them, of course. I don't need their money.'

'But they're not likely to take no for an answer,' Genevra supplied.

'No. I do believe we'll be encouraged to rethink our position.' Ashe understood all too well this visit had been a warning and a chance, a last chance to throw in with Henry's plans or face his cousin's revenge.

Chapter Twenty-Four

This was how they'd do it: Henry would send a note to the house for Ashe. He wanted to talk and clear the air. Would Ashe please meet him at the mausoleum? The tone of the note would make it obvious this was to be a confession. If Ashe had no idea what Henry wanted to confess, all the better. But Henry very much feared Ashe would have at least an inkling. His cousin had spent too much time holed up going over ledgers not to suspect something was wrong even if he didn't know exactly what it was.

It wouldn't matter after today. He could tell Ashe he'd stolen the crown jewels among his myriad sins and there'd be nothing Ashe could do about it. Ashe would be dead before he left the mausoleum. A paid man would be waiting in the foliage to take a prime shot and catch Ashe unawares while he and Henry talked. Then Trent would quietly kill the man who had shot Ashe and no one would be any wiser. People didn't come looking for men who could be hired for murder. The shooter would not be missed and Ashe's death could be ruled as many things: suicide, a gun handling accident, perhaps even an accident perpetrated by his crazy brother. Henry liked that option best. It would give him an excuse to put Alex back under the care of Dr Lawrence.

The note had been sent. Even now, it should be sitting on the front table at Bedevere, waiting for Ashe's attention just as Henry would be waiting for him. Plans were in motion, even a little surprise Ashe would know nothing about if all went well. In a few hours this would be over and Bedevere would be his.

Ashe was late. Alex checked his watch again and paced the foyer. It was a languid pace, a stroll really. He wasn't upset. They were supposed to go walking this afternoon, a chance for brothers to talk. But Alex had seen him sitting on the lawn with Genevra enjoying a day of rare weather. When he'd looked out later, they'd been gone. He didn't mind. His restless brother was happy at last. And in love, although Alex didn't think Ashe even knew it. He would realise it soon enough and that gave Alex great comfort. Ashe would be content and that contentment would make him a fine trustee of Bedevere and a fine earl.

He'd not spoken of it with Ashe and hadn't planned to until he absolutely must, but he thought he didn't have long left in this world. There'd been a young doctor at the place where he'd been kept who'd confided his opinion of Alex's condition to him. Dr Lawrence hadn't agreed with such a bleak prognosis and had banned any further discussion, but it had made sense to Alex. The nervous breakdown had been a prelude, a sign of something larger. The depression, the despondency, the fits of forgetfulness, all typical. The young doctor had called it a disruption of his neurological system. He wasn't crazy. That was the good news. It had sustained him the months he'd been away. But his condition would eventually lead to death. With luck he had a year.

Alex could feel the small changes already. It was nothing drastic, but he could feel his energy ebbing throughout the day. Some days, he could feel his thoughts slipping away before he could grasp them. Some days, his speech slurred on occasion. Some days his hand shook.

And some days, like today, he was just fine. Today was a blessing. He worked hard on those days. He'd worked hard today, writing everything he meant to tell Ashe against the days and the times that would come when he wouldn't remember the answers his brother was looking for.

Alex paused by the front table. A folded note lay on the silver salver. Invitations were a rare commodity at Bedevere these days, but he imagined a time not far off when Genevra and Ashe would inspire a plateful of invitations. Bedevere would thrive again and Ashe's children would run up and down the halls and sail their boats in the fountain.

Alex picked up the note. It was addressed to Ashe, but there was no postmark to indicate it had come from

London or elsewhere. Whoever had written it had been local. No one in the house would write a note when they could just as easily speak with Ashe at dinner.

A fearful intuition pricked at him. Henry. Henry was out of the house now, driven off by his anger over Ashe's impending marriage. A note would be the only way for Henry to directly reach Ashe. Before his conscience could cause too much trouble, Alex flicked open the note. His eyes scanned down to the signature—*your cousin, Henry.*

Alex read each line carefully. The weasel was up to something. Henry wanted to talk? To confess? There wasn't enough hours in the day to hear that confession. The request seemed uncharacteristic. Henry wasn't exactly the penitent type. Alex carefully refolded the note and put it back. Whatever Henry wanted with this meeting, he was up to no good. His coal-cartel colleagues must be getting nervous. Henry had to know his 'business partners' would turn on him if he didn't deliver on his promises. He would have to give them something.

Thoughts clicked. Henry would give them Ashe. With Ashe dead there would be no more contest for the trusteeship of Bedevere. Only Ashe and Henry held any shares in Bedevere. A cold chill rushed through Alex. Ashe was walking into a trap. Henry didn't mean to confess. He meant to do murder.

Alex made a quick decision. He would go in place of Ashe. Henry didn't want him dead. Not yet, anyway. But first, he had to get something from his room.

Forewarned was forearmed. A 'crazy' man with a gun was bound to scare anyone and Henry had always been a coward.

'Sir, your brother has gone out walking alone.' Ashe nodded. Alex had been well since his return, but Ashe had made it explicitly known he wasn't to roam the estate alone. It was his fault. He was late. He was supposed to have gone out with Alex. He'd thought Alex would wait.

'Do you know which direction?' Ashe asked. The receipts could wait. 'How long ago did he leave?' Alex couldn't be that far ahead of him, he was only twenty minutes late.

'Ashe,' Genevra said tersely, 'read this.' She passed him a note. 'It was here on the table, but I think this might explain where Alex has gone.'

Ashe read the note, his fist clenching around the paper until it crumpled. 'Gardener, find my pistol.'

'Bring one for me, too, if you have them to spare,' Genevra said matter of factly. Gardener didn't flinch at the request. Gardener was doing better than he was.

Genevra turned to him. 'I'm going with you. If Henry plans to do evil out there, you will need me.'

'No, Neva. I cannot risk you,' Ashe said firmly. He would not put Genevra in harm's way intentionally. 'I need you here in case Alex comes back.' He couldn't quite give voice to the rest of the reason. He needed her here to be witness to the circumstances if he didn't return. If Henry had something horrible planned and he didn't come back, Genevra would be the one who had to seek justice.

Gardener clattered the down the steps, guns in hand. Ashe gave Genevra a final glance. Her grey eyes were dark and the stoic set of her jaw suggested she guessed at the unspoken reasons. She put a hand on his sleeve. 'Be careful.'

Ashe felt as if he was riding out to do battle. When had it become so ugly? When had this become so sinister? Henry's malice ran deep, far deeper than anyone had given 'lazy' Henry credit for.

His horse covered the distance to the mausoleum in no time. He dismounted a fair way from the destination. If something nefarious was afoot he didn't want to risk announcing his presence. He approached quietly, his pistol in hand discreetly at his side. If he'd guessed wrong and Henry had honourable intentions, he'd look utterly foolish coming armed.

But Ashe saw immediately his initial assumptions were correct. Alex stood in the clearing facing Henry, his voice carrying in the clearing before the mausoleum. 'You're surprised to see me.'

'The message wasn't for you.' Henry was nervous. His eyes darted everywhere and his feet shifted anxiously from foot to foot. Something was wrong. Ashe looked about trying to see what Henry hoped to see. Was there someone hidden in the bushes?

'I know.' Alex began to circle Henry. Alex had always been able to manage Henry. Watching him now brought back memories from childhood when Alex had been the only one who could bring Henry to justice for his cruel pranks. 'It made the message that much more interesting. What in the world did you need to tell my brother that it had to be done in private out here, so far from the house?'

Alex prowled like a cat. Henry's eyes followed him around the circle. Alex did not relent. 'Did you mean to tell him you forged your uncle's signature on several bills of sale? Or perhaps you wanted to tell him you forged *my* signature on the funds you took from Bedevere for the Forsyth investment?'

'You're a raving lunatic, no one will believe you. Dr Lawrence will say it's part of your paranoia,' Henry snarled. 'All the knowledge in the world won't save you.'

'And nothing will save you.' Alex brought his arm up, levelling a pistol at Henry. 'We're both lost souls, Henry. How does it feel?'

Henry paled. Ashe watched in fascinated horror. Alex had seemed almost fragile since his return, but today he was strong and commanding, the way Ashe remembered him, except now there was a cold edge to that command devoid of Alex's usual compassion. Ashe waited, not wanting to intervene until it was necessary.

'You won't shoot me,' Henry challenged, but his voice wavered as if he didn't believe it himself. Ashe didn't believe it either. Alex would shoot him. The coldness in him left Ashe in no doubt. The bigger issue was whether Ashe should let him do it.

'Of course I will. I'm "crazy". A crazy man with a

gun is a very frightening thing. One can never tell what they'll do.' Alex paused, his eyes narrowing in consideration. 'Or maybe I'm sane after all. Which is more terrifying because then you can be sure I know exactly what I'm doing. I will give you one chance, Henry. I want a signed confession from you about the forgeries and I want you to resign yourself from any attempt to control Bedevere.'

Henry looked petulant. 'Maybe you're not the only one here with a gun. Maybe there's a man in the woods waiting to fire.'

'On me?' Alex made an exaggerated show of amazement. 'I'm a peer of the realm. Is that what you'd planned for Ashe? To have someone shoot him unawares when he came to meet you in good conscience?'

Ashe looked about the grove. If a shooter recognised him, that could still happen. It was becoming imperative for all their safety that the elusive hidden man be found. There was a slight movement on the periphery of the clearing and Ashe saw what he'd been looking for.

Within in moments, Ashe had manoeuvred behind the would-be assassin. It was the work of seconds to render the man unconscious. Ashe decided it was time to show himself. He picked up the man's gun and stepped forwards.

'Your man has been neutralised, Henry.' Ashe smiled. 'I have personally rendered him useless. It hardly seems sporting of you to have planned such an unpleasant surprise for me. Now, about that confession

Alex has offered you. I suppose that offer is looking better and better.'

Henry was deathly pale now, all his plans in sudden shreds. 'That confession is my death warrant. You know the penalty for forgery.'

'As did you when you began all this,' Ashe reminded him.

'I'll shoot you now if you prefer,' Alex offered.

Ashe wondered if his brother would do it. He seemed in deadly earnest. He didn't relish watching Henry gunned down in cold blood at the family grave site. 'I think he means it, Henry. Come to the house, write out the confession,' Ashe urged.

Henry's face suddenly lit with something akin to hope as if he'd just remembered something. 'That might be difficult.'

'Why is that?'

'Because Bedevere is burning,' Henry said with malicious glee. 'You can smell it.'

The wind shifted and Ashe smelled the smoke for the first time. Alex vaulted up behind him on Rex and they were off, Rex driven hard by Ashe's own panic.

They saw the dark billows of smoke looming over the house as they took the last rise. 'Dear Lord,' Alex breathed, his grip on Ashe's waist tightening in horror.

It was only part of the house, Ashe noted. Already, he could see the workers from the road rushing towards the house. If he could get a bucket brigade going, there was still time to save the main wing. There had to be. Everything he loved was down there. Genevra was down there.

* * *

'Mrs Bedevere, there's a man here to see you.' Gardener found her in the music room where she'd taken up vigil after Ashe had ridden out. All she wanted was for Ashe to come back safely, for the issue of Henry's perfidy to be resolved once and for all.

'Who is it, Gardener?' The last thing she wanted was to receive guests and make small talk while she worried over Ashe.

'He is one of the coal people, madam.' Gardener's voice carried a tone of disapproval. Clearly, Gardener felt the man was not fit company. 'He called here once before to meet with Lord Bedevere.'

Genevra fingered the smooth butt of Ashe's pistol. She did not want to worry Gardener with other suppositions. Genevra had kept the pistol with her—the afternoon had been strange. What if this was a man who'd come with news about Ashe or some new threat from Henry? She hurried downstairs, the gun hidden effectively from view in the folds of her gown.

She didn't like the man on sight. He introduced himself as Mr Trent, a man of business, but he didn't look respectable in spite of his expensive clothes. He didn't carry the air of a successful businessman—there was something too sinister about him for that.

'What do you want?' she asked unkindly.

He chuckled at her coldness. 'You must be Mrs Bedevere. Mr Bennington told us you were quite the spitfire. He was right. Bennington knows his women. My business is with Mr Bedevere. Is he here?'

'You know he is not,' Genevra guessed. 'He's with Bennington. There was a note, as I am sure you're well aware.'

Trent leered with satisfaction. 'If he's with Bennington, he's dead already.'

Genevra held her ground. She would not give in to the fear those words invoked. This man meant for the words to upset her. She wouldn't give him the satisfaction. Henry wouldn't kill Ashe, he wasn't that brave. 'I doubt it. Mr Bennington has shown himself to be a fool on more than one occasion.'

'Don't worry, Mrs Bedevere. Henry didn't have to do the shooting. We hired a professional to do that. You're right, Bennington doesn't have the ruthlessness to do it in cold blood.'

Genevra's bravado faltered. Did this Mr Trent know that Alex had gone as well? A professional would not hesitate to shoot both of the handsome Bedevere brothers. There was a moment when she could imagine them lying dead at the mausoleum, taken by surprise with no chance to defend themselves. But then she thought of the night she'd gone to wait for Ashe there, how fluid his movements had been when he'd pulled his knife from his boot, how he'd sensed her presence before she'd announced herself. Surely no one would take him by surprise.

'I don't believe you,' Genevra replied smoothly. 'Mr Bedevere is a tough man to kill.'

'If you're right, he'll be in time to save you. If you're wrong, then you can both be together in the afterlife.'

He raised his hand in a signal and Genevra watched in dismay as three other men filed into the hall. 'I'll manage the chit, you fire the building. Make sure it takes.'

'No! You cannot burn this house,' Genevra protested, her anger rising.

Trent struck a match and watched it flare. 'I assure you I can. It's my match.'

No one was going to burn Ashe's beloved Bedevere while she lived and breathed. With a steady arm, Genevra raised the pistol from its hiding spot against her skirts. 'It's my gun.'

'You've only got one shot and I've got a hundred matches.' Trent was a cool customer, unfazed by the pistol barrel. Her eyes held his. She let him see every ounce of her determination. She'd give him no reason to doubt this woman would fire the weapon and at this range she would not miss.

'You can't light matches when you're dead.'

'Then my men will light the match. You can't shoot us all.'

'Are you so eager to die for a stick of wood?' Genevra challenged.

But her bravado was short lived. 'I've had enough, boss.' One of the men spoke. 'I've got a pistol, too. Let me shoot her and be done with it.'

'Cunningham.' Trent swivelled his oily gaze towards the man who'd spoken. 'Always the thinker. Well, what do you say, Mrs Bedevere? Are *you* eager to die over a stick of wood?'

Everything that happened next seemed to slow. A

shot rang out from above in the stairwell and Cunningham fell, a rose of colour blossoming on his chest. Another shot fired from Trent's men, she turned to see Gardener fall in answer. 'No!' Genevra screamed. She remembered too late to fire her own pistol. Trent rushed her, grabbing for her gun arm, his hand imprisoning her wrist until the gun fell to the floor.

Trent dragged her upstairs past Gardener's prone form. She screamed, she kicked, she struggled, but there was no one to hear, no one to help. The day labourers were working on the fences along the road. The aunts, thank the lord, were in Audley Village and it was cook's day off. There was only Ashe and Alex if they were still alive.

Trent shoved her into a bedroom and slammed the door. He looped a length of rope over her hands and secured her to a bedpost. 'Hopefully, Henry will prove as foolish as you believe and Mr Bedevere will come racing home in time.' He laughed harshly. 'But then I'll be here, waiting on the front steps, and I won't fail like Henry.'

Genevra spat at him. It was a vain gesture. He swiped at the spittle on his cheek. He leaned close, his breath fetid with garlic, and took her mouth in a bruising kiss. 'I wish there was time for more. I could teach you the merit of obedience, my spitfire. You'd be worthy of my bed.'

Genevra glared. He laughed at her defiance. 'We'll see what you think about that when the smoke reaches you. My bed might sound like a good bargain for your life.'

He slammed the door behind him, but not before Genevra caught the smell of smoke rising from downstairs. Bedevere was burning and she was alone. She tugged at the bonds around her hands, assessing their strength. The bonds held. If she couldn't break the ropes, maybe she could break the bed post. She threw weight into it, but the strong mahogany that had served generations of Bedeveres held firm.

It wasn't until the first fingers of smoke curled under the door that she truly began to panic. There was a real possibility she'd die before she could tell Ashe she loved him.

Chapter Twenty-Five

Ashe flung himself off Rex, his pistol at the ready, Alex beside him. It reminded him of all the times they'd fought imaginary foes of the Round Table, Alex always at his back. But this was no child's game.

A man stood sentry at Bedevere's entrance. Before Ashe could speak, Alex raised his pistol and fired. The man fell, but not before Ashe saw a second too late what Alex had seen in time. The man dropped a knife, his arm arrested in the early stages of a throw. If not for Alex's cold-blooded assessment, he'd have died on the steps.

Another man rushed them from the side of the house. Ashe swept up the dropped weapon and sent it into the man's shoulder. The man sank to the ground and Ashe wasted no time pressing a boot to his neck. 'Where's Mrs Bedevere?'

The man growled and Ashe pressed harder, reaching for the knife in his own boot. The knife had the desired effect. 'She's in the house, on the second floor.'

The man coughed. 'But you'll be too late, for all the good that will do you.'

Alex was beside him. 'I'll take care of this swine, Ashe. Get Genevra, I'll be behind you in a moment.'

Ashe left Alex with his pistol and raced into the house. A body lay on the floor of the hallway. Another of Henry's so-called friends, he guessed. The smoke was rising fast. He was on the stairs and already choking. There were flames from the small front parlour. They must have set the curtains on fire. That posed a danger. Those flames would go straight up through the ceiling and into the second floor.

There was another body at the top of the landing. What had happened here? Then Ashe recognised the form. Good God, it was Gardener, shot straight through the heart. Who the hell had shot the butler? Rage tore through him. Ashe fell to his knees, impulsively looking for signs of life. It seemed incredible that, two hours ago, Gardener had fetched his pistols and now lay dead in a burning house. He had to find Genevra. She would not die for him, too.

'Genevra!' He staggered to his feet, struggling for breath. If she was hurt, she might not be able to answer. Ashe threw open each door he passed. The third door revealed success.

The smoke was thick in this room and Genevra had fallen slack against the bed frame, overcome. 'No, no, no, no, no.' Ashe fumbled at her neck for a pulse. 'Neva!' He shook her. He would not be too late, it wasn't possible. 'Neva!' He took his knife and sliced the ropes. She fell into his arms, the merest groan escaping her lips.

Ashe slid his knife into his boot and lifted her into his arms. The staircase was engulfed in smoke. He hoped there were no flames at the bottom yet. There was no other choice.

He heard someone call his name. 'Up here! Alex, I'm up here.' His voice was fading. With the last of it, he managed a warning. 'Get out, Alex, it's too dangerous. The stairs won't last.'

Something nearby cracked and crashed. He couldn't see it. Ashe hurried on to the smoke-shrouded staircase, Genevra heavy in his arms. He turned her head against his chest trying to protect her from the smoke.

Alex emerged on the stairs, having disregarded the warning. 'We'll take the servants' backstairs at the end of the hall. There's no chance this way. The hall below is engulfed.' Alex pushed him back up the stairs just in time. They'd gained the landing when the whole case gave way, effectively trapping them on the second floor. Alex led the way down the long hall, fearless and sure. The air was clearer here. The backstairs were as yet untouched. Alex held the door and ushered Ashe before him.

'You're a crazy fool, Alex, coming in like that.' Ashe panted as they reached the bottom and spilled out into the vegetable garden. He laid Genevra down, relieved to see signs of life as she stirred in response to the clean air.

Alex doubled over, catching his breath. 'I could see

the staircase was in jeopardy of collapsing. I knew you would try it. You didn't know the other way was clear and it was the shortest path to an exit.'

'You could have been killed,' Ashe scolded.

'You still might be. In fact, I think it is a surety.' Ashe turned. Henry, the cousin of nine lives, stood in the gateway, gun in hand. 'I think it's time I did my own dirty work.' There was madness in Henry's blue eyes. Pale and bedraggled, he'd managed to find his own way back to the house. Ashe had no doubt his cousin meant fatal business. It was the only way this could end now for Henry. His cartel was shattered, Henry's secrets exposed.

Ashe bent for his knife, but he knew it wouldn't be fast enough. Gun would beat knife in this contest. He had the knife in his hand and threw from a crouch, hoping the throw would be accurate. A shot fired. There was a yell, a scream. Neva! Then he was falling, thrown off balance. He waited for the burning sensation of the ball to take him. None came.

Ashe scrambled to his feet, searching, but there was no enemy. Genevra was scrabbling to her knees, half-crawling, half-falling towards a form on the ground.

'Alex!' Ashe rasped in horror.

'He threw himself at you when Henry fired,' Genevra gasped. She was tearing at Alex's shirt. Henry lay still a few feet away, Ashe's knife in his chest and Henry's bullet finding deadly purchase. His brother had given his life for him. Ashe knelt by Alex, closing his hands over Genevra's where she'd pressed a hastily made pad to the wound. His throat tightened.

'Ashe.' Alex's voice was a mere whisper. Ashe bent forwards, his ear to Alex's lips. 'You're the earl now, little brother.' Alex coughed.

'We'll get help.' If he was talking, maybe there was some hope, Ashe thought wildly.

'No, just stay with me. It won't be long now.' Alex was calm. 'I've written it all down for you if the fire didn't take it. You know most of it already.'

Ashe gripped his brother's hand. 'You shouldn't have done it. You shouldn't have thrown yourself away like that.'

'I hadn't long left, Ashe.' Alex struggled for a breath. 'It's much better this way.' He managed a smile. 'Father loved you, he forgave you for leaving. Make sure you forgive yourself.' His grip tightened on Ashe's hands. Pain and fear flashed in his dark eyes.

'Remember what we used to say when we played, Ashe? The king is dead, long live the king.'

'I remember.'

A lone tear trailed out of the corner of Alex's eye. 'The earl is dead, long live the earl.' Then the fear was replaced by peace as Alex breathed his last.

'So passes the fifth Earl of Audley,' Ashe said solemnly. Genevra held his gaze, unbothered by the tears on his cheeks. 'Long live the earl,' she softly echoed Alex's words.

He pulled her to him, revelling in the feel of her body, of life. 'When I saw the smoke, all I could think of was I was too late to tell you I loved you. I should have told you weeks ago, but I was too stubborn to admit it.' He pushed his hands gently through her hair, tilting her face up to his.

'I love you, too, Ashe. I think I loved you from the first.' She kissed him softly.

Ashe laughed. 'No, you didn't, Neva. You slapped me across the face for insolence.'

'Well, maybe you're right about that.' She smiled wearily and didn't protest when he bent to carry her away from the heartbreak that lay in the garden and into the future.

One year later

Ashe paced the back terrace, surveying the expanse of parkland and gardens. Rebuilt, redecorated, Bedevere had never looked so well, or perhaps it was his own happiness that painted everything with a rosy veneer these days. Ashe could not recall having ever been this content in his adult life, not even when he'd been playing piano in Vienna. He shifted the bundle in his arms ever so gently.

'Fatherhood becomes you,' Genevra said softly, shutting the veranda door behind her. 'Is he asleep?' She peered into the blanket at the little face. 'I missed him too much today.' It had been her first day out of the house since little Alexander had been born two months ago.

'How is Seaton Hall?' Ashe asked. It had become operational a few months ago, Genevra's dream of a place for women to run their own business fully realised.

'It's fine. I am happy to say they're ably running things on their own. They hardly need me at all.'

'That's good.' Ashe bent to kiss her. 'There are plenty of us who need you here.'

'That reminds me, I have a surprise for you.' Genevra smiled. 'Come walk with me.'

Baby in one arm, his wife on the other, Ashe let Genevra lead him through the garden to the fountain. It still wasn't working. After the fire, there'd been plenty of projects to oversee that took precedence in order to make Bedevere livable again.

Genevra gave a nod of her head and the fountain sprang to life. Water plumed high into the air, arcing gracefully into the wide basin below. 'Happy birthday, Ashe,' she whispered. With a gesture of her hand, people began to emerge from behind the trees—the staff were there, his aunts were there, Markham Marsbury was there.

'I'm sorry we missed it last year. I didn't know.' Genevra shrugged apologetically. She moved to take the baby from him, but he declined.

'No, I want to hold him a while longer.'

'You'll be the only lord in England to actually raise his own child,' Genevra teased.

Ashe grinned.

'What are you thinking?'

'I'm thinking what a difference a year makes.' Last year had been full of loss. He'd lost his father, his brother, even a chance to make amends, but he'd found Genevra and he'd found peace. The future lay in his arms and stood by his side.

'I have a gift for you.' Genevra reached for an awkwardly wrapped package at the base of the fountain. 'Now you'll have to let me take the baby.'

Ashe obliged and undid the wrapping. Beneath the paper was a model four-masted schooner. He was speechless for a moment. 'It's perfect, Neva. Does it float?'

'Put it in the fountain and find out.'

There were those who believed Ashe Bedevere was the greatest pleasure of the Season, but he knew better. The best pleasure was being loved by Genevra through all the seasons to come, and there would be plenty of them if he had anything to say about it. Ashe Bedevere was home.

* * * * *

COMING NEXT MONTH from Harlequin® Historical
AVAILABLE OCTOBER 16, 2012

SNOWBOUND WEDDING WISHES
Louise Allen, Lucy Ashford, Joanna Fulford

This Christmas, as the snow begins to fall, wedding dreams are made against a beautiful Regency backdrop. Enjoy three wonderful tales you'll never forget.
(Regency)

UNCLAIMED BRIDE
Lauri Robinson

After stepping off the stage in Wyoming, mail-order bride Constance Jennings waits for her husband-to-be, who never shows up. Single father Ellis Clayton must be the only man in town *not* looking for a bride. But his young daughter's habit of rescuing wounded critters means he ends up offering Constance a temporary shelter. One that he quickly wishes to make more permanent!
(Western)

HOW TO SIN SUCCESSFULLY
Rakes Beyond Redemption
Bronwyn Scott

With his comrade rakes-in-arms succumbing to respectability, wicked Riordan Barrett might be assumed to be next. Until Riordan finds himself not only an earl...but father to two young wards! This rake needs help—and hiring sweet, innocent Maura Caulfield as governess won't be such a hardship. He'll show her just how much fun sinning can be....
(1830s)

RETURN OF THE BORDER WARRIOR
The Brunson Clan
Blythe Gifford

Once part of a powerful border clan, John has not set eyes on the Brunson stone tower in years. With failure *never* an option, he must persuade his family to honor the king's call for peace. To succeed, John knows winning over the intriguing beauty Cate Gilnock holds the key....
(Tudor)

You can find more information on upcoming Harlequin® titles, free excerpts and more at www.Harlequin.com.

HHCNM1012

REQUEST YOUR FREE BOOKS!

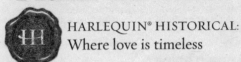

HARLEQUIN® HISTORICAL:
Where love is timeless

2 FREE NOVELS PLUS 2 FREE GIFTS!

YES! Please send me 2 FREE Harlequin® Historical novels and my 2 FREE gifts (gifts are worth about $10). After receiving them, if I don't wish to receive any more books, I can return the shipping statement marked "cancel." If I don't cancel, I will receive 6 brand-new novels every month and be billed just $5.19 per book in the U.S. or $5.74 per book in Canada. That's a savings of at least 17% off the cover price! It's quite a bargain! Shipping and handling is just 50¢ per book in the U.S. and 75¢ per book in Canada.* I understand that accepting the 2 free books and gifts places me under no obligation to buy anything. I can always return a shipment and cancel at any time. Even if I never buy another book, the two free books and gifts are mine to keep forever.

246/349 HDN FEQQ

Name	(PLEASE PRINT)	
Address		Apt. #
City	State/Prov.	Zip/Postal Code

Signature (if under 18, a parent or guardian must sign)

Mail to the **Reader Service:**
IN U.S.A.: P.O. Box 1867, Buffalo, NY 14240-1867
IN CANADA: P.O. Box 609, Fort Erie, Ontario L2A 5X3

Not valid for current subscribers to Harlequin Historical books.

Want to try two free books from another line?
Call 1-800-873-8635 or visit www.ReaderService.com.

* Terms and prices subject to change without notice. Prices do not include applicable taxes. Sales tax applicable in N.Y. Canadian residents will be charged applicable taxes. Offer not valid in Quebec. This offer is limited to one order per household. All orders subject to credit approval. Credit or debit balances in a customer's account(s) may be offset by any other outstanding balance owed by or to the customer. Please allow 4 to 6 weeks for delivery. Offer available while quantities last.

Your Privacy—The Reader Service is committed to protecting your privacy. Our Privacy Policy is available online at www.ReaderService.com or upon request from the Reader Service.

We make a portion of our mailing list available to reputable third parties that offer products we believe may interest you. If you prefer that we not exchange your name with third parties, or if you wish to clarify or modify your communication preferences, please visit us at www.ReaderService.com/consumerchoice or write to us at Reader Service Preference Service, P.O. Box 9062, Buffalo, NY 14269. Include your complete name and address.

HH11B

HARLEQUIN® HISTORICAL:
Where love is timeless

Explore a land as wild and beautiful as the men
who rule it with author

BLYTHE GIFFORD

WORD IN THE ROYAL COURT HAS SPREAD
THAT THE WILD SCOTTISH BORDERS
ARE TOO UNRULY AND ONLY ONE MAN
CAN ENSURE PEACE....

Return of the Border Warrior

With failure *never* an option, John Brunson returns home
to persuade his family to honor the king's call for peace. But the
Brunson Clan will kneel to no one....

To succeed, John knows winning over Cate Gilnock, the daughter
of an allied family, is the key. But this intriguing beauty
is beyond the powers of flattery and seduction. Instead, the painful
vulnerability hidden behind her spirited eyes calls out to John
as he is drawn back into the warrior Brunson clan....

Available from Harlequin® Historical October 16.

www.Harlequin.com

HH29714

*Read on for a sneak peek of the final installment in
Bronwyn Scott's witty and sexy trilogy,
Rakes Beyond Redemption.*

HOW TO SIN SUCCESSFULLY

Arguing with one's employer on the first day was no way to
start. "I should call you Lord Chatham." She smiled again,
looking for a better subject of conversation. What had her
governesses done on the first day? She sipped her tea and
racked her brain for an appropriate next step.

"Lord Chatham?" He arched a dark eyebrow in query.
The expression drew attention to his eyes, twin blue flames
flickering with life and mischief.

"I think that would be best, under the circumstances." She
knew that would be best. He was a dangerous sort of man
when it came to a woman's sensibilities with his good looks
and penchant for informality. A half hour in his company
had proven it. He hadn't even bothered to put his coat on or
tuck in his shirttails.

To her surprise, he laughed and leaned forward,
smiling wickedly over his teacup. "You weren't under any
circumstances on the porch, you were under me."

"Lord Chatham! There are children in the room." But
the children didn't seem to mind. They were laughing.
They did that a lot, she noticed, no doubt encouraged by the
irrepressible audacity of their guardian. Laughter was well
and good but they would have to learn to control it just a bit.

"So there are." He rubbed at his chin in thought for a
moment, although she had the distinct impression he was
teasing her. "If we are to be formal, I'll need to call you
something more than Six." He was smiling again, flirting

outrageously with his blue, blue eyes while saying nothing technically objectionable at all.

From her perch on a chair, Cecilia looked crestfallen. "I want to call her Six. It will ruin the joke if we don't."

Lord Chatham quirked another eyebrow in Maura's direction, a little smile hovering about his lips while he waited for her response. Good heavens, the man was a handsome devil. Cecilia's lip began to quiver. Maura felt a moment's panic. She didn't want to be the governess who made her charge cry within the first half hour. Her next words came rushing out to forestall any tears. "Sex is fine."

Sex is fine? Maura clapped a hand over her mouth but it was far too late.

"Is it? That's good to know." Lord Chatham's smile widened in good humor.

Maura blushed hotly in mortification. What had happened to her tongue? It had done nothing right since her arrival.

Don't miss the final installment in Bronwyn Scott's witty and sexy trilogy, Rakes Beyond Redemption.

HOW TO SIN SUCCESSFULLY

Available from Harlequin Historical November 2012.

Copyright © 2012 by Nikki Poppen

HHEXP1112TRIL

HARLEQUIN *Presents*®

Find yourself
BANISHED TO THE HAREM
in a glamorous and tantalizing new tale from

Carol
Marinelli

Playboy Sheikh Prince Rakhal Alzirz has time for
one more fling in London before he must return
to his desert kingdom—and Natasha Winters has
caught his eye. He seizes the chance to discover if
Natasha is as fiery in bed as her flaming red hair,
but their recklessness has consequences.... She
might be carrying the Alzirz heir!

BANISHED
TO THE HAREM

Available October 16!

www.Harlequin.com

HP13103

HARLEQUIN *Blaze*™
red-hot reads

Double your reading pleasure with
Harlequin® Blaze™!

As a special treat to you, all Harlequin
Blaze books in November will include
a new story, plus a classic story by the
same author including…

Kate Hoffmann

When Ronan Quinn arrives in Sibleyville, Maine, all he's
looking for is a decent job. What he finds instead
is a centuries-old curse connected to his family and hostility
from all the townsfolk. Only sexy oysterwoman
Charlotte Sibley is willing to hire Ronan…and she's about
to turn his life upside down.

The Mighty Quinns: Ronan

Look for this new installment of The Mighty Quinns, plus
The Mighty Quinns: Marcus, the first ever Mighty Quinns
book in the same volume!

Available this November wherever books are sold!

www.Harlequin.com

HB79723

Love Inspired **HISTORICAL**

celebrating
15
YEARS

Author

LYN COTE

brings you kindred hearts in a wild new land.

No one is more surprised than Sunny Licht when Noah Whitmore proposes. She's a scarlet woman and an unwed mother—an outcast in her small Quaker community. But she can't resist Noah's offer of a fresh start. Noah, a former Union soldier, sees Sunny as a woman whose loneliness matches his own. He'll see that she and her baby daughter want for nothing...except the love that war burned out of him. Yet Sunny makes him hope once more—for the home they're building, and the family he never hoped to find.

Their Frontier Family

Available November wherever books are sold.

www.LoveInspiredBooks.com

LIH82939